REVOLUTION FROM ABOVE

REVOLUTION FROM ABOVE

India's Future and the Citizen Elite

DIPANKAR GUPTA

RAINLIGHT
RUPA

Published in Rainlight by
Rupa Publications India Pvt. Ltd 2013
7/16, Ansari Road, Daryaganj
New Delhi 110002

Sales centres:
Allahabad Bengaluru Chennai
Hyderabad Jaipur Kathmandu
Kolkata Mumbai

Copyright © Dipankar Gupta 2013

All rights reserved.
No part of this publication may be reproduced, transmitted, or stored
in a retrieval system, in any form or by any means, electronic, mechanical,
photocopying, recording or otherwise, without the prior permission of
the publisher.

ISBN: 978-81-291-2460-9

10 9 8 7 6 5 4 3 2 1

The moral right of the author has been asserted.

Typeset by RECTO GRAPHICS, Delhi

Printed at Replika Press Pvt. Ltd, India

This book is sold subject to the condition that it shall not, by way of trade
or otherwise, be lent, resold, hired out, or otherwise circulated, without
the publisher's prior consent, in any form of binding or cover other than
that in which it is published.

To André Béteille,
Friend, Philosopher, Guide and Critic
(most of all a friend!)

Contents

Preface

In the years leading up to 2010, I was reading extensively about the advances in western democracy and was impressed at how certain members of the privileged strata contributed to these. My reading aroused reflections in me, but of the idle kind. As India's near past had nothing in common with the glorious period of nineteenth-century Europe, I could only admire what happened there from a distance.

During those years, members of the elite class, landlords and rich merchants together advanced British democracy with the most profound consequences. It is therefore fitting that these historical personages are retrospectively referred to as the Victorian Radicals. Similar instances occurred elsewhere in Europe too, but I came to that realization much later. Citizenship was deepened, rights were granted of the kind that would have been unthinkable earlier, and gradually the 'public' became a vibrant reality. I also concluded from my ruminations that much of this had become possible because the welfare state kept growing in size, and yet these advances had little to do with the shameful way these countries behaved in their colonies.

King Leopold of Belgium is an archetypal example of this duality, but the fact remains that internally Europe began to experience greater democracy. The delivery of welfare services, or public goods, such as universal health and education, started haltingly, but over time became an essential ingredient of what it means to be European today. It was almost as if these features had taken on a cultural dimension and had become identity markers of sorts.

As I ploughed on I also came to another somewhat startling conclusion. Not only did Europe's investment in social welfare happen in spurts, these moments coincided with periods of economic constraints. This may perhaps be old hat for specialists in this area of study, but it is not something that is widely known or appreciated. Now I began to question the argument that our spending on universal social welfare projects must necessarily be limited because India is a poor country. Statements of this kind not only make up much of our public rhetoric on the subject, but are pretty loudly pronounced in the Planning Commission too.

At this time, I was fortunate to be appointed a Visiting Professor at Deusto University. This institution is in Bilbao, the most vibrant city of Basque Spain, and one of the most beautiful places I have ever been to. I met many Basque nationalists, who took enormous pains to further my understanding of how their part of the country grew out of poverty to prosperity. They took me around to visit some of the most interesting institutions of the region and even introduced me to people who actually changed the Basque country. They were the first-generation Basque politicians who created a miracle when they came to power in the 1980s, post General Franco. 1980? Yes, it is that recent, just three short decades ago. Unlike the Victorian Radicals, these people were all there in front of me, patiently answering my questions and showing me how they did it all. It was the treat of a lifetime!

It is then that I realized that democracy needs 'an elite of calling' if it is to be pressed to deliver to citizens. Ordinary politicians will not do; it requires people of substance, training, foresight and, most of all, the willingness to forsake their immediate class interests for a social good. The individuals who initiated and campaigned successfully for a fully functional and efficient public delivery system in the Basque region were people of this kind. This is why this province is high up today on the index of health, education and innovation and competes with the best in Europe. It has left the rest of Spain well behind.

Basque Spain usually arouses images of terrorists, of the ETA, or the Euskadi ta Askatasuna ('Basque Fatherland and Liberty'). But today terrorism is long gone from here and it has become a place totally different from its past. Prominent banners hang from many of the region's public buildings announcing in bold: 'ETA, No!' There could be no more evocative a way of showing how much this part of Spain had changed. The first generation of Basque leaders, after Franco's death, had the passion and zeal of ETA activists, but also possessed democratic sense and technical expertise. It is this combination that decimated ETA, not a superior police force or repression.

In the period before the 1980s, photographs of Bilbao show a grim and grey place with a polluted river running through it. There were ugly chimney stacks along the banks and just a single bridge connecting them. All that is now in distant history. As if to signal this transformation, the spectacular Guggenheim Museum has been built on the riverside, with clean air above and sparkling blue water below. This transition from the old to the new was so quick and decisive that it leaves one with nothing but admiration for those who initiated the change and saw the process through. When I heard their stories, I wished we in India could say something like that some day soon.

I then began looking at India closely and found that we once had our elite of calling, but since then have had more politicians and leaders. In this book, my principal aim is to demonstrate that it is not by elections alone that democracy prospers. It requires active interventions to take democracy forward and that push can happen only from above. In this we should not let our poverty come in the way, but use it to galvanize our country to take up challenges.

As all of this requires bold, but not reckless, planning it needs an elite of calling to dig deep and bring out democracy's many potentials. The people who constitute this elite are of the kind that work for a future, which may even appear utopian, without fearing economic reversals in their personal lives. They set the pace and think big and, invariably, over a period of time, they win over public opinion. As members of this elite category allow voters to judge them every so many years, they often lose elections. Just as often, they also make a comeback and when that happens they force history to look ahead. Many of this breed are dead, some are alive, but the best, I hope, are yet to be born.

As this book is inspired by such people, it is only fitting that the words 'citizen elite' figure in the title of this book.

I would have learnt none of this had not Ion de la Riva, former Spanish Ambassador to India, been the prime mover in getting me started on Basque Spain. He introduced me to Mikel Burzako, who immediately took me under his wing in Bilbao and went out of his way to introduce me to the people and institutions of the Basque region. His knowledge of Basque history as well as his grasp over current affairs in the region were of invaluable help to me. Along with Paul Ortega, a close friend of Mikel Burzako, I got to know a wide range of people, from politicians to businessmen to activists in the cooperative sector. I cannot thank them enough.

David Corral and Jon Ocio took pains to read through sections of the manuscript and corrected a few important factual details. I am grateful to them for that. I must also thank Professor Julia Gonzalez who, as Vice-Chancellor of Deusto University, made me welcome and did her share of connecting me to intellectuals in the city. Soledad Aizpurua helped me through some of the official details that one inevitably encounters in a foreign land with patience and forbearance. Finally, Gipson Varghese was always there, ever helpful, always obliging and willing to drop everything and come to my rescue whenever I needed him in Bilbao.

This book is almost entirely about India, but it would not have been written had I not visited Basque Spain, when I did. This in no way undermines the friendship, camaraderie and intellectual inspiration I gained from my colleagues and teachers in India. The time I spent in Jawaharlal Nehru University (JNU) as a student and then professor was of the kind I would not trade for anything else. During this period I realized that it is only by meeting the exacting standards of democracy that we can actually deliver to citizens. Democracy does not come in the way of overcoming poverty and ethnic strife; it actually shows the way out of these circumstances, and the most efficient one at that.

A few of the arguments in this book were earlier tested in my columns in *The Times of India* and *Mail Today*. I am grateful to the many readers who commented on them, as their views helped me to recast my positions on some of these issues.

In between my years in JNU, I had the opportunity of working for a while in the corporate world, which was very educational. When KPMG, India, asked me to head a group on Business Ethics I really had no idea how much I would learn from this experience. This engagement allowed me to understand how business and labour interact, especially in small-scale enterprises. My trips to universities outside India allowed me to take a close look at several existing social welfare systems, warts and all. What little I have learnt from all of this over the years would not have been possible had my intellectual colleagues and friends in India not provided the context.

I must also thank the National University of Education, Planning and Administration (NUEPA) for granting me a Fellowship in 2011-2012. During this period I tried to understand as much as I could about educational policy and, along with it, about health delivery too. Also, as I was located at NUEPA, I had the good fortune of meeting many of India's best-known educationists and spending long hours learning from them. Pairing health and education together helped me get a clearer view of what universal delivery of social welfare is meant to be.

In the end, only I am responsible for what appears in the following pages.

CHAPTER I

The Mirror or the Hammer: The Quest for India's Citizen Elite

Democracy is very difficult to practise for its basic tenet flies against popular constructions of reality. While fraternity demands that we see the 'us' in the 'them', human beings are predisposed towards separating cultures on a natural basis. This is an unfortunate anthropological failing that cuts across space and time, and is democracy's first great hurdle. The title of this chapter is important, for it metaphorically highlights the fact that democracy is meant to change reality and not submit to it. If it had been compliant with the given, none of the major advances in democracy would have happened. Also, if democracy were bound only by what the people want, then the best that could be delivered would be a reworked version of what they already have. This is why whenever democracy has enlarged fraternity and deepened citizenship in practice, the inputs have come from the 'elite of calling' or the 'citizen elite'. Thus, while the general belief is that people make democracy, the fact is that a select few actually contribute much more. Leaders take the first step and voters either accept or reject what is being proposed.

'Art is not a mirror held up to society but a hammer
with which to shape it.'
—Bertolt Brecht

Democracy, at its best, does not reflect reality, rather, it shapes
it. True democrats do not need a mirror as much as they do
a hammer. Likewise, in a democracy, leaders must not aim to
represent reality as much as to change it. Democracy was put
in this world not just to alter 'given' social conditions, but also
'given' human nature.

Look back at all that democracy has bequeathed to us over
time; in nearly every case it needed individuals with a hammer
to make that difference. Rarely, in the introduction of many
of these programmes, has there been a majority voice, or a
mirroring of the given. Instead, from establishing universal
health and education (as in Europe and Canada), to abolishing
child labour and limiting the maximum hours of work (as in
most contemporary societies), to fighting slavery (as in the
southern United States), to the abolition of untouchability (as
in India), in not a single case did democracy begin by reflecting
popular will, but by shaping it. It was not the mirror but the
hammer that did its job.

Just because something is not around today does not mean
it cannot happen. What once seemed unthinkable suddenly
becomes routine. Remember, nobody believed the gold standard
would ever be lifted, but it was. Till then, it was impossible to
imagine that money could function without a gold backup.
Who would have thought, before it happened, that the Soviet
Union would collapse one day? Who could have imagined
that credit cards would rule the world of shopping, even just
a few years before this piece of plastic became unremarkable?
Who would have ever imagined that IPads would make paper
unnecessary? Just because something does not exist at a certain
point in time this should not mean that it cannot happen. This
is equally true in the political realm.

Democracy Contests Reality: Fraternity as the Guiding Thread

Why do we need leaders to make a difference? This is because reality everywhere runs contrary to the principles of democracy. The human tendency, as anthropology has taught us, spontaneously distances cultures and peoples into 'us' and 'them'. Not just that, we tend naturally to separate humanity in such a way that the 'us' can never be the 'them'. A society can be economically advanced or backward but people everywhere happily, and without provocation, indulge in the 'us/them' polarity. The credo of 'fraternity' that is so central to democracy consequently finds little resonance in popular cultures across the world.

It is easy to imagine the Hindus of Aryavarta, or the Chinese of the Middle Kingdom, demonstrating such swagger; indeed, their sense of superiority is much commented upon. But prejudices of the same genre also hold for the near 'stone-age' Kung people of the Kalahari, the Kachins of Burma, the Pueblo Indians of Nevada—just about everywhere. In a number of instances those who belong to other cultures are not even seen as being fully human. While we all know that 'others' exist around us, they are somehow found wanting in our esteem.

Each of the categories that differentiates humankind is amenable to further divisions but every slice will possess the vigour that the first-order prejudice contains. For example, full-blown distinctions are made between not just Hindus and Muslims, but between Hindu Bengalis and Hindu Punjabis and Hindu Tamilians and so on. It is as if each of these communities is genetically programmed to be the way they are. The 'us' and the 'them' are the twain that will never meet.

So the Punjabis view themselves as industrious and consider the Bengalis and Tamilians effete incompetents. Then there are takes on Punjabis which are far from being complimentary, and it just goes on all the way up, sideways and down. Not a single community that is known and knowable is able to escape the naturalization of differences. That this happens so extensively is because different contexts set up different sets of 'others' for the 'us' to consider. This also explains why ethnic and sectarian politicians find it relatively easy to stay in business even though they have little by way of a concrete programme.

Only democracy strains against this popular conception of reality and, instead, advocates fraternity. Simply put, fraternity is all about seeing the 'them' in 'us'—and this is the single most important tenet of democracy. When this nugget is encased in popular franchise, peoples' representation is truly at work. Dr B.R. Ambedkar, for example, argued that without fraternity, neither equality nor liberty would amount to much (see Shiva Rao, 1968). Quite clearly, fraternity projects an alternative where passions that spontaneously separate people from one another get little, or no, purchase; but it takes a lot of hard work. It also takes leadership!

Human beings, in general, are unhappy with thoroughgoing fraternity and are comfortable instead in bracketing others with cultural tags. It does not take long to scratch the surface of such attitudes to discover a pseudo-biological reasoning behind them. While differences in religion, language and race can be 'naturalized' easily, we must remember that even vast economic differences can set these juices flowing.

As a matter of fact, economic differences take on a 'naturalistic' attribute more often than is generally acknowledged. Though this does not come through quite as starkly as in the case of race, language or religion, it is, nevertheless, surprising to see how closely it can mimic them. If there is a tragedy in a poor household then that does not seem to be as painful to those who come from a more fortunate background. A labourer dying in a construction accident is not as moving to the better-off as when one of their own is crushed by a speeding car.

Examples of this sort can be multiplied: a bus falling off a cliff carrying villagers will not hit the headlines as much as when a small chopper meets with an accident. When cancer patients wait interminably in line it is not quite as devastating as when a person of substance is denied medical care. Such category divides do not spare children or old people either; somehow the pain of a loss does not bridge the economic barriers that exist.

It is almost as if those others are not as human as we are, as if they do not possess the complete complement of emotions that we are blessed with.

Limits of Mirroring Reality: Democracy Constrained

Sadly, all of this is reality too, but must democracy mirror this miserable plenitude? Or should democracy use a hammer and chisel and shape this reality along the lines of liberty, equality, and, most of all, fraternity? Empathy, which follows fraternity, is not easy to generate unless social conditions that favour its emergence are in place. But they are never in place from the start; they need to be realized by deliberate practice which denies the superiority of the given. Failing that, sympathy can be in abundance, for it is gratifying to affect a gesture of condescension—rather like *noblesse oblige*. For empathy to be dominant, the given will have to change.

It needs to be kept in mind that a democracy is not an un-interfering form of governance. It intervenes in the given so as to change society in the direction of greater fraternity. This also brings out one of the significant differences between a democracy and the most benign form of colonial rule, which might ladle out dollops of *noblesse oblige*. British domination in India is often praised by some for its tolerance towards Indian customs. In fact, William Jones by all accounts meant well when he said, in a lecture delivered in Kolkata on 15 January 1784, that 'British Subjects resident in India be protected, yet governed by British Laws; and the natives of these important provinces be indulged in their own prejudices, civil and religious and suffered to enjoy their own custom unmolested' (http://eliohs.unfit.it/testi/700/jones/Preliminary_Discourse.html; accessed 7 July 2012). Such a position would, however, be anathema to any self-respecting democracy.

In India, caste is an in-your-face social fact and so are community differences, but a state that acknowledges them as rock-hard reality should not call itself a democracy. The Mandal formula, which increased the scope of reservations, is supported by all political parties on the grounds that we must accept the reality of caste. Consequently, in the past two decades and some, India has become much more caste-conscious in its political life than ever before. Rather than examining the causes behind poverty that affect us all, special provisions are made along caste lines that only exacerbate intercommunity relations.

Likewise, who can deny that minority religious communities feel a sense of deprivation in India? From there to make the jump and play the Muslim, Hindu, Sikh, Christian or caste card, in the name of reflecting reality, is certainly not warranted. Far from taking democracy forward such political moves actually impede its progress. It openly fractures 'fraternity' into several competing groups that find their ultimate rationale in the idea of 'naturalized' differences.

Or take another, less egregious example. The bulk of India lives in the countryside, but that does not mean that villagers must be marooned there without a chance of leading a non-rural life elsewhere. If policymakers were to put themselves in the place of the poor villager in the spirit of fraternity, they would soon realize that rural life, in truth, is not uplifting at all. Nevertheless, a strong current of opinion believes that Indians are happiest in villages and best express themselves in community huddles behind mud walls.

No doubt the reality of rural numbers is indubitable, but that does not warrant that the poor rustic farmer should be abandoned in the countryside. If the principle of fraternity is put to work, and policymakers place themselves in the shoes of the villager, the urgency to find an alternative non-rural life would gain momentum. If the same principle were to be applied in the case of poverty, it would soon be clear that the poor can have ambitions like the rest of us.

In which case, we are really not doing the poor a favour by fashioning rescue packages that are in the nature of doles; what we need to do is to eradicate poverty. Those who believe that the reality of the given can only be ameliorated in a piecemeal fashion would rather keep the poor alive, for removing poverty appears far too ambitious a project and would take too long. Try telling them that there are countries in one's short-term memory which have planned slum-free urbanization and eradicated poverty and be prepared to be met with disbelief.

If political mobilizations abide by the distinctions and values of the given, of the here and now, then regardless of the popular energy they might generate, they would still be contrary to the spirit of democracy. On such occasions, the partisans might argue that their cause reflects reality and that this is what people want, indeed, this is how the majority have voted. Such claims are, more often than not, accurate, but that still does not make them democratic.

There have been dictators in many nations who have come to the top riding on hysteria. Hitler, for example, rose to power through a popular mandate, but his Third Reich was built on xenophobia. It recognized equality only among those white German Christians who were happy to exterminate Jews, Communists and Gypsies as national threats. It was majority opinion all right, but not a democratic one.

A Hammer for Fraternity: Shaping Reality

The majority is always happy to see its face in the mirror, but it needs hammer-wielding craftsmen to shape a democracy. For that to happen democracy must not think short-term, or within the confines of the given. It must project social goals where citizenship is the fundamental driving force and, in this process, must necessarily combat existing structures and attributes. Democracy now needs to institutionalize an alternative setting from that which already exists, such that the principle of fraternity gets a chance to exercise its magic.

The areas that need to handled first are health, education and access to energy resources. Once these sectors are made culture- and class-blind, fraternity begins to manifest itself in demonstrable terms. Universal health care gives people the confidence to tackle the unforeseen present while universal education strengthens the resolve to face an aspirational future. Those in power do not always see the value of these fraternity-inspired interventions because they are privileged in terms of their access to health, education and other facilities for a good life.

Therefore, the commitment towards achieving an end of this kind requires a vision that looks beyond the given. Even the poor themselves cannot envisage these measures for they do not know what they mean or what form they will take. Only after such projects are actually realized will their appreciation spread amongst different classes and the worth of fraternity be truly understood. But to achieve something so beautiful, where the present and the future are protected universally, requires the imagination and determination of an artist. E.P. Thompson's history on the making of the British working class is largely about how a class comes into being (a class for itself), but has little to say about how the poor get the intellectual and political ammunition to take them beyond the given (Thompson 1963: 9).

The democrat who is driven by concerns of fraternity must necessarily have an artist's temperament. Only an artist will have the temerity to contradict the given even while everybody else bows to it. When such fraternal projects are inaugurated the stock argument against them is to draw attention to the lack of material and human resources. If one accepts this as a binding fact then there will never be the necessary wherewithal. To make things happen, the hard, crusty shell in which our routine lives are trapped has to be forced open. Only then will democracy reveal to us a new world that was hitherto not visible to popular perception.

This would halt the reproduction of naturalized differences, as the 'them' could easily be one of 'us'. It would also raise the level of what is 'given' to heights that were unimaginable before. If the many brilliant minds and hardy spirits that are today wasted in poverty, ill health and neglect could contribute their potential it would raise standards for all of 'us'. Remember Thomas Gray's lines in 'Elegy Written in a Country Churchyard': 'Full many a flower is born to blush unseen, And waste its sweetness on the desert air.' No true democracy can let that happen.

There have been charismatic religious leaders who have enjoined their followers to believe in the oneness of humankind, but the unity central to their teachings died with them. Paradoxically, while Jesus, Mohammed, Nanak and Vivekananda, to name a few, wanted to erase cultural and doctrinal differences, their followers soon formed warring sects. This is where the democratic notion of 'fraternity' makes a difference. Once set in place it becomes a way of life because it is bolstered by state policies aimed specifically at removing distinctions of privilege and creed. Little, if anything at all, is left to the emotional forces of love, charity and the desire to be good.

Planning, constructing and engineering societies with this in mind cannot obey the sounds of 'mournful numbers', but requires the democrat to be an artist at work. Failing that, there can be no forward movement as the confines of the given will remain forever binding. In politics and statecraft the inspiration behind such visions is always spurred by the sentiments associated with 'fraternity'. Mistakes will occur on the way, but they will be of the kind that are not motivated by sectional considerations. Once people become citizens, and not just passive voters or passionate nationalists, democracy acquires an aura that is beguiling.

From then on, democracy stops reflecting the given, but makes a new reality that brings out the best in us. Till the 'elite of calling' make a difference, the difference is never made. From health, to housing, to social insurance and workers' rights, none of these advances of democracy could have been foreseen in advance. In fact, there were bitter struggles over them, many of which will be recounted in later chapters.

What is, however, noteworthy for now is that 'the people' consolidate their force behind these programmes once they realize their positive impact on their lives and circumstances. They had little premonition of what these measures could achieve in advance and reacted to them only when they were in position and their effects in full view. In a democracy, the hammer-wielding artists first shape a new reality and then let people judge them at election time. If their interventions pass the popular test, they are firmed up in administrative practice and become essential ingredients in decision-making.

This is the true circuit of democracy, and it is never the other way around. People, by themselves, can only tinker with the givens and adjust them for short-term sectional advantages, claiming all the while that they have their feet on the ground. The force behind the hammer is not the simple additive power of the people, or crude majority opinion. Real democrats are answering to a higher call, for they are fired by the ideal of citizenship whose core attribute is that of fraternity.

Citizenship guarantees equality of opportunity so that aspirations to excel can be realized at all levels (see Marshall 1963: 87). To serve citizens as a collective is very different from reflecting sectional opinions where those who have the numbers, or have the wherewithal, win. It is not as if citizenship erases differences, it rather harnesses them to increase the social potentials of the whole. This requires vision but also an element of sacrifice; immediate gratification of vested interests is being swapped for the long-term good of citizens.

Why Democracy is Difficult: Going against the Given

Democracy is fragile and requires eternal vigilance. It does not yield to the here and now, does not make concessions to the privileged, nor does it pander to our primordial prejudices that separate people on a 'natural' basis. Our natures must be tamed to respect democracy, and it should never be the other way around. Left to ourselves, without a grand vision, we tend to maximize the given, justifying our targets as pragmatic and realistic. Routine science with its routine technology is always at hand to justify the fidelity to that which exists.

In fact, nothing in the real world can assert the need for fraternity, for its social basis is almost non-existent. In such a situation it is quite natural that tools that maximize the given should be put to use. This elevates the routine scientist for such a person is faithful to the here and now. Science can, however, also help in setting up a democracy where fraternity counts, but it cannot initiate it. For that to happen we first need the vision of the artist which will be the raw material for science to work on. This is quite unlike the situation when politics reflects social reality and the artist just does not get a chance to imagine a new world.

Democracy can be best understood as an art that has scientific possibilities. It begins with a commitment to shape a world that does not conform to what is but to what should be. Though its starting point is omnipresent reality, it has no intention of succumbing to it. When that is the case, democracy finds it difficult to realize its ultimate values. If it needs science at this point to fashion a new world it is no different from the way a sculptor must respect the laws of gravity or a painter the quality of colours.

As democracy in its truest sense requires the union of art and science, it is obviously a very difficult exercise. Democracy took decades to attain working order but it still retains its contrived and delicate nature. Like every fragile object, built of the rarest material, it must be watched over night and day. It cannot let itself be compromised by the continuous threat that chauvinism, racism, or, indeed, unbridled economic favouritism pose.

Not surprising then that all other forms of political order, such as monarchy, ethnicity, dictatorship, apartheid and theocracy are so easy to practise. As none of them have fraternity on their agenda, they can crisscross geography and history with such facility. If there was slavery in Greek times, it appeared again more recently in pre-Civil War America. For those who are not the favoured 'us' of these societies, there is just one option. Accept the supremacy of the current dispensation and make oneself as inconspicuous as possible.

This is why Bruno Bauer, a Jew himself, advised in his famous tract, *The Jewish Question*, that those of his faith ought to behave like Christians, or the Gentiles. In a similar fashion, Hindu sectarians advise Muslims to merge with them by dropping their Islamic ways. The blacks and coloured people of South Africa could not change their physical features to look like the whites and hence the apartheid regime ordained strict separation. Doubtless these labels and attitudes had enough approval behind them to make them work, but democracy would have none of it.

Democracy has been made to look easy, as most countries in the contemporary world flaunt this designation. Some of the most odious and non-representative governments give themselves very democratic nomenclatures. They either call themselves a constitutional republic, or a democratic republic, or a peoples' democracy, or use some other cognate term. If challenged, they would either demonstrate their credentials by the fact that they can gather multitudes in the public square; or stage elections when there is no opposition party in sight; or point to the hero leader on top as the object of popular veneration.

No wonder democracy appears so ordinary and simple to work. By this logic there is democracy everywhere, from Syria to Libya to Egypt to North Korea, China and Iraq. The question that still remains is: why do the leaders of these political orders want to be known as democrats? Why do they not take pride in what they actually are: ethnicist, theocratic, monarchic, dictatorial and so on? Why should they insist on calling their regimes a democracy when 'fraternity' is farthest from their agenda?

Though these regimes would deny it, they are actually most envious of what democracies in the western world have been able to achieve at the material and human level. This makes it impossible for them to attack democracy openly without losing face everywhere. So the best they can do is to declare that theirs is also a democracy, albeit of a different kind, one that mirrors the facts on the ground. Assad, Mubarak, Gaddafi, Castro, the Kims of North Korea and several others took this route to justify their claims to being democratic and 'of the masses'.

The success of western democracies is difficult to ignore. Contrary to the opinion that is gaining ground in some quarters today, efficiency is an outcome of democracy. Look at most police states. The potentate has no idea that an overthrow is imminent till it walks in through the main gates of the palace. In these regimes there is loyalty but little efficiency. Democracy's successes are there to see, even at the economic and organizational levels. Unfortunately, those who have benefited from all of this often forget their own history and the amount of hard work it took to make western societies look the way they do now. If civil rights, universal health and education and social insurance are taken for granted today in these countries it is only because they once had artists, and people of vision, who carved them into the social edifice. The hammer was constantly in use to break free from the initial conditions that these democracies found themselves in at the start.

John Rawls, the late Harvard philosopher, once said that liberal democracy works best in a situation of mild scarcity (Rawls 1971: 127). He did not push this point as hard as he should have. If he had, he would have realized that it is not the absolute content of poverty that defeats liberal democracy but the lack of security that citizens enjoy which undermines proper democratic political representation. One might say that a poor country will always have poor public services, but that is not a necessary axiom. Poverty as a starting point does not mean that it should be the end point as well. The only way to beat this vicious cycle is to hope that one day we will have statesmen who will think democratically and set up high-calibre public institutions that would make patrons look silly and out of place.

Neither Europe, nor America, nor Canada, nor Singapore, were prosperous to begin with. Sweden was desperately poor in the 1930s when it suddenly came up with visionaries who charted the route to prosperity. Most people think that Sweden was always rich, but this is historically inaccurate. Neither did anybody give the Basque region of Spain a chance after Franco died. Once again, visionaries came to the fore and made Basque rise from the ashes. This is also the story of Tommy Douglas of Saskatchewan, Canada, as well as of the Victorian Radicals of nineteenth-century England. This is what human agency is about in true historical terms. In most contemporary discussions this aspect is cast aside in the name of 'expediency' (or the pragmatism of the given). In the Stalinist years, human agency was ignored while structure and necessity were exacted (see Thompson 1958: 92-3).

The Artist as Elite: Democracy's Visionaries

For every true artist there are legions of imitators, followers and disciples who deepen the furrow that is already made by their leader. In a democracy too, it is the people with vision who open up fresh territories for lesser ones to consolidate after them. Such pathfinders come rarely; many of us may dream of being one but lack the gumption, determination and dedication for the purpose.

There is no clear reason when and why such exemplars appear on the historic stage, but when they do, posterity worships them with undiluted adoration. No amount of science, statistics or philosophical speculations can inform us of their arrival in advance, but once they make their mark, their presence is unforgettable. They are the 'elite' of democracy for without them none of the advances that we cherish today in our public life would have been possible.

Just as the hammer-wielding artist changes our ideas of aesthetics, democracy's elite fashion social institutions that would not come up naturally in the minds of people. Though there is so much of the artist in such leaders, yet there is one attribute that sets them apart. Unlike the pure artist for whom a painting or a sculpture is 'art for art's sake', a kind of 'purposefulness without purpose' (as Kant would suggest), democracy's elite has a clear purpose. Their goal is to establish a regime where fraternity rules, even if this is not easily appreciated at first sight by the majority. In addition, unlike some artists, they relish the thought of winning a popular mandate for their contributions.

It might seem unwarranted to transform the architects of fraternity from artists to the political elite. The two are not alike, and we have just pointed this out, yet to appreciate the boldness and the conviction of fraternity's vanguard it helps to begin by thinking of the artist. They are legitimately members of the elite because their urge to transform the here and now in line with the principles of fraternity do not rise naturally from the soil. Only after they have accomplished their tasks do ordinary people, the electorate, see the light.

What made these visionaries a success was that they thought independently, even loftily, but let themselves be judged by the people at election time. Those who do not find this proposition attractive are the ones who are spoilt by their own ideas of self-importance. They consider others no better than dumb, driven cattle who must conform for their own good. Such leaders are not democrats, but potentates and dictators who will suffer no course correction. For those of this kind, the world is their will and idea (as Schopenhauer would have it) and the rest had better conform.

A democrat with a vision is of a different genre. Such persons would seek popular sanction because they believe that if their measures are not finally accepted by the masses there must be something wrong with their prescriptions. Or perhaps, they have not tried hard enough, for it takes grit to go against hardened positions and values of the past. This is why these leaders, the artists of their times, are not afraid of facing the voters because they know that their programmes are only as good as their appreciation at the popular level. Thus while they contest the hardy logic of the given, their aim is to supplant the existing with something superior that wins the hearts and minds of the people. If this requires course correction, then so be it.

All of this is possible because those who are democracy's elite have an added refinement which must not be overlooked. While they strive to see the 'them' in 'us' and establish policies that influence events in that direction, they are not like the rest of us. They stand apart even as they despise strata differences; they lead even as they aspire to make their followers much like them. It is their extraordinary ability to empathize on a collective scale that makes them democracy's elite and fraternity's vanguard.

Democracy needs its elite to make people realize that aspirations for the future are grander than the needs of the present. Maximizing the given will not bring in fraternity, though it might help one section get the better of some other. Maximizing the given can do well with journeymen, but to address aspirations where no flower is born to blush unseen requires a political elite. Such a class of elite is democratic not just because they have a 'fraternal vision' but also because they are committed to periodic elections where others can judge their worth.

It is this combination that makes the elite of democracy very different from other kinds of elite. Neither Nietzsche's Superman or Overman, nor Pareto's lions, nor also the Proletarian vanguard of Lenin would subject themselves to a popular mandate. As this elite of democracy must necessarily combat what is present and yet carry enough conviction to face an electorate, their functioning must be transparent. They are above the rest but with nothing to hide.

We have already mentioned some of the great contributions made to democracy by those who swung a hammer at reality instead of merely mirroring it. To revive our memories, I shall here mention only two such transformations that were brought about by the interventions of such an elite force. The first is the abolishing of untouchability by law in India. The second is the establishment of adult franchise in democratic societies everywhere.

To understand the magnitude of the contribution that Indian leaders made to democracy by abolishing untouchability, keep in mind the conditions that had to be overruled. The given reality in the period till India became independent was one where certain castes were not permitted to access certain spaces, or to gain socially valuable skills. Yet, from Gandhi to Nehru to Ambedkar we needed an elite brigade to fight against this given social reality. They were not daunted by the fact that untouchability had the sanction of the scriptures or that it had been a recognized practice among Hindus for centuries.

Democracy was a familiar word by the early nineteenth century in Britain, but was for long confined to certain affluent classes. Today, it is hard to believe that this could have ever been the case. Yet democracy suffered this ignominy for decades without knowing any better. It needed the nineteenth-century Victorian radicals, the elite of that period, to bring in universal franchise and put to an end the privileges of the propertied classes. Like Gandhi and Nehru who had nothing to gain personally by eradicating poverty, neither did British leaders who sought to universalize privileges hitherto limited to a few. In both cases, the elite had no taste for maximizing their fortunes, political and otherwise, by flogging the given.

We are now ready to acknowledge the final move that converts the routine journeyman of democracy into an elite force and fraternity's vanguard. The given only tells us about needs that have to be met in order merely to reproduce the conditions of yesterday, perhaps at a slightly higher level. This is the ground that most politicians are happy to play on, which is why they harp on 'needs'.

The elite, however, are thinking more in terms of 'aspirations' that are not to be found empirically in everyday life. They are in the minds of people and can be accessed through empathy. Aspirations give an indication of the forward movement that is waiting to happen should the elite of calling dare to put them in practice. When these aspirations become nodes of inspirations, democracy gets ready to accept fraternity in a full-blown form.

Schematically then,

1. Democracy is challenged at the start because human beings lack the spirit of fraternity in their given state. Instead, they spontaneously divide among themselves and tend to project these distinctions as 'natural';

2. Democracy must necessarily contest these popular perceptions of reality for it is founded on the principle of 'fraternity' that cannot suffer the naturalization of cultural and economic differences;
3. Therefore, the given must not be mirrored or pandered to, which is what makes democracy so delicate and difficult to practise;
4. Consequently, it will need exceptional people with vision who can break the stranglehold of the everyday givens and the knowledges they carry;
5. For which reason, democracy has always relied on elite interventions in order to realize the potentials that are embodied in fraternity;
6. This elite is driven by people's 'aspirations' and is not satisfied with merely meeting 'needs', as they want to go beyond what exists;
7. None of this would be possible if one were only listening to the people or serving the given or even hoping to maximize it;
8. Because fraternity is their guiding credo, the elite must be one of calling, disinterested in personal aggrandizement, and hence committed to being judged in periodic elections;
9. Democracy was put in this world to alter human nature and not pander to it.

Plan of the Book: Advocating the Hammer

In the following pages, the consequences of elite interventions in democracy will first be elaborated upon. In doing this we shall roam the western world to demonstrate that what we consider today to be the given conditions of these societies were not always that way. After that we shall concentrate our attention primarily on India, beginning with how Gandhi made a difference to the way we thought about society. I shall show that Gandhi, loincloth notwithstanding, was the kind of 'elite citizen' that India could not have done without.

From then on, this book will elaborate on the many instances when the Indian state succumbed to the politics of the given in the name of democracy. The attempt all the while is to prove that democracy needs leaders to show the way, even as it needs the people to evaluate them. It is a balance of these two forces that makes democracy worthwhile or else it descends to a play of numbers, or a dull obedience to the rule of law. In both cases, politics becomes the prisoner of the given.

From time to time we shall return to the significance of establishing fraternity through the universalization of health and education. The reason these two aspects of social welfare are singled out arises from the belief that they make the maximum contribution towards establishing fraternity. Also, there is a need to counter those intellectuals who believe that the cost-benefit calculus can serve in these domains as well. Their arguments have a scientific gloss but they forget that democracy's first commitment is to fraternity. Further, it is also often argued that we can have two systems of medical care and education: one for the rich and the other for the poor. The dangers of this will be dilated upon later, but it is necessary to warn readers that we compromise 'fraternity' once we allow this kind of dualism to colour our perspective.

It is for all these reasons that the impact of democracy's elite can best be seen in the way societies have handled health and education. One could add to that other public facilities like energy, transportation, housing and so on, but health and education will still stand above all else in their importance. Without health facilities, as we shall see in a later chapter, the poor live in perpetual fear and can slide into abject poverty with a single episode of illness. Without universal education and access to gathering socially valuable skills, the past of a family will repeat itself, leaving little room for individual excellence.

Important as health and education are, we cannot allow issues such as migration, informal labour, urban squalor and community tensions to remain as our givens. Even if it is conceded that the universalization of health and education is the leading factor it is necessary to make special provisions for these other issues too. Slums need not be a necessary accompaniment of migration; neither must caste and religious wars be the first-order referents for sorting out disparities. Health and education should receive primacy but they should be accompanied by a thoroughgoing rejection of the given on a variety of fronts.

The domain assumption in placing health and education at the fore is that if these aspirations are met, labour degradation, slums and rural squalor will be gradually eased out. It has been repeatedly recorded, and we shall return to this later, that illness not only forces millions into poverty every year, but that they live on the edge in fear of their future. Poor education too lowers the earning capacity of people and they cannot perform upto potential. This too is a much recorded fact. Put in place universal health and education policies as twin drivers of social reform and watch backwardness cede ground. Nothing happens at one go, nor is it that there will be no mistakes and failures on the way; but that is the route to take and one can learn as one goes along.

Hopefully, this exercise will put in perspective the low calculations of those who gain legitimacy by claiming that they are listening to the people. From caste and religious politics, to piecemeal measures for keeping the poor alive, to tinkering with the economy, the larger vision of 'fraternity' is blanked out. The reason such political maneouvres get by without too much opposition is that they appear to fall in line with efforts people make to maximize their given location in the social structure. Democracy, however, comes into its own when people emerge as citizens and when the given is transformed to serve 'fraternity'.

CHAPTER II

By the Elite, For the Citizens, Of the Citizens: The Vanguards of Democracy

If democracy is meant to change the given and if we postulate that the prime movers in this direction are the 'elite of calling', it is necessary to substantiate this controversial argument. The empirical details, for this purpose, originate in Europe, primarily Britain, and we in India are familiar with the history of the country that colonized us for over 150 years. When we recall the personages who contributed most to the enlargement of fraternity and formed its vanguard, what is of note is that nearly all of them hailed from an affluent and privileged background and initiated policies that were not in their immediate interests. They were also the far-sighted visionaries who established universal health and education in Europe. It is because such basic welfare services were provided to citizens that, over time, prosperity came to these societies and a middle class emerged. Consequently, the role of patronage was undermined as citizens could now access basic social goods directly. Interestingly, in all these cases, the 'elite of calling' initiated such moves and sometimes persevered till these ideals were accomplished in practice.

For all those who believe that in a democracy it is people, or the masses, that make a difference, ponder over this one. There is nobody in the world who likes to pay income tax, unless, of course, the person is a shaggy-haired, tweedy professor or Warren Buffet. But income tax exists in every democratic country; it is that one thing which is as certain as the inevitability of death.

Nor have people, for that matter, clamoured for the legislative reforms that democracy has given us. There were no loud voices from the ground level against child labour, or for minimum wages, or for public education and health. When these measures first saw light in Europe and Britain, it was not because of popular pressure or mass mobilization. They came into being because leaders, many of them aristocrats and business magnates, fought for them. By thinking of society as a whole—not just of the poor, or the rich—the elite in these countries actually brought about a revolution.

. This sounds contradictory. How can the elite deliver to the masses? Yet, as I will try and explain, this is exactly how the best democracies in the world evolved. All elites, obviously, don't qualify. I am only thinking of those members of the elite who believe that the best way to handle poverty is not to devise special programmes for the poor, but to include them in the ambit of citizenship. Once this happens, rich or poor, everybody has quality access to public goods such as health, education and energy. When education and health are delivered at quality levels, the training of doctors and teachers improves tremendously. The poor, of course, benefit from this enlarged pool of realized talent, but so do the better-off. It is only then that a country can legitimately claim to be developed; democracy, after all is not just about the vote, it is also about citizenship. This is an aspect we often lose sight of in India. We might be the world's largest democracy, but sometimes this accolade distracts us from thinking clearly about our future as citizens.

Thinking Big, Thinking Society: Democracy by the 'Elite of Calling'

In the previous chapter we questioned the popular view that democracies are made by the people. We now hope to take this argument further with empirical substantiation. The advances that citizenship made in history were not on account of pressure from the demotic masses but because Europe was fortunate in producing an unusual class of elite.

Comfortable and assured of their status, many members of this elite could rise beyond their birth and privilege and think big in politics. Their concerns were much larger than those dictated by specific personal class, status or economic interests. There have been disagreements about whether their policies were right or wrong, but what cannot be controverted is that they did not allow the administration to nurse sectional claims. In most accounts, those who belong to this section are either considered soft and effete snobs, or dictatorial hardliners drawing inspiration from Nietzsche and other think-alikes and, in most cases, that is true. This should not blind us to the fact that there are other kinds of elite too—the 'elite of calling'. If we rejoice in our freedoms, in our modernity and our democracy, it is because the nineteenth-century British and European democratic elite made them possible. These have been their gifts to humankind and all because they were motivated by the idea of the 'public'.

The truth is that poor people cannot revolt on their own. If they do, such expressions of rebellion are short-lived. The last great uprising of this kind in Europe was the Captain Swing rick-burning incidents of early nineteenth-century England. This movement was ruthlessly crushed in a matter of weeks and its leaders were jailed, exiled or hanged. Numerical superiority does not always guarantee success. When the sans-culottes of France joined the revolution, it was well after Louis XVI had been undermined and discredited by a combination of nobles and clerics. The poor lacked the staying power, even in Paris, which is why Danton wondered in despair, 'Where have the sans-culottes gone?'[1]

The reason democracy is the best system of governance is not just because people can vote, but that they participate as citizens. What then is a citizen that is more than being a voter? T.H. Marshall put it rather well when he said that citizenship confers the status of equality to all citizens as a rock-solid foundation, on which structures of inequality can then be built (Marshall 1950; also Marshall 1975). In simple words, citizens should be able to overcome the accidents of birth in order to equally access socially valuable assets. For this to happen, in concrete terms, an ordinary citizen from a poor family should receive education, health care and infrastructural supports in order to have a fair chance of competing against those born in more affluent homes.

What separates the 'elite of calling' or the 'citizen elite' from being just privileged is that they force the state to deliver public services like health, education and energy, at *quality levels,* to every citizen regardless of class. They know that any programme that is aimed to benefit only the poor is bound to perform poorly, whether it is the Antyodaya of yesterday, or the Mahatma Gandhi National Rural Employment Guarantee Act (or MGNREGA) and the Public Distribution System (primarily designed to provide food and fuel to those below the poverty line) of today. Ironically, in all such cases, the more deprived and impoverished a region is, the more wanting the performance of these programmes (Khera 2011; see also Rothstein 2006). Nor would this 'elite of calling' subscribe to chamber-of-commerce-like recommendations that benefit only the moneyed and the

---

[1] Sans-culottes were the urban poor who formed the bulk of the French Revolutionary Army in the initial stages of the uprising but lost in importance after 1795. They were called 'sans-culottes' because they could not afford the silk breeches, or culottes, that the wealthier bourgeois partisans of the French Revolution wore. The best that the sans-culottes could do was to wear mended pantaloons (or trousers).

privileged. Instead of advocating that wealth should 'trickle down' they would rather it be 'pushed up'.

The elite, for the purposes of our argument, come from well-to-do backgrounds, if not actually rich. They are influential from the start and may derive this also from being professionally successful. When democracy calls out to the elite for furthering its cause, the ones that answer are those who are willing to 'destroy the conditions from which they sprung' (Williamson 1961: 394). There are many elite theories from Nietzsche to Pareto to C. Wright Mills, but they do not explain a Russell, a Grey, a Peel, a Disraeli, or even Louis Bonaparte and Bismarck.

The members of this elite category are not do-gooders of the philanthropic kind. Nor are they the same as those who are renowned in their professions as lawyers, accountants, engineers, intellectuals or any other. The elite of calling are different. They contribute to social development because they believe that in the fullness of time it is to the collective advantage of all citizens, themselves included. To steer society to this stage they are willing to forgo gratification over the short term.

No doubt, the 'citizen elite' will be drawn from the ranks of the established elite, yet they are exceptional individuals in that they can see the big picture. They may be philanthropic, well connected and affluent, but that does not define them entirely. In fact, middle-class individuals can also be elite of the kind necessary for forwarding citizenship if they were to go against the tendencies of most people of their background who prefer the given, provided it is tweaked in their favour.

This 'elite of calling' does not come into being from the ordinary laws of society or politics. It is not a pre-existing group, but as individuals they often combine their energies because it is the calling that summons them to assemble. While the activities of the professional, administrative and intellectual elite can be plotted sociologically, the elite of calling cannot be understood in the same fashion.

There is no law, for example, that can explain the compulsions that prompted the nineteenth-century British elite of calling to act the way they did; or indeed the actions of Louis Bonaparte, Otto von Bismarck or even Mao Zedong. What, however, differentiates the democratic elite from the radical elite is that the former is committed to furthering democracy and would not accept power under any other circumstance, least of all in a totalitarian regime. Contrary to the usual notion of elite (from Nietzsche to Pareto, Mosca and Mills) who ruled for themselves, the elite of calling rule for others. Members of this 'elite of calling' dedicate their lives to the people, but they are not made by the people. Yet they are not autocratic patrons for they allow themselves to be judged periodically by the electorate. Contrast this with what Louis XVI said: 'It is legal because I wish it.'

To go against one's immediate interest can only happen when a mission, a calling, captures one's imagination. Only this can help us understand why certain members of the elite acted the way they did to enlarge democracy. They were answering to a higher voice: a drum was beating inside their heads but their cousins couldn't hear it. History does not routinely throw up privileged people who are willing to go against their family and class interests.

As democracy is willing to challenge the established given it forces us to think differently. This is why democracy has to be treated very carefully for it goes against all previous forms of governance in history. While leaders in a democracy set the pace and the agenda, their respective policies are always on trial and could be voted out. This is why if any advance is made in a democracy it is always because of the leaders, never the people. If leaders come up with bland policies, the masses can do little about it. Therefore, if some countries have gone ahead and advanced fraternity, while others have failed to do so, the blame should fall squarely on the rulers and not on the backwardness of the people.

Walt Whitman once said: 'Produce great men and the rest will follow.' This adage has certainly passed the test of time.

Here is a list of some great people, 'elite of calling'—just consider what they have achieved.

Historical Reminiscences: The Contributions of Europe's Elite of Calling

Without Earl Grey, the Factory Act in Britain would have failed in 1833; without Robert Peel, the aristocratic British prime minister, the Corn Law would have lived longer; without Henry Brougham, the Education Bill would not have made a beginning in 1837. These efforts were energized in later years by Disraeli, William Forster, Richard Cross and so on, and they all came from the privileged bracket.

The list actually is of course much longer. But what is remarkable is that none of these laws and provisions were in the immediate interest of the 'elite of calling'. They believed in them and fought for them for the sake of society. As a consequence, for the longest time now, quality public health care and education are holy cows that no European government would dare sacrifice: not even under American pressure.

European democrats, both conservative and liberals, fought for this outcome, step by step, from the nineteenth century onwards. They put in place the first templates of citizenship which were later filled out in two big bursts: one between the wars, and the other after the defeat of fascism. But without the early contributions of these nineteenth-century democrats Europe would not look like what it does today. Many of them were members of the elite but had to go against their own kind to set in place the first principles of citizenship.

It is because of the exertions of such people that to be European today implies quality access to health, education and social welfare benefits. India is not Europe, but we can have a life-changing dream run if we learn from Europe the values of citizenship. Europe, after all, was not always so developed. Nor was Europe as efficient and, on the whole, as corruption-free as it is today. Nor is it true that the advances in developed parts of Europe were on account of working-class radicalism or because of a popular groundswell from below (see Rothstein, Samanni, Teorell 2010). One might refer to cobblers and tavern-keepers in nineteenth-century England and France who ruminated about revolt and were often 'crowd leaders' (Hobsbawm 1998: 47). Effective though they may have been as rabble-rousers, they were unable to provide political leadership.

Elites make good revolutionaries too. Lenin's father, Iliya Nikolayevich Ulyanov, was a near-aristocrat with an important position in the Russian court. Angel Castro was one of the biggest sugar planters of Cuba who did brisk business with America; he was also Fidel's father. Mao Zedong was a middle-class professional, but he was buoyed by true-blue elites like Ye Jiyaning, Lin Biao, Nier Rongzhen and Zhou Enlai.

The Suffragette Movement of the 1870s, which advocated, sometimes violently, women's voting rights, was also headed by well-to-do activists who could have stayed home, sitting pretty after attending finishing schools. Millicent Fawcett, an important suffragette leader, came from an affluent background and had a rich father who was the owner of an enterprise producing agricultural equipment. Emmeline Pankhurst—a proponent of using violence, if necessary, for this cause (the much written about 'Matchgirls' Strike')—was a daughter of a rich merchant and was sent to the prestigious French academy École Normale Supérieure to complete her elitist education. After her return to England, she was all set to play the role of the society coquette, but changed plans midway. Her parents had friends in intellectual circles and had once participated in anti-slavery movements, but the family's turning to politics was not dictated by self-interest. Nor were their many friends—from Eleanor Marx to members of the Fabian Society and the Bloomsbury Circle—dictated to by similar concerns.

When the 1831 Reforms Act was eventually passed in Britain it benefited the ordinary people: the tradesman, the farmer, the worker and the middle class who were fed up with aristocratic privileges. Yet, let us remember that those who gained most from the passing of this Act, or later the repeal of the Corn Law, were not the ones who initiated this process and saw it to its fruition. The Corn Law, for example, clearly helped the rich landlords of Britain for it protected the price of agricultural produce from external competition, particularly from Europe.

Even the withdrawal of the Poor Law of the Speenhamland system[2] was 'advocated by the intellectual few, and not demanded by the popular voice' (ibid.: 385).

The 1833 Factory Act in Britain came into force under the prime ministership of none other than Earl Grey, with the able help of Michael Thomas Sadler who was an industrialist. Along similar lines, Lord Russell, a Whig aristocrat, fought to abolish the Corn Law, though it benefited large landowners, including members of his family. In fact, Robert Peel, another well-born prime minister and Russell's predecessor, had to pack up his cabinet and leave for he fought too hard against the Corn Law.

However, it was Robert Peel's conservative government that passed the 1844 Factory Act, which limited the use of child labour and spelt out the conditions under which women could be employed. Lord Canning, a rich barrister's son, repealed an earlier Labour Act that did not allow agitations which combined the demand for higher wages, better working conditions and shorter hours. Samuel Plimsoll was the son of a rich coal-miner, but that did not stop him from devising the famous Plimsoll line that ships had to bear so that they would not sink from being overloaded. When the advantages of this became clear, Plimsoll's popularity soared; he almost destabilized Disraeli.

Or let us take the example of Disraeli himself. He was a conservative, half his cabinet was packed with lords, yet he steered the Factory Act of 1875 through Parliament, as well as the Artisans Dwelling Act and the Public Health Act. With these laws in place Disraeli's government made sure that workers would not be subjected to more than fifty-six hours' work per week, that they would live in decent dwellings, and, with the general citizenry, be able to access health services. Richard Cross, the architect of the Public Health bill, was himself a large landowner from Lancashire.

---

[2] The Poor Law of the Speenhamland system refers to the decision taken in late eighteenth-century Britain to provide relief to impoverished families in proportion to the price of bread and the number of children. It derives its name from the fact that this matter was debated in the Pelican Inn in Speenhamland, Berkshire.

Need we recall the efforts of Louis Bonaparte who set up public hospitals and amusement parks for the poor, or Baron von Bismarck who is considered to be the father of social insurance the world over?

The poorer classes cannot represent themselves successfully. They are far too impoverished to pursue their case beyond the here and now. The middle classes usually plot it right, but it is only their wheel that gets the grease. The elite, however, have the potentiality to take history forward. Did the workers complain against how children were put to work, even sent to toil in mines? Did they set up barricades to limit the exploitation of women workers? Not really. In fact, workers actually resented some of these measures when they were being contemplated, most glaringly, in the instance of child labour.

It was the elite that legislated on most of these subjects. These were people of aristocratic backgrounds or bred on industrial and commercial wealth. Indeed, many of them were also members of conservative parties, and yet as elites they realized that they had a social responsibility that went well beyond their sectional welfare.

The sentiments of the people count when they are asked to judge a policy on Election Day. Lord Grey came back as prime minister in 1832 after his Reform Bill was thrown out in 1831 because the popular cry on the streets was: 'The Bill, the whole Bill, and nothing but the Bill.' Once again, the people reacted to a leader's initiative. While votes do matter, they are always cast after the politician has made the first move, never before it. In fact, Disraeli's support of the 1867 Reform Act was aptly likened to a 'leap in the dark' (Rich 1977: 152). He took the risk and acted. The Education Act in 1870 was not an outcome of popular pressure either, though it made the first big move to provide quality education for all.

The leaders of the Third Republic in France took a similar leap in the dark when they decided to give the concept of laicite a firm foundation in the country. The term 'laicite' is a much more uncompromising version of 'secularism' for it absolutely prohibits demonstrations of religion in the public domain.

Therefore, when performing their stated social roles, from politicians to bureaucrats and from teachers to students, nobody is allowed to wear anything that is religious in connotation. This process began in France by banning all demonstrations of religious adherence from public life. The Catholic Church was the target but neither the Pope nor the Catholic people of France were consulted before this measure was introduced.

Voters not Citizens: Advancing Fraternity in India

Therefore, whether it is the left or the right, it is the elite that call the shots. If we are convinced in contemporary India, as we seem to be, that democracy is the best way to get ahead, then we must take a leaf out of the European experience. We must be careful not to take the whole book, for there are many blots in the history of Europe, even Western Europe. Surely, with the gift of hindsight we can avoid them. Why should we imitate the west when we can learn from them? Once the signboards are up, why should we fall into the same holes and booby traps that they were victims of?

If Europe had not been fortunate enough to have this class of elite, their democracies would have been in a primitive state, with a thin rendition of citizenship. In fact, had such dramatic developments not taken place when they did, most people would not even imagine that democracy was capable of so much. Today's welfare state in Europe is an outcome of such elite interventions. It has grown over the last hundred years, but the major breakthroughs started in the nineteenth century. The view that the state should be citizen-centric and provide for public goods is no longer just a political statement in Europe. For most contemporary Europeans this attribute of the state also stands out as a cultural marker. Today, whether conservative or liberal, being European is to accept this heritage that culminated in the welfare state.

When we think of India, the question of whether it is possible to be a voter and yet not a full citizen takes on a much starker appearance. Citizenship is about quality of life, and of being able to improve one's life chances and realize one's ambitions in a free and open system. Citizenship cannot be real if the majority of our voters go to bed hungry. We need not get into statistics at this point for they make even more depressing reading. It is possible then to be a full-fledged voter and an underserved citizen. It is this dichotomy that we need to overcome in a hurry. While on this subject, a Muslim victim of the 2002 ethnic carnage in Gujarat tellingly remarked, 'If taking away our right to vote will bring us peace, we would prefer that right now.'

The fundamental law of politics is that rulers act and the ruled react. This truth has held in all hitherto existing societies: it is carbon-dated, weather-proofed and tropicalized. The difference democracy makes is that it lets the people judge its leaders, though only after they have already acted. When an elected leader advocates a policy in the name of popular will, it nearly always is a big lie. By using people as a cover, ungainly politicians have found happiness in parliaments everywhere. India could be a good example of this fact.

So, if it is political leaders who decide almost everything, it is they, and not the masses, who should take the blame for a dysfunctional democracy. The people can only change allegiance from one set of political masters to another and have no other choice. To make a difference we need an 'elite of calling', or the 'citizen elite', to emerge from the rubble. How much longer must India wait for that elite revolution?

What puzzles most observers about India is the continuing existence of such grinding poverty though the poor vote in impressive numbers in every election? Why can't the majority of the poor vote the bad people out and get the good ones in? As numbers count in a democracy, the sheer numerical preponderance of the poor should make a difference. However, that is not a fair statement, for a voter can only choose between what is available. The price of entering politics in India and many other underdeveloped countries is very high. It is not just money power but physical power too that makes it nearly impossible for the right kind of candidates to fight elections. Consequently, we do not get the leaders we deserve. In the final analysis, the leaders must deserve us. That is the true test of a democracy.

Society, and least of all politics, is not arithmetic. It is not just about numbers. The choices we make at election time parallel our consumer behaviour in the marketplace. Just as monopolists raise the price of a commodity through advertising, the entry price into politics today has been raised by the ability to use violence, ride violence and handle large sums of money. If monopoly practices rule out our dream car, the price for entering politics effectively rules out our dream candidate.

This in turn encourages patronage-based politics where things get done for loyal and lucky clients if the benefactor looks kindly at them. Universal norms are not attractive for it takes too long to deliver to the poor what they urgently require. They cannot wait for the revolution to come, or for files to be bureaucratically pursued. This is where patrons can make a difference. The poor, therefore, really do not deserve the leaders they get, and nor do most of us.

Here then is the problem: how do we in India get a start in truly realizing citizenship? If the poor are incapable of fighting for themselves, if the rich can only act as patrons, and if the middle classes are too self-obsessed and constantly threatened by real or imaginary assaults on their status, then where is the alternative? Moreover, our middle classes consist of a very thin crust, and not an independent one either (see Gupta 2000). They are not like the poor, but they know that they are precariously positioned on higher, but still shaky ground. Come to think of it, a society gets a broad-based middle class only after true citizenship is secured across strata and occupational groups.

Who would not like to see a healthy, happy and prosperous India where the poor are not just kept alive, but, instead, where abject poverty is abolished? The difference lies in what we believe would be the best way to arrive at this desired state of affairs. Some might advocate a laissez-faire, trickle-down approach, others may believe that the electoral process would bring about this transition, others might even think of a violent revolution. There indeed should be a revolution, but of a different kind. It is one that is led by the 'elite of calling', which takes fraternity as its lodestar. It is not as if such a person should be rich or laden with family inheritance. Though they often come from such backgrounds, that need not always be the case. Think of Mahatma Gandhi and the situation should clear itself. Undoubtedly, the very poor would hardly ever be able to fill the ranks of the elite of calling; but if democracy enlarges fraternity, poverty will become a thing of the past—at least, the wretched poverty we see in parts of India and Africa.

'Elite of Calling': India's Record

Believe it or not, there was a time when India had a true elite of calling. Nehru and many of the early leaders in India were members of this class, though most of us do not recognize them as such. When a 'mixed economy' and non-alignment were the pillars of our national policy, nobody consulted the people. Nehru, in fact, went against many Congress members in pushing the Hindu Marriage Act. Come judgement time, the voters seemed to prefer this mix over others on offer and that is why the Congress kept getting elected. Nehru was not just asking grown-ups to eat their vegetables, he was giving them a lot more to chew on.

The early Indian national leaders need not have initiated social reform the way they did, nor woven such programmes into the Freedom Movement. It is not as if struggles against colonialism always bring in a democracy, in most cases they do not. So if it happened in India, it is because we were fortunate to have an elite of calling during that fateful period leading to our Independence. In later years, several prominent politicians rose to eminence, became 'elite' too, but they did not have the 'calling'. Instead, they operated on the logic of immediate political gratification and they stooped to the here and now of the next election.

Nehru's grandson, Rajiv Gandhi, did not consult Panchayati Raj representatives either when structuring the 74th Amendment Bill. Did the BJP listen to the people of India before demolishing the Babri Masjid mosque? It did not; it only hoped to capitalize on the given ethnic sentiments of the Hindus. Is the MGNREGA scheme (guaranteeing minimum rural employment) in place because of popular will, or is it there as a test of administrative will? In a true democracy the outcomes of all such initiatives are tested in elections, but they do not begin their careers in town squares, bus stops and tea shops, not even in village chaupals.

Interestingly, when a policy goes well then the credit for it redounds on the leader. Yet, popular will and too much democracy are blamed for every piece of botched politics and administrative inaction. When Rajiv Gandhi neutered the court judgement on Shah Bano, it was, he claimed, because of the popular will of Muslims (those 'other' people); when the lock on Babri Masjid was broken, it was on account of the will of the majority; when riots in Gujarat happened, it was because the Hindu masses rose spontaneously.

Or take the Commonwealth Games. The people of Delhi were never consulted about its feasibility, yet when preparations fell behind schedule, the blame for it was on the 'excess' of democracy. The truth is that when slums have to be demolished and if there is pecuniary gain in sight, then it gets done right away—sometimes even just to facilitate the starting of a private school. A quick look at the map of Delhi will show resettlement colonies miles away from the centre of the capital. Not just slums, if it is in the interest of politicians and the price is right, even better-off people are not spared.

When it comes to caste politics the tendency to blame the people is the greatest. The main reason politicians get away with this lie is that most intellectuals believe it to be true. But once again, politicians have set the stage and arranged all the props to conceal the fact that in terms of pure numbers no caste has enough votes to win an election to the legislature or Parliament. In which case, sheer empirical reality tells us that it has to take more than caste to swing an election in somebody's favour, but this detail goes unnoticed.

Caste might work at the Gram Sabha level, but not in larger constituencies where there are just too many jatis, of roughly the same size, jostling for power. Yet, as this simple factual detail is little known, it allows members of nearly every political party to endorse the role of caste in election strategizing. On this point at least, Lalu Yadav of the RJD, Digvijay Singh of the Congress, and Ravi Pratap Rudy of the BJP think alike. For all of them, when it comes to politics, caste is the hero. Sadly, many dalit leaders like Sushil Shinde, now home minister, and Mayawati, till recently chief minister of Uttar Pradesh, flog this caste formula as well. In the case of ethnic killings too politicians put the onus on the people, but not as convincingly as in the case of caste. This is because there is a mass of evidence, collected by national and international scholars, that reveals how religious riots in India begin their innings in political pavilions.

What separates colonialism from democracy is not that the former doesn't consult the people while the latter does. In both cases, it is the rulers that act. What, however, sets the two apart is that under foreign rule subjects cannot choose between leaders. This is where democracy makes a difference. Further, in a democracy there is at least another 'legitimate' political force in the wings: the opposition, both in fact and theory. In colonialism such a situation would be a contradiction in terms. But make no mistake: in neither case are people consulted.

Remember the tales of the Panchatantra and those of Akbar and Birbal. Recall also the fables of the Ramrajya when the king listened to his subjects. The fact that these are fables is simply because such cuddly things never happened. The king consulted his ministers, but as in all such arrangements, it was ruinous to oppose the monarch. Every piece of advice had to be aligned to the sovereign's will. That courtier did the best who understood the mind of the throne better than others. No prizes for guessing why this should sound familiar in India today. Human beings have identical failings across time and space.

India has a large elite class; there are the business elite, the professional elite, the real estate elite, the old moneyed elite, the new moneyed elite, but they are all busy looking after their own interests. That, in itself, is quite understandable, but so ordinary. Many members from this tribe are also in politics, some are even parliamentarians. Yet they do not qualify as members of the 'citizen elite' because they lack one critical attribute. They are either unmindful or unaware of how crucial fraternity is if one is to advance citizenship. There may be a few exceptions, very few, but that does not contradict the rule. Generally, they are of the kind that would play safe, maximize their given assets, and protect their position in society and not risk a thing. What a waste!

Had they been 'citizen elite' they would have acted and thought differently. They would have taken advantage of their starting position and striven to merge their horizons with those of the common person, particularly in the realms of health and education. This would bring about a greater identity of interests across classes enabling people to respect one another without a proper introduction. Citizenship is not just about voting; it is also about gaining access to state resources on an equal basis, both in law and in practice. This, as one might recall, is exactly what T.H. Marshall had in mind (Marshall 1950, 1975).

The Solar Economy and the Welfare State: Waiting for the Indian Elite

As the elite of calling are not people who think of the short term, they have a vision and are ready to go the distance to make it come true. They are prepared also to take the slings and arrows of their outraged relations as well as the frequent incredulity with which their views are initially received by the broader public. They do not expect an immediate return on their political investment because they are confident that such rewards await them in the long run. If we have not already

38 *Revolution from Above*

belaboured this issue enough, let us turn to Georges Bataille's discussion of the 'solar economy' to give it a seal of finality.

By the 'solar economy' Bataille was referring to a source of wealth creation that, like the sun, gave without thinking of what it could get in return. The sun shines even behind the clouds, even as the earth rotates on its axis. It just gives. This solar economy, like the rays of the sun, 'loses itself without counting, without consideration' (Bataille 1991: 75). He contrasts this with commonplace economy (ibid.) where ledger books are constantly being adjusted, as counting and cost-benefit analysis are continuously being pursued without a break.

When the sun shines without counting its good deeds then life emerges and 'lavishes without reason' (ibid.). When the state gives like the sun, citizens flourish, but when the state succumbs to commonplace economy, citizenship does not get the indulgence it requires to grow. In a commonplace economy if an investment does not yield returns in the short run, it is unwise to go ahead. If the state were to think 'commonplace economics' then Europe would not have had the universal health and educational system that it is so proud of today. Bo Rothstein (2010) demonstrates most persuasively that those states where welfare programmes work best are also the most prosperous ones. In contrast to the 'smallest size fits all' Libertarian notion, it is the stronger and more effective states that invest in the common good. Good governance, as many studies with global data have shown, is positively correlated with the size of government. This is not simply in terms of the number of functionaries it supports, but relates rather to how much it is willing to spend on social welfare (La Porta et al., 1999; Besley-Perrson 2011).

Clearly, citizens must first benefit from the largesse that the solar economy of the state provides in order to give back to it. This causality is clearly unidirectional as many European societies, from Sweden to Spain, grew in prosperity with the establishment of the welfare state. As all of this is recent history, even popular memory can testify to this. This is where the 'elite of calling' come in, to bring in some of the sunshine.

It is necessary for the state to provide health, education, a living wage and housing such that the standards of performance and skills go up in the long run. Commonplace economics that is concerned primarily with immediate returns in the short run is not suited for this purpose.

When ill health and unemployment can strike any time, the workers are ready to work for anything, even below minimum wages for hours on end. How can we justify the fact that about 76 per cent of health costs in India are borne by individuals (also known as 'out of pocket' expenses)? This is about the highest in the world. When workers are so vulnerable it naturally tempts entrepreneurs to flog cheap labour rather than innovate and raise levels of productivity. Sadly, the rate at which the formal sector is sourcing out its operations to the informal sector only goes to show how attractive a low wage option can be (*Report on Conditions of Work...2007*). To make matters worse, the skill sets of the working class are still at a low level (*Manpower Profile of India* 2005: table 2.3.1:143). This is not just a human resource statistic, but tells us a lot about how much work remains to be done in order to realize citizenship.

Even in the highly glamourized IT sector it has been noticed that the reason why Indian IT firms get international customers is because they charge 40-50 per cent less (NASSCOM-IDC 2006) than what their global competitors would. In fact, the Planning Commission in its approach paper of 2006 put on record that we need five times more PhDs in science and technology than we have today ('Towards Faster and more Inclusive Growth: An Approach to the Eleventh Five-Year Plan' 2006: 59-65). The same document also accepts the fact that government schools and hospitals do not function owing to lack of funds, amenities and sheer neglect.

Clearly, all the conditions are ready for the 'elite of calling' to emerge and take India forward. But where is this elite? Will it come up soon, before India records her 100th year? It is not possible to state when this 'elite of calling' will coalesce into a unit and have an effect on the democratic functioning of our society. But when it happens its effect can be felt like the rays of the sun in a solar economy (see also Robson 1957: 16).

It is not as if we are giving in to subjectivity when we admit that there is no sociological law that can predict when such an elite group will become active. The contributions of the elite can be measured objectively by the real advances they bring about in the content of citizenship. This is the real test and its results are out in the open and under the sun. What is critical is that members of this elite class spurn commonplace economics. Unlike merchants and book-keepers, the elite of calling rarely ask the question: 'Where is the money?' They know their priorities and will do what it takes to get there. The given does not constrain them as much as it challenges them to act. They know that it is only by addressing social problems on a grand scale that advances can happen.

India today has an elite class, but not the elite of calling. Members of India's favoured population do not yet realize that the best way of getting richer is to make society as a whole much better off. But to make this happen they must have a kind of missionary zeal for it is quite likely that they would not personally benefit from all their efforts during their lifetime. Sadly, India's elite today have committed themselves to commonplace economics and have no patience for the principles of the solar economy.

So for India to do better than what it is doing today we should not let growth figures mislead us for they do not always translate into development. But for that, India must somehow conjure up an elite of calling who would take our society into a regime where the solar economy rules. This would make it easier for people to access social assets such that the premise of equality of status (not income) that citizenship promises can be realized. People would be healthier, better educated and better trained. As a consequence Indian business people would have to change their ways. They would no longer be able to take advantage of a low wage economy to make a mark at the global level. They would be compelled to behave like entrepreneurs and raise productivity levels by investing in Research and

Development. Only then would our economy be truly developed and world-class.

When the solar economy is in full force its glare makes us colour-blind, race-blind and ethnically blind. It creates a kind of reciprocity that does not spring naturally in the human breast; fraternity, as we argued earlier, is not a natural condition (see also Rothstein 2011). As the solar economy shines abundantly and equally, differences between communities cease to be political resources that can be exploited at will by interested parties. The assumption here is that a solar economy is not worth a candle if it does not enforce universal laws universally.

When it comes to religious wars, ethnic strife and caste atrocities we must remember that these egregious incidents happen not because they are fired by popular will, but because politicians play on cultural cleavages to win votes. Though they do all this in the name of the people, let us remember that people are not professional Hindus, Muslims, Maharashtrians, Brahmins or Yadavas. They are worried about jobs, schools and food on the table. The politicians are professional ethnic and cultural chauvinists who use cultural differences to their advantage. That they often succeed in making nightmares come true is because the solar economy is not yet in operation. This allows great differences between people on account of the accidents of birth, and these often overlap with their cultural background. If a correlation such as this be made into a legitimate political weapon, then ethnic clashes are bound to emerge as if they had been ordained by culture.

It all depends on leadership and how it makes the administration function. Does it support the solar economy; or does it line up behind the politics of the given where each class and strata maximize their own advantage at somebody else's cost?

The Iron Law of Dystopia: Legitimizing the Politics of the Given

'The Politics of the Given' is a call for pragmatics where, even at the best of times, each section is furthering its own interests.

In an ideal situation, such endeavours could perhaps be carried out without stepping on the toes of others. Even if such a perfect scenario can be dreamt up, the fact is that if fraternity is not kept alive then society stops moving, or proceeds like an amoeba.

India cannot afford the luxury of such slow progress for then the forces of inertia catch up and stall any challenge to the given, in the name of order. The predictable takes over, in which case dreams have to be abandoned. Without dreams there is little hope of, first, establishing fraternity and then, second, of furthering it.

Let us not think of utopia as a fluffy, pointless concept especially after Karl Manneheim gave it body and substance with his masterly work on the subject (Mannheim 1936). A programme for the future is a utopia only if it is realizable, or else it is a fantasy. Utopia is not day-dreaming or whistling for the moon; it is about making a better future possible by deliberate interventions in democracy. In the ultimate analysis, a utopia is only as good as it takes fraternity forward, not lazily, but with determination and drive.

In this connection it is necessary also to remember that for Karl Mannheim an ivory tower scholar is no scholar at all. He did not dignify them by calling them ethereal specialists, 'heads in the cloud' aspirants after true knowledge, or anything like that. He was very blunt about it: any scholar who does not engage with reality should be exposed and shown the door. But this engagement with reality does not simply mean that the intellectual should join a political party; in fact, Mannheim believed that this step, though superficially attractive, might impose a rigid form of thinking that would hardly be worthy of a scholar. A true intellectual then is the one who can think beyond the given and works towards making utopias realizable. Only politicians who are among an elite of calling would be attracted to such people. When that happens, democracy is once again on the move.

We may now add another proposition. Though democracy made great advances in Europe, why is it that today we can hardly find anyone there who could be termed as belonging to an elite of calling? Is it because once the contributions have been made and the everyday lives of ordinary people have improved beyond what they could have imagined, complacency sets in? This then acts as a disincentive towards utopian thinking, preferring pragmatics instead. This is probably also the reason why many Europeans have forgotten the contributions of those who made their lives so prosperous and free. Indeed, so many advocate policies for the poorer parts of the world which their own democratic forebears fought against.

Democracy, therefore, has a hidden caveat. If it is not periodically surcharged with utopian impulses, there is a high likelihood that dystopia will set in. We may call this the 'iron law of dystopia'. As dystopia is the negative of everything that utopia stands for, it is a state of affairs that privileges the given in the name of caution and pragmatics. The way to combat dystopia is by keeping the utopia live and recharging it continuously through a critical perspective.

We are today no longer thinking as Thomas Moore did or as George Owen or even Karl Marx when we speak of utopias. True, these thinkers still set our imaginations on fire, but, as Mannheim clarified, vision that cannot be realized is mere cant or chicanery (ibid.: 182). Contemporary utopias need no longer be imaginary, for we now have a sound principle on which to stabilize them. Our subsequent discussion on Gandhi will arm us with the realization that for utopias to be credible today, fraternity must be twinned with non-violence. Earlier, history had not prepared us for such wisdom, but now it has, thanks to democracy and the many 'elite of calling' who took it forward.

When our utopian spirit slackens with the passage of time, it is not peace, the routine and the humdrum, that take over: actual dystopia steps in. When that happens, there is a slide backward and the gains of earlier utopias can be easily lost. Initially, there is a clear perception of this loss, but as dystopia deepens and consolidates itself, hope and optimism give way to the acceptance of the less than ordinary. This is why we must remain aware of 'the iron law of dystopia' before we run down those who think big and think society. If dystopias are to be kept at bay it is important never to let utopias wander into meaningless political sands.

It is true that certain utopias will not succeed. It would be foolish to deny this possibility. However, if they are imbued with the spirit of fraternity, then in spite of some drawbacks, they will take citizenship forward. To give up on utopian visions and to let the logic of the given take over is a sure recipe for inefficiency and sloth. We are already seeing this in India in the form of corruption, administrative sluggishness, and the unwillingness to bite the bullet and do what is right for society. Consequently, what we see everywhere in India is the tendency to play safe; we play safe on health and education; we play safe on innovation and industrial entrepreneurship; we play safe in our political calculations. Unsurprisingly, India offers us an example of dystopia on a grand scale, but we are conditioned by pragmatism not to object to it.

It is rather unfortunate that after Europe made such important advances in citizenship from the mid-nineteenth century onwards, not much has happened in this respect in the western world in recent decades. Why has a new generation of the 'citizen elite' not emerged? Europe illustrates what happens once dystopia sets in, for those who are in public life get easily complacent about their prosperity. They take the advances of the past for granted and forget the conditions that brought them about. Though there is no sociological way of forecasting when the elite of calling will emerge anywhere, one can at least articulate, when the conditions are ripe for such people to emerge. India certainly needs them urgently—but where are our 'elite of calling', our 'citizen elite?

CHAPTER III

Mahatma Gandhi: Ahimsa as an Elite Intervention

Without Gandhi, India may still have become free from the British, perhaps even earlier, but it would not have been a democracy. On many occasions Gandhi had to go against the popular mood and stand firmly by his beliefs and convictions, which were, in essence, liberal democratic in character. By overemphasizing his 'fakir' persona one tends to ignore Gandhi's influence on the major Articles of our Constitution. This document was not produced after discussions with the masses, or the people, but was essentially an 'elite' document. This is another reason one should look at the Mahatma as a 'citizen elite' or an 'elite of calling'. He changed the given conditions of India by fighting against untouchability, for women's emergence in public spaces and for minority protection, to name a few. While discussing Gandhi's emphasis on ahimsa we must accept his important contributions to the theory of democracy, particularly in terms of the importance of debate in the public sphere. For this reason, I have included a dialogue between Gandhi and Habermas in this chapter.

Mahatma Gandhi's image is so laden with references to his many eccentricities that we tend to forget that he was modern India's most eminent member of the 'elite of calling'. By highlighting Gandhi's many quirks and fads, by making him into a kind of fakir who strayed into politics, and by portraying him as an enemy of the modern state and of industrial machinery, I believe a grave injustice has been done to his legacy. Sociologically, it is more important for us to analyse the unintended consequences of Gandhi's life and works, rather than to be strict adherents of what he said, on which front, and frankly, he often contradicted himself. Yet many advocates of Gandhi blanch out these inconsistencies in order to present him as a simple-minded moralist who preferred a traditional solution to practically everything. But ironically it is this tendency to box in Gandhi that leads his interpreters to overlook his contribution as a modern liberal democrat who led from the front. Inconsistencies did not bother him; the larger message was his main concern. Gandhi, in fact, proudly proclaimed his inconsistencies and made no apologies for them. To quote him:

> I must admit my many inconsistencies. But since I am called Mahatma I might well endure Emerson's saying that 'foolish consistency is the hobgoblin of the little minds'. There is, I fancy, a method in my inconsistencies. (quoted in Sen ed., 1995: 43; see also Gandhi 1960: 52)

Gandhi, quite obviously, saw himself as a man not to be measured by ordinary standards. In fact, he even refused Sarvapally Radhakrishnan's request to provide a systematic account of his own thought. Gandhi believed that he was more committed to doing things and that if a coherent account of his thought needed to be presented it should be attempted by Radhakrishnan himself. For instance, Gandhi believed that to 'give [swaraj] one definite meaning is to narrow the outlook, and to limit what is potentially limitless' (Gandhi 1967, vol. XXXII: 553). As he said in the *Harijan* of 1 May 1937:

'My writings should be cremated with my body. What I have done will endure, not what I have said and written.' (Gandhi 1971: 271) As Nirmal Bose records, Gandhi once turned to him and said:

> 'You have drank up all that I have written... But it is necessary that you should observe me at work so that you can understand me better.' (Bose 1953: 77)

Here we have evidence of a leader who was quite prepared to put himself above the rest, quite impatient with those who saw him in bits, but not as a whole.

Gandhi as India's Elite of Calling: Leading from the Front

Gandhi was a leader who thought differently without giving the impression that he was actually marching into virgin territory. This is the key to his success as well as the reason for our misreading him. Obviously when one is intent on portraying Gandhi without contradictions there is an overemphasis on presenting what he said as systematically as possible. What is more, as in any content analysis, the number of times a person hits on a word gets greater preference over what is unintentionally left unsaid, and which is probably much more significant. It must also be admitted that in such interpretations the quaint and the unusual get greater preference over the non-exotic. Consequently, if it lacks sensational content, there is a tendency then to gloss over what has sedimented as social practice. Hence we see a greater emphasis on Gandhi's many oddities and not on his very modern and liberal democratic contribution to the making of our nation-state. It is this imbalance that this chapter attempts to correct. While doing so, it should become apparent that Gandhi was an 'elite of calling' who did what he thought was right and persuaded others to follow him.

It is often argued that Gandhi is no longer relevant in India. We have given up the charkha, gone in for industrialization, and lapsed into communal frenzy on more occasions than we would like to remember. What happened to all those Gandhian exhortations to stay close to simplicity, truth and non-violence? On the face of it, it does appear that Gandhi was yesterday's messiah whose band of worshippers is dwindling fast. Those that remain are aging moral soldiers, disillusioned yet carrying on, in the few eponymous foundations and samitis that bear Gandhi's name.

But Gandhi's legacy is much more than the reinforcement of tradition, or of difficult moral values which are impossible to uphold. In fact, his influence is boldly written into our laws and in the fundaments of our national policies. Harold Gould is the only scholar I know who has in recent times made this point forcefully (Gould 2000). This Gandhi is not the Gandhi of mudpacks and prayer meetings, but a person who, through all of this, made the single greatest contribution towards giving India a modern, liberal democratic state.

So if we must respect Gandhi, let us acknowledge his role in this regard and not cast him as a man of the past obsessed with impractical fads. With a little care in studying Gandhi's works and speeches it can be shown that there was indeed another Gandhi: a Gandhi who has always been prompting us to be modern, secular and democratic even if the bulk of us were looking the other way. Gandhi forced us to reject untouchability, embrace fraternity, protect minority rights, give equal space to women, and question unchecked industrialization. Where did he get these ideas from? From his own experience, from his reading of Emerson, Thoreau, Tolstoy and the Gita, but very little from 'people', not even from his many disciples.

Without Gandhi, India may well have become independent, perhaps even earlier, but would we have been a liberal, democratic nation state? This question should give us pause before we make little of Gandhi's legacy. Uncertain and imperfect though our democracy may be, it is still the world's largest, and it functions for the most part. All of us who value this form of governance ought to remember that we owe it to Gandhi, more than to anyone else, for giving us a start in the right direction. If Gandhi is to be measured in terms of charkhas, frugality and prayer meetings then certainly he would be of little consequence today. But a sociological appreciation of Gandhi would take us beyond these emblematic acts to the unintended consequences of what he did and stood for. It is only then that we realize the gravitas of Gandhi's living legacy.

The Troubled Mahatma: Gandhi's Response to Industry

No doubt, Gandhi was a great advocate of the spinning wheel, of khaddar, and was in some senses against mills and machines. Here again, one must proceed cautiously for there are at least two Gandhis we are talking about. Quite true to his position of staying away from a systematic philosophy but insisting more on practice, Gandhi said:

> Opposition to mills or machines is not the point. What suits our country most is the point. I am not opposed to the movement of manufacturing machines in this country, or to making improvements in machinery. I am only concerned with what these machineries are meant for. I may ask, in the words of Ruskin, whether these machines will be such as would blow off a million men in a minute, or they will be such as would turn waste land into arable land. And if legislation were in my hands, I would penalize the manufacture of labour-saving machines and protect the industry which manufactures a nice plough that can be handled by everyone. (Gandhi 1991: 367; see also 401)

As will be easily noticed, Gandhi equivocates. To turn waste land into arable land, or to make high-quality ploughshares requires a fairly advanced degree of technology and science, outside the reach of an ordinary cottager. Yet, on many occasions, Gandhi seems to weigh in against the pursuit of such knowledge. But true to his contradictory method he also argues a little earlier in the same article in *Young India* (14 September 1919) that:

> Pure swadeshi is not at all opposed to machinery. The swadeshi movement is meant only against the use of foreign cloth. There is no objection to weaving mill-made cloths. (Gandhi 1991: 366)

Or, in the *Harijan* of 22 June 1935:

> I would prize every invention of science made for the benefit of all. There is a difference between invention and invention. I should not care for the asphyxiating gases capable of killing masses of men at a time. The heavy machinery for work of public utility which cannot be undertaken by human labour has its inevitable place, but *that would be owned by the State* and used entirely for the benefit of the people. (ibid.: 402; emphasis mine)

However, when pressed on the subject of machinery he often professed ignorance. He even admitted on occasions that he had not thought through the matter and all that he knew something about was the humble Singer sewing machine (Gandhi 1991: 348-9).

Charkha and khadi should therefore be seen as symbols of swadeshi and non-violence (Gandhi 1967 LXXXII: 358; Gandhi 1967 XXIV: 248) and, as Gandhi cautioned, one should not make a 'fetish of the spinning wheel' (ibid.: 309). Indeed, he warned that if he should 'see that it (charkha) is an impediment in the winning of swaraj, I shall immediately set fire to it' (ibid.). This in spite of stating somewhat categorically that 'all the members of the various representative bodies of the Congress organization shall...regularly spin for half an hour every day' (Gandhi 1967, vol. XXIV: 266).

Gandhi is not done yet and there are more contradictions waiting. Though he advocated spinning, Gandhi did not want 'to make every one of the boys and girls in the villages of

India spinners or weavers, but...whole men through whatever occupation they will learn' (Gandhi 1967, vol. LXVI: 342). This led him to argue that the wheel was not meant for those with 'remunerative employment... The message of the wheel has to be carried to people who have no hope, no initiative left in them...' (ibid., vol. LXXXII: 25). In the same contradictory vein Gandhi said that in his *Nai Taleem* schools there 'should be no place for books' (Gandhi 1967, vol. LXXXII: 142), but he also urged elsewhere that for true education 'some people may feel the need for a study of literature, some for a study of physical sciences and others for art' (Gandhi 1991: 296).

Neither was Gandhi steadfast in his opposition to socialism. He inveighed against socialism on several occasions and this is the Gandhi some people refer to, particularly in the context of the Ahmedabad textile strikes. He opposed socialism for two reasons. First, he felt that workers should understand that their labour was a kind of capital, and capitalists should acknowledge that capital is a form of labour (Gandhi 1991:401; Gandhi 1967, vol. LXXXII: 335). Gandhi had clearly put himself in a definitional bind. This compelled him to seek a way out which, without temporizing on his sentiments, would uphold the principles of amity. His second objection to socialism was much more reasoned. In his view, socialism was impossible in its current articulation without resorting to violence (Gandhi 1991: 401). But it was Gandhi again who believed that in real socialism both truth and ahimsa can come alive (ibid.: 413), and that this concept is not a new discovery but can be found in the Gita (ibid.: 408).

Nehru's advocacy of socialism was thus not contrary to Gandhi's, as Nehru too thought of it in non-violent terms. Many of course would argue, and quite legitimately, that Nehru's socialism was not socialism at all, but at least it was Gandhian to the extent that there was no violence attached to it. Socialism for Gandhi, if achieved through non-violence, can be 'as pure as crystal' (Gandhi 1960: 314). In a manner reminiscent of the

Gospel, Gandhi said that the 'rich man, to say the least, did not advance the moral struggle of passive resistance as did the poor' (Gandhi 1991: 95).

Truly, Gandhi was a man of many contradictions and he was the first to recognize this trait in himself. As mentioned earlier, he was never keen to systematize his thoughts, and instead demanded that others take that extra trouble and learn from how he conducted himself in practice. And as we have just found, apart from his insistence on non-violence, which was an 'eternal principle' that brooked 'no compromise' (Gandhi 1991: 190), he was open to persuasion on practically everything else. Gandhi's main object was independence from the British through non-violence, and he made sure that those who opposed him within the Congress stayed marginalized in the organization. It is not surprising then that Gandhi did not want to be called a Mahatma (Gandhi 1967, vol. XXIV: 232). But because he stayed true to his *eternal principles* we must address him as one. He was a Mahatma; but more than that, he was an 'elite of calling' as he stayed close to the principles of democracy and fraternity. In fact, in many ways he was ahead of many of the more contemporary political philosophers on such subjects.

Gandhi before Habermas: Non-Violence and Liberal Democracy

If contemporary sociology can still call Gandhi a Mahatma it is not because he was temperamentally an ascetic, or a religious obdurate. These qualities may have encouraged the sobriquet at the time when he first earned it, but they do not explain the man's lasting legacy in a harsh, irreligious world. Without Gandhi, India might have looked like some of the other autocracies and dictatorships that characterize so many newly independent states. They too fought against colonialism and many of their leaders made heroic contributions. Yet the political dispensations of these countries either bear no trace of democracy, or, if they do, it is just a façade. Gandhi may not have always been self-conscious about his contribution to liberal thought; but his practice of, and bold insistence on, non-violence made all the difference for us in India between democracy and dictatorship. In advocating non-violence he often stood alone, but he did not waver. There were those in his camp who felt constrained by his uncompromising non-violence; but that did not dent Gandhi's commitment to the cause.

Gandhi's non-violence has to be rescued from spirituality and religion for a rounded assessment of his legacy. It was not something that sprang from the popular imagination, which is why he had to be so insistent on this issue. When Gandhi insisted on disciplinary rule it should be seen in the context of the just laws of a constitutional democratic state, and not as a variant of spiritual tapas and self-control (Hardiman 2003:26). It is quite correct that Gandhi was indebted to pacifists like Tolstoy and Thoreau, and perhaps to all pietistic religions of the day. But what needs to be recognized is that Gandhi's adherence to non-violence did not hold fast to a scriptural course as much as it was directed towards a mass movement. As Gandhi's ahimsa was not just a divine, spiritual predisposition, but actually put to use in the struggle for Independence, the understanding of his legacy too should be adjusted accordingly. We thus need to acknowledge Gandhi's non-violence not so much as a religious expression but as a signal contribution to the theory and practice of modern, liberal democracy.

So if we find Gandhi's influence pervading our Constitution we should not be surprised. The spirit of democracy and the most prized Articles on Fundamental Rights and Duties have found their place in our Constitution largely because of Gandhi's insistence on non-violence as a political precept. By not yielding an inch on non-violence, even when there were severe pressures to do so, he was able to claim the whole nine yards of democracy. For Gandhi non-violence did not just mean physical non-violence, as is often assumed, but equally non-violence in words and in the way one conducted an argument.

Well after Gandhi, Jurgen Habermas and the theorists of the Frankfurt School have also emphasized the power of debate, provided violence and manipulation are kept out of its purview (see Habermas I and II: 1987). Like Gandhi, Habermas too believed that the reason we argue is because, in principle, we believe that consensus can be arrived at (Habermas 1981: 10). For Habermas, democracy brackets away all considerations of power, pelf and wealth so that debates can be dominated by reason alone. Given the close concordance this position has with the Gandhian stand on political ahimsa (see also Parel 2007: 109), it is indeed surprising that Habermas never quoted him. What is even more surprising is that contemporary theorists of democracy do not see how Gandhi preceded Habermas in all the essentials. The Mahatma clearly paid the price of being painted as the 'other-worldly' political ascetic.[1]

The Centrality of Non-Violence: Intolerance as a Weapon of the Weak

Gandhi was upset when his own followers did not appreciate why he often suspended the freedom movement because violence had crept in. As he said:

---

[1] Gandhi was ahead of Habermas at practically every step. Gandhi did not see a problem conducting debates between people who did not have a shared definition of the situation as long as violence was kept out. Habermas, however, is uncomfortable with the idea of debating with somebody whose arguments cannot be validated by a set of criteria that passes the communicative rationality test (Habermas 1987 I: 13,: 15, 17, 70; see also Habermas II: 124 and *passim*). The strength in Gandhi's position is that as long as non-violence played a pivotal role it did not really matter if the views expressed were not rational, or certifiable on objective grounds. After all, one should also be able to discuss matters of faith without which human life would be impossible to conceive. At the end of the day, we need to recognize that in the most critical moments of life and death, one cannot, and does not, rely on validity claims of communicative rationality.

It has not yet been understood: my suspension of
Satyagraha after Ahmedabad and Viramnagar tragedies,
then after the Bombay rowdyism, and lastly, after the
Chauri Chaura outrage. (Gandhi 1967, vol. XXIV: 139)

But if Gandhi had not acted as he did on those occasions,
instead of debate and democracy, the Indian Constitution might
well have valorized some other doctrine. It is so easy to stray off
course, as democracy is a highly cultivated political preference.
For Gandhi, freedom by itself was not an unqualified good.
According to him, 'the attainment of freedom whether for a
man, a nation, or the world, must be in exact proportion to the
attainment of non-violence in each' (Gandhi 1960: 32).

In fact, the ultimate rationale behind debate and democracy
lies in the principle of non-violence. If this were absent, the
public sphere, where individuals can interact freely and without
fear, would be impossible to conduct. It is not as if we must all
agree all the time, but in order to relate to one another through
differences, the credo of non violence is absolutely essential.
It is this that allows people holding diverse views to see each
other as equal citizens, deserving equal space and consideration.
This is why Gandhi could live with disagreements provided life
went on non-violently. This is why he was able to intellectualize
consistency, even belittle it.

What mattered most to Gandhi was that every dogma, every
argument, every strategy be burnished by undergoing the test
of non-violence. Instead of stressing a rationality, Gandhi
argued for non-violence; instead of rebuke and abuse, he
chose 'sweet persuasion' (quoted in Heredia 2007: 157). Else,
he warned, satyagraha can become its opposite, duragraha
(for an extended treatment of duragraha see Bondurant 1964:
76). Gandhi wrote: 'Anger proves our intolerance. We shall
lack the capacity to bear one another's criticism. This is a very
important quality of *public life*' (ibid.: 249; emphasis mine).
Note, it is public life that is being stressed here and not religious
mysticism, or tapas.

From a pronounced liberal tradition Bertrand Russell also echoed Gandhi's sentiments when he wrote: 'If an opinion contrary to your own makes you angry, that is a sign that you are subconsciously aware of having no good reason for thinking as you do' (Russell 1958: 136). For Gandhi, the evolution of democracy was not possible unless we give the other side a fair hearing, otherwise we 'shut the doors of reason when we refuse to hear our opponents...we run the risk of missing the truth' (see also Terchek 2000: 154).

In line with his liberal values Gandhi argued that 'democracy dreads to spill blood' (Gandhi 1971: 79). As he said in a meeting at the Satyagraha Camp in Nadiad in 1918: 'We are not to boycott or treat with scorn those who hold different views from ours' (Gandhi 1991: 311). Satyagraha must therefore 'not be violent in thought, word or deed towards the "enemy" or among ourselves' (ibid.: 324). But Gandhi could be more specific than that. In the *Harijan* of 26 March 1938, Gandhi wrote:

> We must try patiently to convert our opponents. If we wish to evolve the spirit of democracy out of slavery, we must be scrupulously exact in our dealings with opponents... We must concede to our opponents the freedom we claim for ourselves for which we are fighting. (quoted in Gandhi: 1971: 73-4)

The fact is that non-violence is also debate and discussion, and should not be limited only to the physical aspect of that term. Although Gandhi no doubt castigated Fascism on a number of occasions for its inbuilt violence, his critique was essentially buoyed by his advocacy of searching for truth through ahimsa-style democratic debate (Gandhi 1960: 68-79). Gandhi argued quite forcefully that in a true democracy 'the weakest should have the same opportunity as the strongest (shades of John Rawls's difference principle). That can never happen except through non-violence' (Gandhi 1960: 114). It was the spirit of fraternity that was pumping energy into his advocacy of non-violence in a fashion that was deliberate, thought out and rich in theory.

It is non-violence again that inspired Gandhi's anti-majoritarian views of democracy (see Terchek 2000:132). Democracy is for all, and not for this or that group. The fundamental tenet of democracy for Gandhi was the ultimate liberal one for under it 'individual liberty of opinion and action is jealously guarded' (ibid.: 157). In 1946, as Independence was approaching, Gandhi said in a meeting in Panchgani: 'What is Independence? Independence must begin at the bottom...it is the individual who is the unit' (Gandhi 1991: 347). The individual is at the centre of Gandhi's thought, not an ethereal soul. And much like T.H. Marshall's notion of citizenship (Marshall 1963:9), Gandhi also argued that his life's mission was 'to bring about an equalization of status' (Gandhi 1967, vol. LXVI: 341).

Independence was not good enough for its own sake unless it was characterized by the strictest rules of discipline (Gandhi 1967: 310). Without this quality of self-discipline and non-violence at all levels, democracy would be impossible. Perhaps a fascist state could be contrived, perhaps a state that is all pomp and splendour, but, for all that, a soulless state (Gandhi 1973: 255). Nirmal Bose records Gandhi telling a delegation from Gorakhpur's Gita Press in November 1946 that unless 'people were conscious of their political rights and know how to act in a crisis, democracy can never be built up' (Bose 1953: 75). He was conscious that this awareness did not come about naturally among the multitudes, but had to be fostered from above.

Gandhi as a Liberal Secularist: Ballasting India's Democratic Constitution

Gandhi's devoted espousal of secularism flows as powerfully from his insistence on liberal, democratic principles as it does from his strong advocacy of non-violence in all forms. If in the Constitution of India we have an unquestioning subscription to secularism, where 'every religion has full and equal place' (Gandhi 1991: 348), it is Gandhi that is most responsible for it. His secularism was even-handed and based on liberal principles, and not on charity and good will. This can be seen from an incident recorded by Nirmal Bose. When some Hindu workers came to meet Gandhi in the communally tense days of 1946 to demand that Muslim officers should be replaced by Hindu officers, Gandhiji remarked that it was an unreasonable and communal demand. 'While putting forward such a proposal, you should ask yourself if the Muslims of Bihar can reasonably make a similar demand. In my opinion, the present demand is absurd and I would personally never countenance it. You can of course substitute impartial officers in place of biased ones, that would be fair' (Bose 1953: 61).

Gandhi's liberal secularism was therefore not one of grand gestures but stemmed directly from allegiance to constitutional and legal norms. A secular society for Gandhi would be one where we could share 'one another's sorrows' (Gandhi 1971:168). Could John Rawls have done better when he asked us to participate in one another's fate (Rawls 1971: 102)? As Gandhi remarked: 'Independent India as conceived by me will have all Indians belonging to different religions living in "perfect friendship"' (Gandhi 1991: 360). It is important for us that for Gandhi 'perfect friendship' was not based on tolerance or equidistance, but on an active involvement in each other's lives as full citizens. Quite in keeping with this position on secularism, Gandhi said:

> The state has nothing to do with religion. The state should look after secular welfare, health, communication, foreign relations, currency, and so on, but not your or my religion (quoted in Terchek 2000: 161).

This should put paid to those who believe that Gandhi saw politics in purely traditional and religious terms. The separation of the church and state could not have been stated in more forthright a manner. The tone of his assertion recalls the great liberal tradition that goes back to Kant, Hegel and Mills.

Much is made of Gandhi's adherence to religion and to Hinduism in particular. But in fact he was extremely wary of

Hinduism, though this was a religion he prized above all others. In the 11 August 1920 issue of *Young India* he had this to say about Hinduism:

> There is on the one hand, the Historical Hinduism with its untouchability, superstitious worship of rocks and stones, animal sacrifice and so on. On the other hand we have the Hinduism of the Gita, the Upanishads and Patanjali's Yoga Shastra which is the acme of Hinduism (quoted in Terchek 2000:180).

In fact, he said at one point that the way in which he saw and practised Hinduism and non-violence led many to believe that he 'was a Christian in disguise' (Gandhi 1967: vol. XXIV: 139). This is not entirely surprising. Gandhi had once also commented that Jesus Christ was 'the Prince of passive resistance' (Gandhi 1973: 273). As for Gandhi's reaction when people described him as a fakir and yogi, we have Gandhi again in his own words: 'Non-violence is not just for yogis, but for *citizens*' (see Parel 2007: 122; emphasis mine). For Gandhi is the ultimate practitioner: 'Nothing can be accepted as the word of God which cannot be tested by reason or capable of being spiritually experienced' (*Collected Works*, vol. 50: 92; quoted in Parel 2007: 105). This is why Gandhi's legacy is so modern and in line with liberal democratic thought. He was not the old, superstitious, stone-worshipping Hindu who we think is closest to the ordinary people. That he was not ritualistic in his observance of Hinduism is no surprise. Had his Hinduism been even remotely inclined in that direction he would have had to forsake his crusade against untouchability.

Gandhi as Myth: How Gandhi Created a Fresh Discourse

Gandhi was an elite par excellence in yet another significant way. Though the essence of Gandhi's non-violence is responsible for establishing our secular, democratic and liberal state, there is yet another side to Gandhi where he in fact succeeded out of his many failures. No amount of object validation could show that the charkha, the practice of being a celebate brahmachari, espousing the value of frugality and so forth were correct beyond dispute. Yet by raising these issues, Gandhi enlarged our public sphere and helped us to discuss openly some of the most tabooed subjects of the time. Perhaps because of his obvious disinterest in capturing power for himself (Habermas's attack on 'steering media'), perhaps also because of his popular image as a person of religious conviction (which has no Habermasian equivalent), perhaps also because of his ascetic ways, when Gandhi raised an issue it had immediate credibility. Nobody could accuse him of concealing a secret axe which he would later grind in the dark.

Gandhi provided the stage for people to openly confront diverse options regarding the role of women in public life, the place of capitalism in a developing country, caste relations, the importance of import substitution, and the significance of village life, of family relationships and of tradition in general (see Gandhi 1991: 319). Gandhi's espousal of brahmacharya usually inspires a smile in contemporary times, but it could also be seen as a way of easing the entry of women into public life. He was not against marriage but only the obsession with 'carnal desire' (1971: 160, 163) which made women unsafe outside their homes. He was against child labour, forced labour and unpaid labour at a time when these were the order of the day. The fact that he raised the issue of child labour is itself quite striking (Gandhi 1971: 127). If children are still employed does it mean that Gandhi failed? On the contrary, it shows that Gandhi was well ahead of his time and that he forced the issue in our consciousness.

Imagine a traditional society, such as India, whose myriad shackles had never been examined for ages. Then Gandhi comes along and opens up some of the most hushed issues for debate. Gandhi was widely acknowledged as *Bapu* (father), and he too accepted this honorific; yet this did not prevent him from saying that if a father fails in his duty then children should have the right to leave home (Gandhi 1971: 133). This is not unlike what Hegel had accomplished in the *Philosophy of Right* when he critiqued Roman law for allowing unrestrained patriarchal control on the part of the father. That Gandhi should entertain such an opinion does not mean that patriarchy was defeated, but he certainly shook the complacency out of traditional ties. Interestingly, Gandhi once wrote a letter to a delegation of Chinese women where he said, 'Women of the world must unite' (Gandhi 1991: 387).

On several occasions, Gandhi did not just fail to live up to Habermas's validity claims; he often refrained from taking a categorical position on many significant issues. For example, he raised the matter of inter-dining and intermarriage between religious groups without clearly giving his views on the subject. He seemed to allow for separation of personal space on religious grounds, but he also believed that marrying or dining within one's caste, or religion, should not come in the way of public interactions (ibid.: 167-8). He also shocked his friends by taking toast from a Muslim (ibid.: 179), but did not openly oppose those who resisted eating with other communities. But at any rate he succeeded in bringing to public notice the testy matter of inter-faith relations in the context of everyday activity. Though there was a lack of unanimity on these questions, nevertheless, now that such concerns were aired in the open it enabled the formulation of liberal policies that put faith and tradition in their place.

To argue then that Gandhi is irrelevant because many of his opinions have been cast aside disregards how through him public debates were conducted that eventually enhanced the democratic content of our lives. It is true that while there were no firm conclusions on many of these issues, that should not lead us to conclude carelessly that Gandhi is irrelevant today. Women are still dominated, child labour is rampant in the carpet industry, workers do not get their dues, scheduled castes continue to face oppression, and parents routinely force their girls into unhappy marriages. But even so, without Gandhi, we would have still been largely unaware of these warts in our culture. He helped us see them by persuading us to talk about them publicly.

In most of these cases Gandhi said he listened to his 'inner voice' (Gandhi 1991: 213). It is hard to argue against money, but even harder against someone's inner voice! Gandhi disdained pecuniary considerations, and actively carried on a dialogue with his inner voice. While these issues were raised by Gandhi's inner voice to him, the way he amplified them allowed us to enlarge our public lives. So what if we do not accept Gandhi's view on brahmacharya; so what if we find it difficult to return to the charkha; so what if we still have elements of patriarchy in family life; Gandhi helped us to move from tradition to modernity by the very act of bringing up these issues for public debate.

Gandhi, in this sense, was like a myth. Through him worrisome issues were brought out in the open for discussion, though they were never quite resolved. As Levi-Strauss remarks, a myth is not misplaced history (1966: 224-238), but a way of contemplating and mulling over imponderables that do not easily yield solutions. Myths discuss questions that have no easy answer, like the beginning of the beginning, or the darkness of death.[2] But humankind must nevertheless reflect on these matters and this is why myths of all kinds endure, even in our time. By taking us to our deepest thoughts myths help us to respond to dilemmas of everyday life.

---

[2] I am explicitly following Levi-Strauss's understanding of myths against Habermas's views on the subject (see Habermas 1987 II: 159). Habermas views myths derogatorily and does not appear to have a good word for them in the sphere of communicative rationality. He also seems to link myths with tribal societies. At any rate, for him myths are a problem as they 'blur the categorical distinctions between the objective, social and subjective worlds, and how they do not even draw a clear line between interpretations and the interpreted reality. Internal relations among meanings are fused with external relations among things' (ibid.).

Gandhi and Public Policy: The Indian Constitution put to Work

There were, however, some issues on which Gandhi was unequivocal and these come through in the pages of the Constitution. This aspect is often overlooked by most of us. The credit for the extraordinary depth, profundity and liberal content of our Constitution is almost entirely handed to the Drafting Committee. It is true that this committee rationally debated, gave a little, took a little, and finally crafted a document that the world will always remember. While none of this can be denied, what escapes attention is the pre-history of such deliberations—a prehistory where Gandhi's influence is inescapable.

This can best be seen in the disavowal of separate electorates in the Constitution. How can we forget Gandhi's insistent commitment, from the days of the Poona Pact onwards, to see this proposal die? This idea was killed again in the Constituent Assembly debates. The abolition of untouchability is all Gandhi, and so are the strictures against sectarian, caste and religious discrimination. He was against untouchability and religious sectarianism, both in word and deed. He relentlessly pursued his opponents on these questions at every opportunity with every weapon in his non-violent armamentarium. If we have unbending laws today regarding caste atrocities and minority rights, we must remember it was Gandhi who compelled us to frame them. If untouchability is outlawed today in the Constitution, then it is primarily because of Gandhi. Imagine the world's most stratified society legally abolishing caste-based discrimination by a stroke of the constitutional pen. It is not just a question of reservations for Scheduled Castes, our entire public attitude regarding inter-caste relations is now grounded in law.

No other leader before Gandhi fought caste and religious discrimination with as much cogency and consistency. For example, when it came to untouchability he willingly performed the 'lowest' of tasks himself; likewise when it came to inter-faith violence, he staked his personal safety and marched straight into the line of fire. This put Hindu activists on the defensive even in the fervid post-Partition days. Remember

Nehru and the Congress won election after election in the first two decades after Independence. Gandhi did not relent even in death. Incensed by Gandhi's assassination Nehru compelled the RSS to change its constitution and accept that India was a multi-religious society. Hindu sectarians acquiesced because they lacked the heart to take on Gandhi's ghost.

Decentralized governance and the significance of Panchayati Raj surfaced once again in our Constitution with the 73rd Amendment in 1992. Where did all of this begin but in Gandhi's strong belief that without local self-governance at the village level, rural interests and aspirations would go unheeded. The Constitution ensures that the Gram Panchayat is directly elected so that the village oligarch can be outnumbered. Since the Constitution first enshrined Panchayati Raj, this provision has undergone several modifications, but none of them dare take away the basic kernel of popular elections at the lowest level of self-governance. Likewise, Gandhi's espousal of working-class rights also contributed to the establishment of Article 43A of the Directive Principles that advocates the participation of workers in factory management.

Swadeshi may not have been a practical solution, especially if the charkha was to be its major weapon in the crusade, but it bred in us the idea of self-reliance, and with it a certain pride in being economically sovereign. If today we have the human and physical resources to be an economic power, it is because the spirit of swadeshi led us to develop the infrastructure necessary for this purpose. When Gandhi campaigned for swadeshi he faced many barbs and slights. He was dubbed a village anarchist, a backward revanchist, but he held course. Today we realize how indebted we ought to be to him, as it was swadeshi that gave us the springboard to participate in the global market of the twenty-first century.

But Gandhi's biggest gift to the nation is the spirit of liberal democracy which is the life and soul of our Constitution. Pages are devoted to the various tiers of elected representatives, to the powers of different wings of the government, and to the modalities of holding free and fair elections. We rarely acknowledge how ahimsa and satyagraha are the bedrock of our democracy—indeed, of any democracy. The fact that Gandhi used thoroughly Indian terms does not diminish their universal relevance for the theory and practice of liberal democracy.

Remembering Gandhi's Contribution to Democracy: Beyond Prayer Meetings or Charkhas

So if we must remember Gandhi let us not devote ourselves to empty gestures like prayer meetings or spinning the charkha for a few mandatory minutes. Nor should we make him out to be, as Richard Attenborough did in the eponymous film, a big-hearted saint who was devoted to swadeshi. To limit Gandhi's legacy to these emblematic acts does grave injustice to the one person who staked his all to fast-forward our backward country towards a modern liberal democracy—and not just to Independence. That is why, in the fitness of things, Gandhi's ahimsa should be remembered as a democratic conviction of a very high order and not as a purely religious or moral affair. That he advocated anti-untouchability, minority rights, democratic procedure and the rights of the poor at a time when none of these considerations were acceptable at the popular level, certainly grants Gandhi a preeminent position as a 'citizen-elite'.

Sadly, we are eroding some of his most outstanding contributions and adhering instead to purely ceremonial acts of memory. After these little obligatory routines are performed, we are back to 'business as usual': money is brandished in the Lok Sabha, members of Parliament shout down their opponents, elected representatives openly espouse sectarian positions, and all of this without a sense of shame of what we are doing to Gandhi's true legacy. Today even Rajnath Singh, of the Bharatiya Janata Party, and Chief Minister Narendra Modi of Gujarat quote Gandhi selectively to suit their sectarian interests.

Gandhi surely does not deserve this. It is for this reason that we must remember, before anything else, the Mahatma's democratic and liberal contribution to our nation-state.

Search Narendra Modi's face when he quotes Gandhi in fulsome praise and you won't find a twitching muscle or a furtive glance! Not just him, there are thousands of Hindu sectarian activists who believe that they are the true inheritors of Gandhi! With a straight face Modi threatens Muslims with certain death in 'Gandhi's Gujarat' if they don't behave according to his lights. Can so many saffron-clad soldiers be so dreadfully wrong? Was Gandhi an apostle of peace, or was he, unbeknownst to himself, the first field marshal of the Hindu army?

What these Hindu activists draw upon are the many laudatory comments Gandhi made about the simple village life, about the Gita and also about Hinduism. But for Gandhi, Hinduism was a religion of love and not a manifesto against Muslims or people of other faiths. Yet, when the RSS and BJP use him they selectively excise the content of Gandhi's Hinduism and use it instead as an emblematic standard of war. Gandhi had many contradictory views on a number of issues, but he was firm on ahimsa and democracy. He was, as we just saw earlier in this chapter, a man of religion but also believed that science and reason should not be dumbed down. He upheld the charkha, but did not want to make a fetish of it. He was against Lancashire cloth but not Indian mill-made textiles.

There is just one thing on which he stood firm and on which he and his inner voice spoke in unison. Gandhi did not countenance any compromise on ahimsa. However, for uncomplicated votaries of the RSS and other like-minded organizations, ahimsa is a minor irritant, best put out of the way. Non-violence for them is an after-dinner topic when the shutters are down and children are safely in bed. Interestingly, during the Ahmedabad riots of 2002, the Gandhians retired early even though the city could not sleep. They woke up later with bhajans, or prayer meetings, but they dared not face the killing mobs like Gandhi did, in Noakhali and elsewhere. If the Sabarmati Ashram that Gandhi had set up in Ahmedabad had become a Muslim refugee camp in 2002, as it should have been, Narendra Modi would not have quoted Gandhi so brazenly to further his Hindu sectarian (or Hindutva) cause.

It is up to Gandhians today to show us where they stand. Would they rather line up behind a 'cultural Gandhi' who can easily be cast as a Hindutva partisan? Or are they going to stand firm and unfazed by the principles of ahimsa? In the first case they would uphold cultural stereotypes, and in the second the dignity of citizens—and all humanity. It is for them to choose.

CHAPTER IV

Jawaharlal Nehru to Manmohan Singh: From Utopia to the Politics of the Given

After Gandhi, Nehru was the next, and perhaps the last great member of the 'elite of calling' in India. His fight against theocracy and communalism, his persistence with the policy of self-reliance, his encouragement of science and technology come immediately to mind. Indian families would also have been bound by traditional laws had Nehru given in to what was the popular view at the time. It is true that Nehru had many faults, and some of them haunt us even today, yet he advanced India's democracy more significantly than most others. He resolutely pushed for the Hindu Marriage Bill, for non-alignment and self-reliance without which some of the things we calmly take for granted today would not be there. In doing all this, Nehru had to frequently go against his colleagues and friends in India and abroad. Nehru did function with a vision of a utopia, of the Karl Mannheiman kind, because he was intent on changing the given and creating a wider fraternity-based democracy. Manmohan Singh, on the other hand, does not draw inspiration from a utopia but is instead intent on maximizing the politics of the given. The contrast between Nehru and Manmohan Singh brings out this feature clearly.

These days 14 November, Jawaharlal Nehru's birthday, hardly stirs any memories. Some time soon after Independence, Nehru's love for children was noticed and he was accordingly canonized as 'Chacha'. As the nation already had a Bapu, only the post of uncle was open.

This title suited Nehru, and India's then new-generation happily endorsed it. As Nehru promised a vital and modern India, the young had reason to dream that as doctors and engineers they would soon banish poverty and disease. This is why for years his birthday was a festive occasion with optimistic children, teachers and parents participating in it. Today Chacha Nehru's birth anniversaries are flat affairs without a vestige of the earlier passion that accompanied them. Nor are we enthused by the utopian visions of our first prime minister. We would rather indulge in the 'politics of the given'.

Nehru's Policies: The Lingering Relevance of Elite Intervention

Is Nehru irrelevant today, or has his legacy been wronged by latter-day politicians and commentators? India is still poor, India still needs talent, and India must have communal peace. On all these counts Nehru's memory should have been kept alive, yet we have to scratch our heads to remember him.

In many ways, Nehru is an uncomfortable memory. He not only believed in secularism but actually practised it. Barely six months after Partition, Nehru had the courage to declare in Aligarh Muslim University: 'I do not like the university being called the Muslim University just as I do not like the Benares University to be called the Hindu University.' By the standards of today's political calculations, this would be a disastrous admission to make.

Though there are some who would grant Nehru his secular credentials, most mainstream politicians today would cast him as a reckless leftist who brought our country to ruination. He is believed to have angered America unnecessarily, foolishly sided with Russia, and taken India's economy to the brink of collapse. Much of this calumny is unfair and inaccurate, which is why it is time to set the record right and return to Nehru his Chacha status.

True, Nehru was not starry-eyed about capitalism, but he was not blind to the shortcomings of the other side either. In Bandung he stated very clearly: 'We do not agree with the communist teachings, we do not agree with anti-communist teachings.' On another occasion he told C. Rajagopalachari— the lawyer, freedom fighter and a leader of the Indian National Congress who served as the first governor-general of India— that 'India...will never go communist because of the inherent communist belief in violence'. This is exactly what Gandhi had said time and time again, years earlier.

His anti-left stand came through as early as 1949 when Nehru's cabinet guaranteed safety to foreign investments in India and allowed profits to be remitted outside the country. Nor did Nehru, in his 1956 Industrial Policy, advocate nationalizing the private sector (as his daughter Indira Gandhi did later). In his opinion such a measure would lead to 'economic totalitarianism' of the communist kind. This should not come as a surprise, as Nehru, by his own admission, 'did not encourage class conflicts as some people do'. Can one still call him a woolly-headed leftist?

But the Nehru-bashers may still not be satisfied. What about his closeness to Russia, they would argue? The truth is that in times of trouble, whether it was the war with China, food shortages, or currency crunches, Nehru's immediate instinct was always to turn to America or Britain for help. When India faced its first foreign exchange crisis Nehru appealed to the World Bank and to the United States for assistance; likewise, when India was starving in the 1950s and 1960s, PL-480's grain (and gravel!) mix was shipped from America to feed our poor.

Recall also that soon after Independence Nehru instructed G.S. Bajpai, then secretary general of External Affairs, to assure the US that India would never be pro-Soviet. Yet it was not just the Americans but Stalin too who was displeased with India's policy of non-alignment. He made this known by refusing to give an audience to Vijayalakshmi Pandit, who went to the USSR as Nehru's emissary. In fact, Andrei Vyshinsky, the Russian UN representative from 1949 to 1953, condemned India for being the 'worst instruments of horrible American policy'.

Stalin had other reasons to be upset as well. During the Korean War, B.N. Rau, India's representative in the UN, called North Korea the 'aggressor'. Even though Nehru got along well with Khrushchev, the Russian premier, particularly after the latter denounced Stalin in 1956, it did not stop the Indian prime minister from criticizing in Parliament the USSR's invasion of Hungary. So the next time the Kashmir issue surfaced in the United Nations, Russia abstained and said nothing in India's favour.

It was the Americans who first caricatured Nehru as a frothy communist sympathizer. That was the only way they knew of showing their displeasure at India for not signing into the SEATO or the Baghdad Pact. Both the Bandung and the Baghdad Pact came up in 1955 and required the signatories to abide by an international treaty which protected American interests against communist advances. As India refused to sign these treaties on the ground that it was a sovereign nation with its own set of interests, the US vilification of Nehru and his foreign policy became intense. It came to a point when the American propaganda on this matter even miffed Rajagopalachari. India's non-alignment was, therefore, suspect in the eyes of both Stalin's Russia and the United States. This itself should be reason enough to believe that Nehru was on to something good.

When after the humiliation of the 1962 China war Nehru did a stock-taking of India's defence capabilities he was aghast at what he found. He sent officials right away to the US and Britain with a shopping list for planes, submarines and everything else in between. Unfortunately, neither the UK nor the US was forthcoming at this point. As long as the Chinese threat was imminent the Americans stood by Nehru, but now they felt that it was payback time. They wanted India to solve the Kashmir issue before they agreed on any weapons deal. The SEATO rejection still stung and America was clearly on Pakistan's side. It was only then, in desperation, that Nehru turned to Russia and that is how the MIGs made their appearance in our air force. Likewise, after being stood up by the Americans in the establishment of the Bokaro Steel Plant, India went to Russia on the rebound.

It is this other side of Nehru that has to be recovered from all the crypto-communist demonology that surrounds his legacy. Nehru was not perfect, far from it, but his feet were not all clay either. It is quite clear that he tried to get the best deal for his country by negotiating between the two cold war antagonists and super-powers. He was also acutely conscious of protecting India's pride and dignity. Like many other post-colonial leaders, he had seen western swagger up close.

Nobody would doubt that Nehru miscalculated on China and perhaps even on Kashmir. But that would hardly be reason enough to paint him as a red devil or a pink pretender. He often bent like a reed, but he was always a patriotic reed. In all fairness, Nehru's ledger should show that he was neither left nor right, and maybe he should be criticized for that; but he did what he thought was best for his country.

Nehru steered India through its most difficult period. He kept it from being Balkanized, and from being a mirror image of Pakistan. If India is often acknowledged as an emerging economic power, we must thank Nehru for it. More than any other leader of his time, he was responsible for setting up the IITs, the All India Institute of Medical Science, the Indian Institute of Sciences, the Indian Statistical Institute, and a host of other major centres of learning.

It is time now to put the ghosts behind us and reinstate Nehru to the status of Chacha, and this time with feeling and gratitude.

Not by Goodwill Alone: Secularism for Economic Development

Our grief at the way Governor Salman Taseer was killed next door, in Pakistan, has a *schadenfreude* aspect to it. We are sad that a brave man died unjustly, but we are happy this happened to our neighbour next door. True, Taseer was part of the establishment, but he had a change of heart when it came to the blasphemy law. It takes a lot to leave your barber halfway through a haircut, but he did that, and paid for it.

The broadband endorsement of Salman Taseer's assassination in Pakistan in 2011 for opposing the blasphemy laws of the country is even more horrifying than the act itself. While rejoicing that we are lucky to be born here and not there, let us remember that even khap panchayats in Haryana and UP can be very hostile to those who flout traditional marriage norms. They can even issue chilling diktats against women for doing something as harmless as wearing jeans. The Ram Sena organization that came up from nowhere in Karnataka earned a quick reputation by attacking couples in coffee shops and vandalizing stores selling Valentine gifts and cards. We are still far from being Pakistan, but not that far.

Secularism, with all its faults, has helped to distance us from Pakistan in more ways than we imagine. While commending ourselves on this let us not forget that if Nehru did one thing right, it was his steadfast advocacy of secularism. It is not just that we are secular and Pakistan is not, but that we are thinking development and they are not. Secularism takes our minds off whether our wives and sisters are behaving, or whether our gods are being upstaged by other gods. In place of such ungovernable passions, it positions issues of economic growth and development instead.

Pakistan's near total obsession with identity politics has disabled it on a number of fronts. Its theocratic character has kept it from bringing about land reforms, curbing the military, setting up institutions of higher learning, and establishing steel mills. That we have been able to do all that—from engineering units to IT giants—is because secularism gave us the space to grow. We had energy in stock to think of poverty removal, economic sovereignty, export promotion and so on.

In politics a kind of zero sum game is at work. Either we exhaust our reserves asserting identity politics or get ahead with developmental programmes. The two cannot be combined. Is it surprising then that theocratic states are nearly always the least developed? Once we open the door to ethnicity, out goes progress and economic well-being.

Those who snigger at India's secularism should perhaps take a step back from the fence that separates us from Pakistan. Only then will they realize how fortunate we actually are. All the forces of primeval passion, let loose by the Partition, were baying for a Hindu state mirroring that of Pakistan: blood for blood, and so on. Pakistan has not made matters easier either. Every time it gets too hot in their kitchen, they open the window and throw junk in our backyard. There have been more times than can be forgiven or forgotten when we have given in to ethnic passions. That we did not go all the way is because secular values are still with us, courtesy the founders of our Constitution.

When the UPA came to power in 2000, we were more relieved than elated. We could now switch off the ethnic engines (they were overheated anyway) and think development instead. Today, that promise the UPA held out is without real legs. It is not because this government has yielded to Muslim- and minority-baiters, but because it has done little to improve the everyday life of everyday people—majority and minorities included. This is why ethnic parties are raising their heads once again. There is no point in condemning Narendra Modi for being communal if Congress-run states elsewhere cannot out-perform Gujarat on the economic front. Secularism has a double burden: it must not only be good, it has to be better than the rest.

This is a lesson that is often hard to drive home. Secularism is not just about minority protection, it is about majority promotion too. Secularism draws our attention away from medieval concerns so that we can think about economic progress. History is a testament to this. When the western world emerged from the religious trap, they experienced economic growth like never before. By not emphasizing this aspect, the promoters of secularism have underserved their cause.

In the period from 1820 till today, the per capita income in Europe and America grew between fifteenfold and twentyfold. Till that time, for centuries, nobody knew anything about growth. It never rang anybody's doorbell. John Maynard Keynes made this point emphatically in his 1930 essay, 'Economic Possibilities for our Grandchildren'. He noticed, as many others did, that from the beginning of the Christian era all the way up to the eighteenth century, the average standard of living remained roughly the same.

Life expectancy till then was extremely low; people died of natural causes that are easily controllable now; epidemics swept the world—even in today's developed countries. How did it all change? There are many reasons for this, but the most important one is that politics changed. It now espoused industrialization, freedom of movement, and rights of children and workers as free citizens. Religion was put in its place.

This is why democracy can reel out a continuous series of success stories that read like fairy tales. Quebec, in Canada, and the Basque province of Spain, made huge strides after they shook off the hold of the Catholic Church. France realized the importance of this very early when in 1906 it clipped the wings of the papal establishment and forced it to retreat. It is only after that that the vision of the Third Republic got a fighting chance of realizing itself. David Brooks, one of America's renowned conservative journalists, made a similar point recently. He argued that when secular ideologies come to the fore, ethnic passions must recede. This is an interesting insight, made more remarkable by the fact that it comes from conservative quarters.

If we want to believe in the things our forefathers did, if we want to tremble at the sound of thunder, if we want to be helpless in the face of avoidable diseases, we should go back to religious passions. If, on the other hand, we want to enjoy the comforts of today, the sciences of today, then we better get secular. There is much more to secularism than mere religious tolerance, religious equidistance, or even religious goodwill. Without secularism there is no development, and that is the hard truth.

The choice is clear. We can either think like our grandparents and go ethnic, or think of our grandchildren, as Keynes did, and become secular. There is no other option!

Consequently, with secularism as a cornerstone of our Constitution, no matter how many times attempts have been made to mangle it, we have been able to achieve successes. They are quite significant, and none of this would have been possible if we were thinking identity politics, or security, most of the time the way Pakistan does.

We now have a unified market, because secularism gave us room to think in terms of economic growth. Remember, neither the Hindu Mahasabha nor the Bharatiya Jana Sangh had a glimmer of an economic programme in the period before and after Independence. If the Congress won repeatedly for twenty straight years after 1947 it is primarily because Nehru's secularism gave room to plan the economy, to think of progress and ultimately development. While we may criticize Nehru for a faulty model of growth, and there will be many who will defend his record, what is indubitable is that discussion would not have been as vibrant, but for him.

There was a time when India's future as a nation-state was threatened, but today this issue is hardly on the agenda. To a large extent, it is because this country now has a unified market where every region depends on another, either for raw material or for labour or both. If we were to discuss India's future as a democracy, many hands would rise to participate in the debate. But not one would doubt India's durability as a nation-state. We need to remember our first-generation 'elite of calling' for making that possible.

The Winding Down of a Utopia: When Nationalism Clouds Citizenship

Today, our own agricultural production, in spite of some ups and downs, can feed India. This is a consequence of the land reforms that India undertook soon after Independence.

Without these reforms the Green Revolution would just not have happened. Imagine a landlord class even thinking about changing their lifestyle and actually engaging in production and supervision. Over time, the abolition of the zamindari system led to a robust class of peasant proprietors who have since become a significant political force in contemporary India. From 1950 to the present day, there are more family farms than before, and old-style landed oligarchs are difficult to find. The fact that Maoism has moved from the agrarian belt of India to the tribal regions is an outcome of this feature.

Nehru was attentive to the other end of the spectrum as well. Not for him, the old guru-shishya relationship where knowledge stayed stagnant. How can we forget his contribution to the establishment of the IITs, the Institutes of Management and the Institute of Science that have made India proud? They were set up under Nehru's supervision and, one may add, his inspiration too. In those early post-Independence years not many were thinking of the big picture, of how India would look decades down the line.

Nehru's impact on urban India too is hard to shake off. Even today Bhilai and Bokaro are important centres for sourcing steel. BHEL and HAL, along with several so-called navratna (or high asset) companies in the public sector have served India well. They were all ideas that emanated in Nehru's time. True, the public sector has since failed to deliver at standards necessary and expected, but that is largely because of political mismanagement. Europe, for example, relies heavily on the public sector for a number of essential services. This is probably the world's best-kept secret, but the proportion of America's investment in the public sector is way above that of India (for an extended treatment of this theme, see La Porta, et al., 1999; Besley and Perrson 2011). The public sector did not answer the call of efficiency and service as it should have, and Nehru must take part of the blame for not insisting on this.

In acknowledging all of this, let us not overlook the fact that Nehru never really paid much attention to universal health and education. This is surprising, since Nehru was an outward-looking person, well aware of global welfare reforms, so how did he ignore the experiences of Europe and Britain in this regard? If only he had laid the foundations for these services, India may well have been different today. That was certainly a leadership deficit on Nehru's part and India needs another round of enlightened political elite to make that happen.

Nehru had other shortcomings too. He was quite happy to allow the pomp and splendour of office, many of them carryovers from the colonial period, to continue during his time. He also caved in and allowed justice to be evaded when some of his close political allies were corrupt. While Nehru performed excellently when he went against the tide and fought old cultural prejudices and shook India out of its ancient forms of knowledge, he failed whenever he became a prisoner to nationalism. He had many admirable qualities, but there is no doubt that when it came to dealing with Kashmiri activists or those in the North East, he came down heavily on them. Even their legitimate complaints against the behaviour of the armed forces in those areas were not entertained because, for Nehru, India's territorial integrity was paramount. He used Preventive Detention freely, even though this was set up in 1818 by the British, to curb dissent within the nation's boundaries. The unfairness with which he incarcerated Sheikh Abdullah of Kashmir is only now becoming rather well-known, but was not so in Nehru's lifetime. On China, he blundered, for once again his nationalist spirit took over his saner side.

Yet when it came to matters that had to do with religion, family, science and the creation of national assets, Nehru definitely set the pace. The contradiction in Nehru arose because he was both an advocate of citizenship as well as of nationalism. Nehru was an exemplar as a citizen, but failed India when he was stoked by nationalism. Even after admitting all these failings, Nehru remains an 'elite of calling' who could stand on his own and challenge established custom and wisdom. He directed India towards secularism, scientific and industrial self-reliance, and kept us from being pawns in the hands of superpowers. Again, he did all this when the social climate around him made no such demands. Because Pakistan failed to perform, or even start up, on such enterprises, it is where it is now. Even America, which was always in Pakistan's corner, does not hesitate to list it as a probable failed state.

After Nehru, India's leaders have not lived up to the role of an 'elite of calling' role but acted rather as politicians and, in fact, enlarged on many of Nehru's flaws. Instead of picking up from where Nehru left us, instead of correcting the inadequacies of Nehru's contributions, they have played the game as politicians do. Without Nehru, India's secularism, its record in agriculture, sciences and higher education, its ability to produce capital goods, would have been seriously wanting. Yet Nehru left several gaps, primarily in the health and education sectors and in the way the legal apparatuses continue to function in this country. Not only are there grave inadequacies in the delivery of health and education, Nehru did not quite free our legal and law enforcement apparatuses from much of their colonial past. For example, our Criminal Penal Code as well as the provisions for Preventive Detention and Emergency can be traced to our pre-Independence days. This has left the field wide open for dystopia to settle in.

This is why we see a plethora of politicians avidly maximizing the given. Catering to short-term interests the policy on reservations has moved from being utopian to dystopian. There is no shame any longer if one is wanting in 'merit'. Urban planning has fallen by the wayside, which is unfortunate, and we shall return to this aspect in a later chapter. Neither excellence in health and education, nor efficiency in urban planning, nor the quality delivery of public services is possible without a commitment to citizenship where the utopia of fraternity rules. While Nehru did inaugurate independent India's thinking on this vital issue and while the Constitution made special provisions for this, democracy cannot afford to idle away. As we argued earlier, democracy needs constant attention and care. It is a delicate plant, even a rare jewel, which we could lose should there be a lapse in our vigilance.

The absence of commitment to the core aspects of democracy became increasingly obvious in the post-Nehru years. Instead of equating the public sector with service, his daughter, Indira Gandhi, made it synonymous with 'nationalization'. Political control, at whatever cost, became the guiding motto of the Congress party after Nehru and, indeed, this characterizes all political parties today.

Who can deny that the rich-poor divide has deepened in India and that our form of liberalized economy is paying practically no attention to research and science? Nor can we turn away from the fact that the majority of our people are disadvantaged because of ill health and poor education. What good is economic growth, if large numbers still struggle under these very un-democratic circumstances? When something as urgent as health and education leaves politicians in our country unmoved, why should they be really concerned when infrastructure projects are behind schedule; when roughly 10 million tons of grain rot because there are no proper storages facilities; when roughly 92 per cent of the working population is unorganized and informal in character; when urban growth is characterized by increasing slums?

For political leaders to be the vanguard of democracy, what must remain uppermost in any strategy move is that society comes before the economy. This, in a nutshell, is how political planning should be envisaged. But to be able to think society, it is necessary to rise above sectional differences and spurn the temptations of playing the 'politics of the given'.

Vision-impaired Planning: Economists of the Given

When we examine Nehru's contributions we must take into account that he did not wait for approbation from his voters before he acted. He was convinced he was on the right track but subjected his government to the popular vote. The electorate returned the Congress regularly till 1967 for Nehru had a Plan and the others did not. Nehru went against the tide, he forced people to decide on issues, and the others did not. The Hindu Right had no concrete plan, other than hating Muslims and avenging Hindu pride, while Nehru had a vision that was citizen-oriented. Right or wrong, Nehru provided India with a dream while the others were only trying to forget a nightmare, namely the Partition and the history of foreign rule.

Our admiration for Nehru grows because he did most of this through the medium of Five-Year Plans. Many of them did not yield the expected benefits—the Second Plan was, for instance, criticized for not paying enough attention to agriculture—but they had a direction. One could attack or praise them and in doing so we make some progress in terms of social development.

Today, our planners are of a different kind altogether. They are afraid to take a position and, like politicians, are non-committal on major issues, hoping that events will make the final decision for them.

Planners should have done better; at least they should have looked ahead and shamed the politicians into action. Yet they too are unable to think beyond the given and are constantly making compromises in the name of being realistic. The documents produced by them are not of the kind that can challenge politicians, nor even make them do a rethink. In most cases, the planners stuff their policy prescriptions with so many caveats that at the end of the day, there are many excuses to stay with the 'given'.

When economists turn administrators, or hope to become administrators, they start to think with their hands—both of them. Their response to problems is nearly always on the lines of: 'on the one hand...and then on the other...' The majority of experts in our Planning Commission are economists, making it the largest employer of the Indian Economic Services. Little wonder that their vision documents are liberally peppered with 'but', 'however' and 'while', or words to that effect. This marks practically every statement they make with deep ambivalence. Consequently, we are unsure about the route to take. Faced with this jungle of options, should we turn left, right or centre, or just stand still? Planners may want to keep their options open because their masters are fickle, but this confuses a country looking for direction.

Before we come to a more recent edition, open the Planning Commission's earlier 'Approach Paper' to the Eleventh Five-Year Plan. Going through it is difficult for we almost instantly stumble into a thicket of qualifiers. This document asserts that the Plan's major component is to spur private investment, *but* substantial increases must be secured for public resources. Likewise, small and marginal farmers need to be encouraged *but* also middle and large farmers. Now this is puzzling. Large and marginal farmers have very different interests, so which way should we turn?

The Planning Commission also promises us a 9 per cent growth rate *but* there should be no sharp disruption in the world economy and no cyclical downturns in oil prices. The 'Approach Paper' recognizes that agricultural productivity must rise *but* no dramatic technological breakthrough is in sight. There is also the need to narrow the gap between actual agricultural yields and those in trial runs, *but* it is hard to get region-wise, crop-wise intelligence on this.

Recognizing agriculture's poor form over the past decades, the Planning Commission wants farmers to think differently, even big. The experts assure the cultivators that their fears regarding the move from agriculture to horticulture are exaggerated. They should diversify into high-value products like fruits and flowers and climb up the value chain. *But*, as food stocks are dangerously low, they must not neglect cereal production either. Under these circumstances what should a simple farmer do? Can crop insurance help? Yes, it can, *but* as it is too expensive only 4 per cent of agriculturists can afford it.

The 'Approach Paper' goes into honest details on how deficient our health and educational services are, especially when it comes to the poor. The admissions made in this document are truly startling. Children cannot read simple sentences nor do elementary sums. This is not surprising, the experts argue, when 30 per cent of school teachers do not have a Higher Secondary certificate. Is there a way out?

Obviously it is very urgent for us to plan interventions in education and health. Schools need to be upgraded, *but* teachers don't work; likewise rural health should be improved *but* doctor absenteeism is rampant. We need high-quality technical education *but* there is a shortage of qualified instructors. No matter which way we turn, for every possible action there is an equal and opposite inaction.

It is not as if the tendency to equivocate is a trait peculiar to the current set of experts in the Planning Commission. Montek Singh Ahluwalia's guru, Dr Manmohan Singh, showed his adeptness in this department when he was in charge of the South Commission in Geneva. In probably his most quoted address, entitled 'Development Policy Research: The Task Ahead', Manmohan Singh's 'buts' were often more categorical than his assertions.

Sample the following from Dr Manmohan Singh's address:

> It is not fair to lay the blame for slow development on excessive state apparatuses, *but* developing countries need to trim their government machineries.

> De-regulation is important in order to de-politicize the economic process, *but* politics cannot be wished away.

> Competition is good, *but* as Adam Smith warned, it requires political control.

> Further expansion of the public sector is not the way to go, *but* the private sector cannot do the job by itself.

> The public sector is not innovative, *but* how can it be for it operates in an environment where monopolies are strong.

> Export orientation is desirable, *but* what will happen if every country drops its local markets and begins to export?

Quite clearly, whether it is Rajiv Gandhi, Narasimha Rao, or the Left Front, there is something in it for everybody. With a format like this, economist-administrators will never have to eat crow. As long as no long-term vision is spelt out, planning is a safe affair. As long as the given holds, the Plans make sense, but if things should change, all bets are off.

Though Nehru-bashing is common these days, a glance at the documents of those times reveals a willingness to take risks and step boldly into the future. The First Five-Year Plan was typically such an exercise. As it took positions and had something definitive to offer, it invited both scorn and praise.

Today our planners are very different. Unsure of their future, they play both ends and the middle. This is why they need their 'hands' to think with. This measure protects them against head-butts, even if their plans are a tangle of escape clauses.

Interestingly, once the same economists-cum-administrators retire, or are retired, their pronouncements become more definitive. This is probably true of many bureaucrats. They turn assertive, even radical, the moment they demit office, but never before it.

If a primer for planners is ever written, it should strongly recommend that words like 'but', 'however' and 'while' should be taken out of their vocabulary. Only then will planners stop thinking with their hands; first 'one' and then the 'other'.

Unfortunately, the just released 12th Plan Approach Paper is a cross between a suggestion box and a cork board. We are first stuffed with good intentions and then subjected to thumb-tacked bullet points. It is clear that our Planners mean well and are kind people, but several walls covered with 'must do' reminders cannot substitute for an action plan.

Yes, we must reduce poverty, get our working class up to speed, improve our health and educational systems, use solar energy effectively, and inoculate our roads against early potholes. But how do we get all this done? Whether it is manufacturing, agriculture or skill development, the text is full of 'why' and 'what', with very little spelt out on the 'how'. True, this document is padded with information, numbers and tables, but they can all be sussed out from standard data sets, if not just good old Google.

All of this, put together, makes it hard to comment on the 12th Plan Approach Paper. Even so it is worth a try. If for nothing else, this might prod members of the Planning Commission to think hard on a deep metaphysical question: why, after all, do they exist at their posts?

To begin with, the 12th Plan draft Approach Paper reads almost like its predecessor, the 11th Plan Approach Paper. This naturally prompts us to ask why and where the 11th Plan let us down. As the Planners are the same, they should have an answer to this. From the looks of it, we have stood still in some of the most crucial sectors of our economy.

We have failed to upgrade our manpower skills and improve the contribution of the manufacturing sector. MGNREGA apparently needs 'barefoot engineers' in a hurry, but where are they? Our infrastructure too is shamefully below par, and even state health expenditure doggedly hovers around 1 per cent of GDP and no more. As much as 62 per cent of land under agriculture is rain-fed at present and this figure might increase. We should really panic because sub-soil water is being depleted at the rate of 4 cm per year in North India's alluvial tracts.

Strangely enough, the Planners talk about village 'commons' coming to the rescue, but where are these open grounds and grazing lands? Oscar Lewis, the famous anthropologist, found the absence of village commons in India quite remarkable, especially in contrast to what he was used to in South America. No wonder our cattle look so starved and have to be fed a disproportionate diet of oilcake fodder just to keep them alive. Where have our Planners been living?

Moving away from agriculture, the draft Approach Paper notes that at best about 12 per cent of the workforce is vocationally qualified. The impressive growth in literacy has not altered this picture much. In fact, even after making it through at middle and senior school levels, most young people find jobs as unskilled labourers. By the end of the 12th Plan period it is hoped that 25 per cent of our workers will have seen the inside of a vocational school, but how do we get to this magic number? So far, the Planners have thought of skill development only with respect to construction workers. Now how limited is that? To top it all, we have nearly half a million school teachers who are blissfully untrained.

There are so many issues already, yet no leads on how we can substantively tackle any of them. Yes, the manufacturing sector must employ 100 million more people, but how? We are also told that Private Public Partnerships work well in telecom, oil and gas where profits are quick, but not so in electricity, railways and ports. How then can a difference be made for the better? Without taking us into confidence on what steps have been taken so far to realize any, or all, of the above, how can we meaningfully contribute to the dialogue?

It is no secret that for the economy to grow at 9 per cent, or 7 per cent, or even less, energy availability has to be raised well beyond current levels. Naturally, oil imports are going to increase and it is a no-brainer that this will strain our financial resources. We must then think of alternative energy sources; who can deny that? But what should they be? The Draft Approach is as clueless about this as you or I. Sample the following statement: 'It is essential to develop *some* mechanism of providing power producers with a mix of domestic and imported coal...' Imagine Planners fumbling for 'some mechanism'!

When in a jam, the document tends to bluster its way out by blaming the administration. If some of the government flagship programmes are not working it is because of corruption. Likewise, if the lack of coordination is hurting plan implementation it is because ministries are vertically managed. Even the holy cow, MGNREGA, is blamed for raising agricultural wages and making farming more unprofitable than it already is.

There is a whole section on 'A New Policy Paradigm' but we find no clue in it either. In fact, the text concedes that there is a need to 'shift from planning as allocations to planning as learning and from budget and controls towards improving processes for consultation and co-ordination'. But is this not the Planning Commission's job in the first place? Are the Planners doing themselves a disservice by blocking off the window view with dirty linen?

Though there are a host of hot ideas in the text, they are all packed in ice. However, there is some life in two of the suggestions in this Draft Approach Paper and they should be thawed out. One is about changing the fare structure in the railways so that we can earn more from carrying freight. This needs finessing, but is a doable suggestion with a somewhat clear action prescription.

The other is to adopt at the national level the model set up by the Tamil Nadu Medical Services Corporation to lower drug prices. This last is not strictly a Planning Commission intervention, but there is no harm in learning from others! It is also a good thing that Professor K. Srinath Reddy is heading a commission to look into Universal Health Coverage.

But such a long journey, such a huge exercise, so many experts, and so much public money, just for this? Centuries ago, Saint Bernard of Clairvaux observed that 'hell is full of good meanings, but heaven is full of good works'.

The Planning Commission, like Dante's Virgil, was meant to lead us out of hell, but we find ourselves quite lost in it. Even the issue of poverty, which is so in one's face, becomes the object of a numbers game. Specialists thrive on poverty studies and there are reams of data on how to measure the poor. But does that really matter! Poverty is so obviously out there that even if one were to cover one's eyes, one would feel it through the pores.

Calorie Count: Keeping the Poor Alive

In India, the official measurement of poverty is primarily in terms of calorie intake: 2,400 calories for the rural population and 2,100 for the urban. By this method, the government believes that roughly 28.3 per cent are Below the Poverty Line (BPL). Reports by other experts, including those commissioned by the government, have, as we shall soon see, added other features to the measurement of poverty. Even so, the official estimate of poverty stands unrevised. To be poor, by this definition, it should be hard to stitch body and soul together. It is a matter of survival.

As with everything else, poverty too is a matter of context. In the United States 4.5 million American households below the poverty line own cars, and 290,000 of them actually own up to three cars.

Faced by the growing criticism that poverty levels are standing still in spite of liberalization, the government changed the method of collecting information on this subject. By adjusting the recall period, the administration has successfully reduced the poverty figures by several percentage points: at 28.3 per cent it is about 9 per cent lower than the earlier estimate of 1993-94. Regardless of its veracity, this figure is in keeping with India's universally acclaimed 'growth' story. It also demonstrates how poverty can be removed by statistics (see also Dreze 2010).

The low official poverty rates look good only if the cut-off figure is fixed at ₹11.8 per day, per person, spending power in villages and ₹17.9 in cities. How rational is this figure? Basically, this would be the price of a local bus ticket, and no snacking on the way. But can a man live on bus rides alone? Should we increase this number ever so slightly, by ₹3 for rural areas and ₹2 for cities, the statistics begin to gather an odour. Now the proportion of those who are poor goes up to about 38 per cent. Slowly raise the bar by another tiny fraction, say to ₹22, and this figure swells to an amazing 70 per cent.

This is why many experts, from Suresh Tendulkar to N.C. Saxena, are unconvinced by government figures on poverty. As just calorie requirements reduce the human being to animal levels, these experts argue that other factors should also be included. To this end, Tendulkar formulates a 'poverty line basket' which among other things also includes health, education and nutrition. Accordingly, Tendulkar and Saxena believe that poverty in India is higher than what is officially pronounced. Naturally, the government is not happy with these reports.

If poverty estimates were like batting averages, then it would stand at roughly 50 per cent. When Arjun Sengupta's committee is at the crease the poverty figure touches 77 per cent, but when the Planning Commission takes over it drops to about 29 per cent. Suresh Tendulkar took the score up to 41.8 per cent and that seemed very impressive till N.C. Saxena hit the average at 50 per cent (for discussions on this see Tendulkar, et al., 2009, Saxena 2009, Rai, n.d.).

These numbers are huge: almost half the country's population cannot purchase the bundle of commodities (technically, the 'poverty line basket') that should go with the minimum recommended calorie requirements. Current consensus is around Saxena's finding for it is believed that Tendulkar probably doctored the pitch a bit. He pegged the minimum calorie intake at a level recommended by the FAO, which at 1800 calories per day is well below (by approximately 300-500 calories) that posted by the Indian Council of Medical Research (Tendulkar, et al. 2009: 2). Still, his analysis showed that 41.8 per cent were below the poverty line.

Therefore, once we step out of the official routine, the numbers of poor become much larger, no matter which way we look. Instead of removing poverty, from the Antodaya scheme of yesterday to the MGNREGA intervention of today, have we only kept the poor alive?

The Numbers Game: Poverty Estimates and Targeted Approaches

The reason we like poverty estimates and numbers so much is because we depend almost solely on *targeted* approaches to removing poverty. But targeted policies work best when they are aimed at a small minority. It is not possible to have special programmes that affect anything between 50 per cent to 70 per cent of the population. Such interventions will cease to be special unless they take in the whole.

Among other failings, targeted programmes are a natural magnet for graft and corruption. According to Saxena, a chunk of supplies from ration shops, meant only for Below Poverty Line families, regularly goes to the wrong addresses.

N.C. Saxena argues that as many as 17.4 per cent of the richest quintile possesses ration cards (Saxena 2009).

The only improvements in the numbers game come from the reports of committees headed by Tendulkar and Saxena. This is because they include the delivery of public goods in their accounts of poverty. It does not take long to discover that as education and health services are in a poor shape in India it is legitimate to include them in our understanding of poverty. Once we enlarge our perspective and add these other merit goods to the list, it is apparent that poverty is much more stubborn than the government would like us to believe. Even by official estimates, given the fact that about 68 per cent of India's population is rural, almost every second villager is below the poverty line.

But do we really need poverty statistics to tell us that India is poor? How does it really help if Arjun Sengupta is a bigger hitter than Tendulkar or the Planning Commission? The fact is that no matter which way you look at it, around 10 to 15 crore families can barely feed themselves. If Abhijit Sen is to be believed, about 80 per cent of rural India faces chronic starvation. The number of stunted and undernourished children in India equals the population of sub-Saharan Africa. With numbers as large as this, how can there be special programmes for a targeted group?

When the Tendulkar Committee first announced the poverty figure at 41.8 per cent, the Planning Commission and the Ministries of Finance and Social Welfare choked at their desks. So much money would now have to be put away for those 'other' people, who are not like 'us'. To cope with Tendulkar's findings the food subsidy would now cost ₹47917.62 crores and not 28890.4 crores, as estimated earlier. That was still high, but the government could probably live with it. Naturally, when Saxena came up with 50 per cent, nobody in the administration wanted to hear about it.

Such exercises in target-oriented poverty removal programmes do not help when the numbers constitute the majority of our population. Of course, one could hide behind our awesome population figures and argue that there is little else we can do. With a billion-plus on the census rolls, the most urgent task is to keep the poor alive. Doubtless, that is an urgent task, but what about removing poverty? Are we then destined to remain poor, for that is what it seems? In spite of National Democratic Alliance's Antodaya Anna Yojana (literally, delivering food to the last person) in 2000, or the United Progressive Alliance governement's MGNREGA (guaranteeing employment to the poor) in 2005, our poverty rates keep stalking us year after year. Isn't it time we changed tacks and thought of the system, and not just the poor? Perhaps that might help.

For social policies to actually have the desired effect, they need to be inclusive in nature. Targeted projects face a problem because those who are supposed to put them in place see no interest in implementing them. This is why social policies should be such that no one class benefits from them exclusively. For any policy to work, it has to have a systemic spread, especially when we are dealing with public goods like education and health and, by extension, to energy and transportation as well. To believe that public goods are to be sold to the highest bidder is a travesty of developmental planning. At the same time, to argue that limited and short-term policy interventions will add up to a systemic change is a denial of reality. Thus, far from being rooted, the policy expert who denies sociology and social theory, is the least relevant.

Under these conditions, the poor would hardly move up the ladder in quick time unless they are attended to under a much broader format than subjecting them to targeted approaches. What we also realize from the above discussion is that growth does not necessarily lead to development. There are a plethora of action plans regarding education and health, but very rarely are they linked to systemic aspects. We are also misled by indicators like 'literacy', 'poverty levels' or 'longevity', but, as we have seen, these numbers can be very deceptive. None of these actually tell us about the *quality* of education, health and development. This is where we need to think beyond 'targets' to 'people'—to make a real difference. Policies should not be about 'others' but for 'us'. Thinking 'poor' is not always good for the poor because state interventions then do not see them as an integral part of society where the non-poor also live. Only when their lives can be linked within a common horizon will social policies make a true difference.

A clear indication that policies that use targeted projects to remove poverty, ignorance and disease have failed can be judged from the International Rankings in Human Development. Sadly, our position on this scale refuses to go up. When we look at Gender Gap indices, even Bangladesh is better than us. We are, however, going up on another scale. Our lack of honesty in public transactions has raised our ranking in the corruption index of Transparency International. We were 72nd in 2007 but rose to the 85th position in 2008. Yes, Pakistan is worse off than us, but is that any source for solace? Hardly, unless we pitch our standards really low.

Political leaders who are anxious to pander to the given are the ones who push for such target-oriented programmes. Anything else that would involve them in the spirit of fraternity with the poor and unprivileged is not quite thinkable. Reality, as they see it, is that there are the poor and the rich; and the poor, if possible, should be less miserable than they obviously already are. But in none of this are they—the leaders, or policymakers—involved. Consequently, schools for the poor are not for their children, and hospitals for the poor are not for their family members. Thus, while it seems that something like the MGNREGA scheme is the outcome of a fraternal spirit, that is not really true. If corruption eats away what is supposed to go to the poor, if grains are pilfered from the Public Distribution System (see Khera 2011), it does not bother the better-off, the non-poor, for none of these schemes are meant for them anyway.

Neither has Manmohan Singh helped to alter the way politicians look at development.

Manmohan Singh: A Man Who Would Not Be Philosopher or King

When Dr Manmohan Singh became the prime minister, there was hope that he would rise above politics and the constraints of the given. It was widely believed that he might be another Nehru (albeit a non-socialist one), even another uncle or chacha to the young, perhaps on a lesser scale.

It is hard to be both philosopher and king, harder still to pull it off for over two decades. Manmohan Singh realized this last year when a few IIT graduates refused to take their degrees from him, in order to mark their support for Anna Hazare. That ended his dream run of emerging as another chacha.

Only the young can be so outrageous; it is their age that condemns them to performative acts. They have not lived long enough to stew their views over a slow fire, like the rest of us. Naturally, they tend to offend old-timers who are used to a soft dict of pulp, mush and double talk.

Had these students turned down a Deve Gowda, a Chandrashekhar or a Gujral, their act would not have caused a public flutter. Why, in the past, Indira Gandhi too has not been spared. But they were now challenging a person whom even Amartya Sen has certified as a virtuoso among economists, and a close friend. How could mere youngsters fresh out of college spurn a scholar like that? This is what made the whole incident newsworthy.

Quite clearly, these young people appear to have forgotten Manmohan Singh's academic past. Instead, they tend to see him today as just another politician. Doubtless, this is a black-and-white cut-out, and quite unkind; but that is how it looks to the young. Why?

Unfortunately, the logic of being a philosopher and that of being a king are not in tandem; it is either one or the other. Superficially, it would seem that an intellectual loses esteem by stepping out of the ivory tower. But the reverse, in fact, is true. As Karl Mannheim or Jean-Paul Sartre or Edward Said have argued, anybody unconcerned with the filth and squalor of the real world cannot be called an 'intellectual'.

Before one gets the impression that this view is held only by radicals, be it known that it was also sponsored by Edward Shils, a mainstream American sociologist. While Manmohan Singh is certainly not perched atop an ivory tower, it is his submission to politics that has damaged his reputation as an independent scholar. A true intellectual, according to Karl Mannheim, must be in the thick of things and yet not belong to any political party. This is a tightrope, all right, but scholars must learn to walk on it.

If 'philosophers' find that difficult, they should either retire into their chambers or enter palaces and rule like kings. In either case, they would have forfeited their right to be called intellectuals. As there is no such thing as a 'private' scholar, the ivory tower can only be a refuge for esoteric exercises. However, to sign up with a political organization would be the other extreme. It makes one card-carriers of the party will, and incapable of independent thought.

Try as hard as Manmohan might, politics and intellectual life function on different principles. While one submits to party diktats, the other scorns consensus. Intellectuals may be bored by established truths, but are obliged to express them in a professional style. Not for them a free-wheeling, invective-hurling ride, but a measured exercise that knocks on all doors, asking people to rethink old certitudes. Though intellectuals answer to no one, they are answerable to everyone.

Intellectual life is at its best when it is able to criticize, especially when the going is tough. While such an attitude does credit to the scholar, it would ruin a politician's career. A party does not need an honest opinion as much as it does a convenient one. A bad intellectual and a good politician have one feature in common: for both, everything is negotiable. It is precisely this trait that separates a true scholar from the power-seeker.

If Manmohan Singh appears to have lost his intellectual starch it is because he has repeatedly aligned his actions with the logic of politics (worse, coalition politics). For a while he was trapped between a Chair and a throne, but then he chose the latter. It is this that led those IIT graduates to be rude to him, even though he had come to felicitate them. That was not quite fair, but in Manmohan Singh they saw a representative of all that has gone wrong in our public life. As the young are less sullied, they are naturally less cautious. They happily speak their minds and call a spade a shovel.

On the face of it, Manmohan Singh should have been their hero. His elevation in public life has been near immaculate. After his PhD from Cambridge he worked in several universities and ministries. For a time he was also governor of The Reserve Bank. In between all this, he spent a good part of his life in the UN system. Finally, as the promoter of 'economic liberalization' he brought India closer to the west.

Every kid in this block, and in neighbouring ones, should be rearing to be like him; and they probably once did. As long as the going was good, before scams blocked out every other news, Manmohan Singh was the toast of the young. If his image has dipped today it is because circumstances have changed. He is now forced to roll up his sleeves and reveal his party hand. Consequently, the young see him more as a politician than as an intellectual. Once that happens, you are easy meat for youthful predators. He has certainly lost his chance to be another chacha of the kind Nehru was.

Scholars, especially the good ones, are much sought after by political parties to bolster their public image. Bad scholars, on the other hand, desperately seek political parties to enhance their personal status. Manmohan Singh did not have to be in politics; he was a good economist, and could have stayed that way forever. Yet, by choosing to walk up the political path, he swapped his philosopher's gown for a kingly robe.

The Congress has certainly gained a politician, but the world has lost an intellectual and a possible 'citizen elite'.

CHAPTER V
A Thousand Tyrants:
One Citizen, Many Masters

While we in India are not tyrannized by a dictator, we regularly face unfair and arbitrary interference in our daily lives from a thousand officials, big and small, who have political patronage. The manner in which our representatives behave, the perks they claim, their unsavoury alliances and their utter disregard for propriety reveal how far they are from being true citizens. Yet, their programmes are ostensibly built around what 'people want', which actually translates into maximizing the given and not of advancing society as a whole. In this process, larger concerns that affect us as a collective of citizens are overlooked. To make matters worse, we have begun to view democracy as an inefficient option—which it need never be at all.

It is true we do not have a dictator who can line us up against the wall and shoot us. While that threat is not there, yet we die a little each time we bribe everyday dictators that surround us. We can sense their presence well before they touch us for a bribe. Even though the average person begins life with an empty cupboard, it soon gets stacked with skeletons, big and small. Fear stalks most homes, for nobody is sure when the next bribe will have to be given and to whom and for what.

People do not trust one another and the idea of reciprocity is consequently a distant one. As we noted earlier, to make people think as citizens requires a fraternal framework, which can only be imposed from above by the state. When the administration demonstrates its fidelity to universal law, corruption recedes almost immediately. In the ultimate analysis, this is the only thing that counts and not culture, history or the democracy of numbers (see also Rothstein 2011).

You have to bribe to get a ration card; you have to bribe to ply your wares on a pushcart; you have to bribe to get your child into school or your mother into hospital. In fact, the hardest thing for the general public to achieve is to be able to lead an honest existence. Getting a legitimate completion certificate for a home built to sanctioned plans is almost impossible without a bribe. At every turn of an ordinary life there is the lurking worry that the latest skeleton will stick out of the cupboard.

Democracy, Indian style, has made all this possible. The political class, as a rule, lives off this ever-present fear that haunts the population. That allows them to act as super-patrons and dispense favours to a select few. To be able to get this far they must accumulate wealth, corner resources and perpetuate their political dynasties. In addition to all of the above, they must be unconcerned about everyday issues of ordinary people. To do otherwise is to exhibit a weakness that no politician of our times, of any calibre or stripe, must ever demonstrate.

Elections only give this political class more reason to flourish. It does not matter which party wins, the political class always triumphs. It is impossible for the good guys to make it to the top, for the short-term interests of the many compel us all to bow to the petty tyrants that line our streets. We are corrupted on our way in and as we go out. Only the most willing in this trade have a fighting chance of making it to that house on the hill.

Opacity is the wall that fortifies this political class best. The existing laws shield them from being tried for misrule, corruption, money laundering and much worse. Naturally, politics attracts people of the kind who can take full advantage of such privileges. And like any dictatorship, the closer one is to this charmed nexus, the more honey-coloured the world becomes.

All of this makes one wonder whether democracy is really a bazaar affair, as Socrates feared it would be. Whether Parliament functions or not makes little difference since nobody is concerned about debating policy matters, for that is hard work. Instead, they fight over issues which require little work but a lot of hot air. To combat terrorism, to upgrade universities, to help the poor and heal the sick you need professionalism in public service. These are technical policy issues that no major party wants to discuss.

Leaders Behaving Badly: A Pastoral Profession for Sale

According to our members of Parliament (MPs) there are two Indias. One belongs to them and to people they deem belonging to their own exalted status, while in the other live lower division clerks (LDCs) and assorted riff-raff. It is on the basis of this divide that our Parliamentarians justified hikes in their perks and salaries in 2011. They were quick to point out that they fully deserve 50,000 local calls and 50,000 units of electricity free per year because, unlike LDCs, their services to the people depend on these facilities.

But will these perks actually help MPs accomplish their job description? With 50,000 local calls, at three minutes per call, MPs would be glued to their phones for seven hours a day. That is a full working day, excluding the lunch hour. So much time for so much talk, but for what? The story does not quite end there. As MPs now want two phones with the same facilities, the total talk time would be around fourteen hours a day, with perhaps a few breaks in between. If from sunrise till well after sunset, telephone signals fill the MP's ear, how will the people get their word in edgeways?

Likewise, 50,000 units of free electricity a year also distance MPs from the electorate. To make full use of this largesse, MPs must spend twenty-four hours a day for 365 days going back and forth between two fully air-conditioned rooms. This will again keep them from visiting their hot and dusty constituencies. Even when it comes to travel allowances, we find that the same pattern repeats: they too are designed to separate the leaders from the led.

With thirty-four business-class tickets for self and companion (disclosed or otherwise), MPs can fly far away from their constituencies roughly three times a month. Note that they must take long-distance flights as there are no business-class tickets in planes that make short hops within a constituency. Even unlimited first-class AC train journeys with companion would involve long-distance travel away from their constituencies and from those who voted them to power.

As these perks encourage MPs to stay away from their people, it is fair for us to question the freebies they have helped themselves to.

But why do most of us balk at the idea of MPs getting a salary hike? They want their pay packet to be heavier than that of the LDCs, but who wouldn't? And yet, when MPs pull LDCs down to make themselves look good, it sticks in our collective throat.

To understand why we feel that way, it needs to be kept in mind that a parliamentarian's profession is principally 'pastoral' and not 'remunerative'. In 'pastoral' occupations, people are not paid for the work they do, but so that they can do their work. In pastoral professions it is impossible to compensate people adequately for the services they give. Their contributions are priceless.

What salary do you think a soldier should be paid when he is out there on the front risking his life so that others might live? It is impossible to make such a calculation. If one were to pay every soldier for the work he does we would be bankrupt in no time with no cash in the till, not even for our lowly LDCs.

On the other hand, it is possible to figure out how much corporate bosses, cricketers, movie stars, builders and architects should make. There are tried and tested formulas for costing them, even if these methods are frequently violated. This is why nobody really faults a business manager or a chartered accountant or an industrialist for making money. Indeed, their success is often measured in those terms. But theirs are not pastoral professions.

Yet, if a doctor, a professor, a policeman, or an MP should say that they have opted for their respective jobs because they had money on their mind, it immediately sounds vulgar. This is why our sensibilities are offended when a doctor overcharges, when a professor joins a no-work demonstration, when a priest demands more pay from his parishioners, or when a policeman gets fat and corrupt. Likewise, when MPs noisily demand a wage hike because of all the hard work they say they do, it has bad taste written all over it.

Unfortunately, the public debate regarding the salary demands of MPs did not distinguish between pastoral and remunerative professions. This enabled our parliamentarians to obfuscate and link their salary demands with that of senior bureaucrats and professionals in the corporate sector.

What they deftly sidetracked is that the stated purpose for which MPs are elected is to serve the people (LDCs included), feel their pain and relieve them of it. Now, what could be more pastoral than that? Perhaps the work of a soldier! Yet MPs complained loudly whenever attempts were made to compare their pay with that of the army jawan. They knew instinctively that this juxtaposition would spoil their case.

This is not to suggest that those in pastoral professions must live like the proverbial church mouse. Yet, come to think of it, if soldiers or priests or teachers do their job well, there is no salary that can equal their contribution. Try putting a price to giving up your life, or saving souls, or imparting education. Members of these 'pastoral' professions are not paid for what they contribute to society; they can never be. Once MPs begin to appreciate that theirs is also a pastoral vocation, they might begin to temper their worldly demands.

According to a 2009 survey, the average asset of a parliamentarian from the Telegu Desam Party is ₹13 crore; from the NCP, ₹30 crore; from the BSP ₹4.76 crore; from the

Congress ₹6.86 crore, and the list goes on. If anything, this is an embarrassment of riches, and, remember, these are only declared incomes. At the same time, many of our MPs are also long in the tooth. The numbers of those aged over fifty have risen from 174 in 2004 to 199 in 2009. So, if one were to apply LDC standards again, the MPs go on, like supercharged batteries, much after these other lowly bureaucrats have retired with their measly pensions.

It is said that several MPs from across parties opposed the hike in salaries, but their voice was drowned by others in Parliament. The MPs wage bill was passed within a week, a record by all standards. Look at the time taken to put in place the Forest Rights Act, or the fact that the Police Reforms Act has not yet been passed though decades have gone by. When placed against this background, one cannot help but be repulsed by the alacrity with which MPs have acted to help themselves. In this all parties are culpable.

This greed hurts public sentiment, not only because MPs want more money, but because they have wholly forsaken the 'pastoral' nature of their chosen vocation.

The Consolidation of the Political Class: Agreement on Fundamentals

Digvijay Singh, a senior Congress spokesman, has said on several occasions that Manmohan Singh 'is an overrated economist but an underrated politician'. In July 2012, the BJP's Yashwant Sinha said the same thing but conveniently forgot to mention where he got the idea from. At least one part of this statement rings true. Our Prime Minister can be ferocious, as with the Nuclear Bill, indeed, some argue that it was his forcefulness on this matter that won him a second term in 2009. But he can also appear very docile and pliant, as he was on the Caste Census issue. When it came up in Parliament, he easily gave in to Laloo Yadav of the Rashtriya Samajwadi Party (RSP), Mulayam Singh Yadav of the Samajwadi Party (SP) and a host of other

'Backward Class' activists. These politicians wanted castes to be counted in the census for they had every intention of playing with the numbers to demand that the reservation quota for the 'Backwards' be raised from its present 27 per cent.

Was it coalition politics that made the cabinet acquiesce to the demand of Mulayam and Laloo? That may have been the case if a weaker man were at the helm. But Manmohan Singh had already proved Digvijay right with the way he handled the Nuclear Bill. He knows his mind and is not an easy pushover. This leaves us with just one inescapable conclusion. Contrary to popular belief, it was not coalition politics that forced the Prime Minister's hand. He relented to caste in the Census because his own party members wanted it that way. The demand for a caste census was as much within the Congress as outside it. But Manmohan Singh successfully underplayed this fact by letting the dogs out and gave the appearance of running scared of the Backward Class protagonists. Untrue though this may sound, there are a large number of casteists in the Congress itself. But with activists of the Samajwadi Party (SP) and Rashtriya Janata Dal (RJD) beating their chest in the open, Congress members could now stay home and yet get their way. Having one's cake and eating it too never appeared so realistic before.

Through this entire period, Manmohan Singh helped his party hold on to its progressive credentials by making himself look weak. Should the occasion demand, the same man could also act very differently. On the Nuclear Bill, Manmohan Singh exuded the confidence that befits the leader of a pack. He clearly broadcast what direction his party was to take, coalition or no coalition. He called the bluff of the Left Front and happily shed them, like dead skin. It was a risky move; the CPI (M)-led group had stood by him against the BJP, but that did not count any longer. He did not want anybody to spoil his tryst with George Bush, who already had one foot out of the door in his own country. What is more, Manmohan Singh had read the mood of his party well and this encouraged him to go ahead. They were all looking for a way to shake off the Left, and now, at last, the tick was out of their fur.

If in the closing months of UPA 1 in 2009, the prime minister could take on the Left Front with 59 members, how can Mulayam and Laloo with a combined strength of only 27 parliamentarians daunt him? As an economist, our prime minister knows his arithmetic well. Why then did UPA II not force its way and call the bluff of the Samajwadi Party (SP) and the Rashtriya Janata Dal (RJD) who support it from outside? Further, as these two parties were bloodied in the 2009 elections, they are in no mood to call for another one in a hurry. Mulayam and Laloo together have only 5 per cent of parliamentarians and with just about 5 per cent of votes polled in their favour. Ram Vilas Paswan, the other North Indian caste activist, could not get a single member from his party to Parliament, himself included.

If one were to take the six major political parties that officially have caste on their mastheads, their presence is not impressive either. In this Lok Sabha, their members constitute less than one-fifth of the strength of the House. Further, as they captured only 19.6 per cent of the votes polled, they fare no better in terms of their electoral base either. Of these six caste parties, only the DMK, with eighteen parliamentarians, is in UPA II.

Since it was Congress MPs who secretly wanted a caste census—just as much as those from the DMK, SP and RJD—it was wise for Manmohan Singh to appear conciliatory. This cleverly gave the impression of a government hemmed in by coalition constraints. Fortunately for the Congress, Laloo and Mulayam played their roles to perfection. Left to himself, the Prime Minister would have probably gone along with P.C. Chidambaram and Mukul Wasnik of the Congress. They were opposed to caste in the Census, but were a minority voice in the Congress. If he really wanted to, Manmohan Singh could have also worked on the leading opposition party to come out differently on this issue. In fact, Gopinath Munde took some time before he supported caste in the Census, while Nitin Gadkari, representing the RSS view, actually opposed it.

Manmohan Singh is, in fact, quite adept at managing coalition politics. He could let his partners take a long walk if they did not see eye to eye with him, yet he could also give the impression that they hold his government on a short, tight leash. It is to his credit that a large number of people believe that coalition partners were responsible for forcing castes to appear in the Census. The truth is that at no stage was Manmohan Singh hostage to coalition arithmetic. If anything, he was a slave to his party's internal chemistry. This is why it was necessary to give the impression of conceding to a bunch of strays even while Congress held the whip hand.

The Congress has drifted away from the original ideals that went into its creation. Indira Gandhi had compromised her party's anti-casteist positions long before the RJD and SP got into the fray. When these latter-day casteists surfaced, they found the atmosphere entirely to their liking. They gave small peasant aspirations a caste colour, aided, no doubt, by Mandal's recommendations.

At this point the Congress could have acted decisively and fought Mandal, as Rajiv Gandhi had once begun to. In later years, the opposition to OBC Reservations waned and finally it became part of Congress's Manifesto. There was now little to differentiate the casteists in the RJD, SP or elsewhere with the many that were in the Congress. Along came the end of one-party rule, and this exaggerated the politics of convenience and the bartering away of values that the Congress once stood for.

Under Manmohan Singh the tactic, for all practical purposes, is to appease caste politicians without actually saying so. Other than capturing and retaining power, there is no larger game plan or strategy regarding the kind of India we should build. The Congress is trying to return to the days when its capacious umbrella simultaneously sheltered a wide variety of interests. It is this aspiration that separates it from many other parties which are either narrowly focused or spatially limited. But in these troubling times, there is room even for casteists in the Congress shade.

Nehru's days were plainer, simpler. It was then unthinkable for anybody from within the party to voice a pro-caste or a pro-Hindu position. But fortunately for Manmohan's Congress, it can easily blame coalition politics today whenever it takes an opportunistic turn.

The reason why politicians get elected in spite of serious criminal charges against them is because we do not discuss fundamentals any longer. This is why they get past the post and succeed in lowering the performance levels in parliaments and legislatures. Democracy does well when politicians oil-wrestle over policies, for that brings in the best public minds to the job. They wrangle, slip, slide and steady themselves in a continuous contest over issues that matter in a deep and abiding way.

Only when politicians differ on policies, you need skill, learning and dedication. If that were the case in India today, the media would delve into issues which are far from frivolous. We would have informed debates on TV and in the press on whether the market should rule, or whether it should be politically regulated and controlled? Should we think of clean coal and diesel instead of nuclear energy? Should we recast agriculture so that farmers can exit the village, or make the village a better place?

Instead, as there is a general agreement on fundamentals, chunks of the great political unwashed find their way into public life. They are incapable of thinking of or acting on any issue other than what is in their immediate petty self-interest, which is why our political life is like garbage in and garbage out. It is time that the UPA and the NDA began to disagree on things big so that they could get together on things small. Only then will we find relief from ethnic wars, floods, terrorism, to name just a few of the many everyday family wreckers.

As anybody can be denied what is legitimately theirs by a petty tyrant who is tied to the bigger one in a great chain of graft, very few have the guts to rock the boat. Even when something as horrendous as ethnic killings take place, instead of coming together to deliver justice, parties relish reaming out the other side in the media. If the BJP is accused of Gujarat 2002, the counter-accusations against the Congress hark back to Delhi 1984. For every concession made to Reliance by one faction, there are charges against the other for favouring Vedanta, Essar, Tata or whoever.

Instances of this kind crowd our political space and we are seemingly helpless at halting this trend. If one chief minister from the NDA is caught with his hand in the till, the tendency is to blame the UPA predecessor for setting the pace. If the BJP accuses the Congress of giving out election tickets to history-sheeters (or candidates convicted of crimes) the Congress can, and does, hit back in the same coin. The blame game goes on— as if to show that two wrongs can make a right.

The media shows little inclination to take any initiative other than following these politicians at high speed, cutting corners to get there before anybody else. If in this process your windscreen is splattered with trivial muck, the journalists are not the only ones to be blamed. Of course, they could do better. They could, for instance, bring to our notice that during the 2012 monsoon season when the 482-kilometre-long coastline of Odisha was ravaged by floods, pathetically little was done by the government to rehabilitate the victims of this disaster. They could also tell us what exactly is going on in Maruti's Manesar car factory between workers and management. It would help us make up our minds on industrial policy if we had a handle on how contract labour and the regular (unionized) labour force interact with management in the automobile industry. On the other hand, from the point of a sensation-seeking journalist, it is easier and more fun to pick up gossip from political headquarters, for what politicos do makes the headlines.

Parliamentarians, legislators and most politicians in India are constantly pressing their knees on their opponents' necks when they should be working together on fundamentals to change the given and get ahead. But these fundamentals require a commitment to fraternity without which it is impossible to frame adequate policies regarding poverty, ignorance and disease. It is precisely because our ministers and politicians do not address the important issues that they have the time to behave badly in public. When the fur flies, either in Parliament or in the state assemblies, it is peculiarly distasteful because the politicians are only attending to their petty interests. When these grown-ups behave appallingly, it is not because they disagree on fundamentals; if that were the case, their excesses would appear more dignified.

In fact, there is more bipartisanship and consensus in Indian politics than is good for democracy. This is because all of it is located at the wrong place. Both the UPA and NDA agree on the basics, such as on economic, nuclear and reservation policies. In all these matters, they claim to represent the will of the people. It seems the people want the 'bomb', of course they do, but does that mean they should have it? The people want caste favours, of course they do, but why does a democracy have to give in to this base craving? The people want immediate relief from poverty and starvation, but does that mean they can only get band-aid solutions?

Politicians also agree on what should be left out. Neither the Congress- nor the BJP-led coalitions are seriously interested in evolving policies on agriculture, urbanization, skill development or health delivery, such that these measures would address the aspirations of the electorate. As tackling these major issues would require too much work, it is easier to address demands from different categories of people who are, in their own ways, trying to maximize the given. Such piecemeal handouts give the impression that not only are politicians 'listening to the people' but also serving them by addressing their immediate needs.

What, however, is happening most of the time is that our political leaders are calculating how to represent different factional interests among them and not thinking policy. To put it bluntly, it is primarily about distributing the spoils of office across partners in the coalition government. For example, very recently Sharad Pawar was miffed at the seating arrangement in Parliament after Pranab Mukherjee left his post as Finance Minister to become President of India. In order to mollify the National Congress Party (NCP) of which Mr Pawar is the boss, the UPA government agreed to appoint members from his organization to various positions as a compensation package.

As a result, Tariq Anwar will be Deputy Chairperson of the Rajya Sabha and will have a say in the appointment of governors.

When the family of democratic nations sits for dinner, India appears uncomfortable and with awkward table manners. We certainly have free elections, but we still look edgy and starved at the high table. The big paradox of India's democracy is that free elections and mass hunger go side by side. To figure this one out we need to first accept the fact that our democracy is different. Sixty years ago a generation stayed up till midnight on 15 August waiting for the day to break. But today, do we have a true liberal democracy or one where patron-client relationships thrive under the cover of democracy?

Corruption and Patronage: Cohorts of the Politics of the Given

Our failure to deal with corruption stems from our overall reliance on the politics of the given. Since our starting point is a situation which is deficient in many essentials, every Indian thinks it is natural, and realistic, to try and maximize what each one of us has, any way we can. In the given situation there is not only a shortage of the best schools, hospitals and such like, but also a shortage of even second-best and third-best institutions. So the urban rich will do their best to stay where they are and get ahead to the extent possible, and this logic works all the way to the bottom of the hierarchy. The poor too do what they can to maximize their opportunities as do the middle class from the lower to the upper reaches.

These are the ideal set of conditions for the patron-client network to flourish. Let us take a simple everyday example. The person who functions as a cook and odd-job man in your house falls sick. The government hospitals are horrible and it is in your interest that he regains his health soon so that he can work for you and you can live the good life. But to get him medical attention in a government hospital is not an easy task. It helps if you know somebody who knows somebody who can help your cook jump the line and get a doctor's attention. So while you are somebody's patron, you automatically submit to a higher patron yourself.

Take another example. Now you want your child to get to a good school. The government schools are atrocious, but getting admission in a good private school is a daunting task. Obviously, you have to do the right thing as a parent. This sets you off in search of a 'patron'—someone who can get your child into a school of your choice because the principal in that institution in turn owes him something from way back when.

Now it is your turn to fall sick. Once again you seek a patron who will tell the much-sought-after specialist in the private hospital that you are not like the other patients in there. Not only do you have the money, you are also now well connected, so a little extra attention is called for. This can often make the difference between life and death. Even fun times can get a lot better with a little help from one's friends. That circuit house in the hills or in the lush forests by the river is all yours for a week if a patron in power puts in a word for you.

What is common in these scenarios? No matter whether one is rich or poor, when public services are woefully inadequate it always helps to have a patron. The main support structure from a patron-client democracy is the lack of public support structures for citizens. This is why both the well off and the poor, from different vantage points, would do well to cultivate a patron, for who knows where the next emergency will come from.

Patron-client politics also corrupts the bureaucracy and the administration by tempting the staff working in these offices with handsome handouts. This allows them to avoid the public health, education, transport and energy systems and build cozy little private nests for themselves. The most important consideration for everybody is how to remain independent of government schools, hospitals and transport systems. The affluent have nightmares imagining themselves in one of these places. Failing a proper universal delivery system, patrons are the best way out.

As patrons are in control, and with our consent, there is little urgency to trim the law and bureaucratic procedures so that they enable rather than disable most of us. From property matters to estate duties to pension funds, one is always at the mercy of incomprehensible bureaucratic procedures forcing one to instinctively reach out to a patron for help. In the patron-client kind of democracy we are all implicated—some of us as better-off clients, and some of us as both patrons and clients. But no matter where we stand in the social hierarchy we are always in a state of perpetual tension because there is no reliable public delivery of public goods that we can turn to in times of need.

In these conditions, each section is doing whatever it takes to get an edge over others in a similar position or, at least, not to slide lower. This is why nearly all of us are driven to patron-client-like social ties. As a result, patrons are always in short supply for that is the best way to beat the odds. Only a patron can help break the law and get you a notch higher, find your mother a hospital, your child a school and you a regular job. Once there are patron-client formations, corruption is a natural corollary; why would one want a patron who would only bat for the client according to law—the idea is to break it. Therefore, as we toil in the attempt to maximize what is given, what is real and what is unshakably there, it is almost inevitable that corruption will follow.

Against this background it is easy to see that once quality public educational and health institutions are established, once social security services are provided to us as citizens, once the most profound uncertainties of our life can be taken care of by a welfare state, the ground slips away from under the patrons and they look a lot like faded cardboard cut-outs, all paper and pulp. The elite of calling can change the circumstances such that the options available are not limited to the current 'given'. Failing that, corruption is here to stay because the existing reality favours the ordinary pursuit of seeking patronage. In this situation, those who are out of it are either brave, or extraordinarily gifted, or just losers. It is the last category that is bound to win in terms of sheer numbers, but who wants to be there?

If, however, a more acute reading of what people want were to be entertained, that would mean addressing their 'aspirations'.

This in turn would require debate on fundamentals, which would spoil the easy calm that prevails between political leaders today. It is not surprising then that all political parties are united in opposing the Lokpal Bill, or any other intervention that makes them vulnerable to charges of corruption. It is another matter that the Anna Hazare team has not covered itself with glory either by playing politics during elections. Yet, what remains unshakable is the united opposition of politicians against the principles of a Lokpal Bill where politicians can be investigated by an independent agency.

Further, the Lokpal Bill also seeks to provide protection to whistle-blowers, and we need that urgently to complement the Right to Information Act. The last important aspect of the Lokpal Bill is to institute a citizens' service bureau to ensure time-bound and graft-free services from the officials in the administration. On the face of it, none of this is objectionable, but our MPs complain loudly against it on a variety of flimsy excuses—the most strident being that ordinary people cannot question parliamentarians as they have been elected and hence reflect the 'voice of the people'! Democracy is limited to a play between majorities and minorities, with no thought to the demands of the law.

The dependence that arises from our general inability to satisfy citizenship aspirations, including such basics as quality health and education makes India corruption-friendly. Corruption is not a stand-alone phenomenon. The root cause behind it is the structured disregard of the public, and no party is willing to change that; they are all too busy maximizing the given. When elected, neither the BJP, nor Janata Dal, nor Congress, has ever opposed an issue as fundamental as detention without trial. They have all agreed to it in one form or the other.

Nor has any government asked for an exposé of the non-performing assets that saddle most public-sector banks. Come to think of it, which party will commit itself to disqualifying any of its elected members if they have serious criminal charges against them? Today there are as many as fifty-three MPs who fall under this category, and many of them are in the opposition.

While we are at it, try this trick question. What was the name of the IIT-trained officer who lost his life for exposing corruption in the National Highways Authority of India (NHAI)? Do the names Lalit Mehta or V. Sasindran ring a bell? They were killed for taking the Right to Information Act seriously. They doggedly pursued their investigations against corrupt officials and eventually paid for it with their lives.

It is not the Congress alone that is complicit in all of this, but practically every party, including those in the front ranks of today's anti-corruption moral brigade. The percentage increase in assets of re-contesting MPs in 2009 has jumped by 289 per cent since the previous elections. As many as 748 candidates in the Bihar polls self-declared that they had criminal cases against them.

These facts reflect the institutional bases of corruption, but they go unaddressed. Mass resentment is trained only towards certain political targets. This is why, once in power, it is anybody's guess what today's anti-corruption activists would do. Incidentally, Hitler was not corrupt, but does it take just that to be everybody's favourite? Corruption occupies a lot of space in our public engagement, but because of the attempts across the board to maximize the given, we will never find a lasting solution to it. The scale of corruption has certainly increased and it is directly related to the dearth, or near absence, of an 'elite of calling' in India. We still remember Laloo's fodder scam and the Bofors scandal, but compared to the 2G spectrum allocation scam or the Commonwealth Games scandals they appear small-time. Under corporate pressure, the government has eased many of the restrictions in setting up telecom towers and in the radiation content of mobile phones, though the health hazards of such concessions are so well recognized (see *Mail Today*, 25 August 25 2012). Before long we might even think that Raja[1] was no more than a pickpocket. Without structural

---

[1] It was during A. Raja's term as minister for telecommunication that the 2G corruption case was exposed. The investigation agency found enough evidence to institute a case against him forcing him to resign from

inhibitors the scale of these public scandals keeps growing. Indeed, when we think back to the years when corruption commissions under Gorwala and Kriplani were set up, in 1952 and 1954 respectively, we cannot help but notice the innocence of those times. When we read those reports today, after nearly sixty years, it is like skipping through a kindergarten text.

Just consider: one of Kriplani's big complaints was that politicians were travelling ticketless on trains to attend party rallies! This, he felt, was not only improper but was also derailing our national resources. Today, the perk package of MPs allows for limitless train journeys by air-conditioned first-class coaches, anywhere in the country. This one example shows just how dated old corruption stories are. The Gorwala report too emphasized the lavishness of official tours and cautioned us against 'durbari'-style politics.

Gorwala's worst nightmares have come true: 'durbari' rule dominates today, complete with guns, guards and sycophants. Playing the politics of the given makes the system naturally prone to corruption, for the following reasons:

1. In a 'durbari' atmosphere, the expectation from political leaders is to act as patrons. A patron, by definition, is a person who can break the law to deliver benefits for somebody else. As we have observed, politicians have first given themselves a whole spectrum of privileges on account of which they can disburse patronage to those who cling to them. This is the first source of corruption and it is a direct consequence of playing the politics of the given.

2. As a result, citizens do not get what is due to them, because inadequate delivery mechanisms force them to be clients to patrons. The most promising part of the Lokpal Bill dealt with the 'Citizens' Charter', which promised time-bound and effective delivery of services. But that

---

his cabinet position. Subsequently, he served several months in prison before he was granted bail. The case has not yet been concluded.

was downplayed even by the leaders of the 'India Against Corruption' movement (also known as the 'Anna team').

3. To be able to tackle corruption, then, the network that thrives on the politics of the given, where each section strives to maximize its positional advantage, by hook or by crook or by patronage, must somehow be sidelined.

There are several policy options that can strike at the heart of patron-client-based politics of the given, but these would need the 'citizen elite' to come forward and put them together in one fell swoop—not in bits and pieces. This is the only way to halt the corruption that we see everywhere in society.

The policy options are:

1. Universal health;
2. Universal education;
3. The formalization of the labour force; and
4. A strict policy regarding urbanization.

Why should these policies matter so much?

Once health and education are universalized, the citizen becomes empowered and is no longer as vulnerable as before to patron-seeking practices. These two areas of public welfare force us into patron-client behaviour, for sickness can land us in serious monetary trouble and, without education, the future of our young is jeopardized. The policy with respect to these public welfare items must be accompanied by the formalization of our labour force. When that happens, it compels entrepreneurs to raise their levels of organizational skills and technological requirements. No longer can they depend on exploiting a low-wage market with the help of friendly inspectors and political patrons.

Finally, we need to curb land speculation—the largest absorber of illicit money. Tackle the real-estate issue and the bulk of the black-money problem is taken care of. The current nexus between banks and property speculation has brought untold misery to many, but huge profits to a few. If urbanization were to adhere to the norms of town planning and were not slave to real-estate manipulators, the health of the parallel economy would rapidly deteriorate. This would cut the wealth of many politicians and their supporters, thereby instantly making them less attractive as patrons. An urbanization policy of this kind is very common in almost every advanced democracy, so why not here?

These measures are resisted by our politicians today for they would require mobilization and standing up to powerful lobbies as well as sacrificing their immediate personal and sectional interests. This is why, though such policies are eminently reasonable by any democratic standard, they find little favour with our parliamentarians and legislators, along with their hangers-on. After all, going by current form, politics for them is not a vocation but a way of disbursing favours such that the patron and the client both benefit at the expense of citizens and citizenship.

It is for this reason that the following chapters will be devoted to examining the issue of informal labour, followed by a close look at the policies of universal health and universal education. Finally, we shall discuss the problems related to urban planning and migration, which too require urgent attention.

Once the gravity that surrounds these topics is fully appreciated, it will become clear that the politics of the given, or even of maximizing the given, will always fall short.

Our understanding of corruption cannot be limited to the egregious behaviour of politicians and their associates: there is something fundamentally systemic about it. This is why we need a reality check on how we have handled labour, health, education and urbanization so far. Without a campaign that addresses these issues at their base, anti-corruption drives will only substitute one set of wicked witches with another. They will all stir the same brew, though some may add a dash of saffron to it.

CHAPTER VI

Taking a Reality Check: The Contribution of Informal Labour to Economic 'Growth'

Without factoring in informal labour's contribution to our economy any understanding of contemporary social changes in India will remain incomplete. As the dependency on informal labour is growing and shows little sign of abatement, India's development model remains rather fragile. It will soon be clear that such a heavy reliance on informal labour encourages corporate corruption and soils the hands of the private sector. But to dismantle such a structure a reality check is called for as India's growth story has many questionable aspects to it which are never fully acknowledged. This allows politicians to pander to the given without considering systemic alternatives. Consequently, the Indian economy finds it difficult to shed its low technology and low wage attributes which in turn undermine attempts to attain world class standards of production. It is not surprising then that this inability to break through the constraints of the given forces different sections of the population to maximize what is immediately available to them.

It is often believed that in the fullness of time, growth will make us all happily middle class without any intervention from above. When our growth rate was a little above 9 per cent in 2008 we thought we had got our model right and before long we would be a world class economy. This early optimism was clearly misplaced as our growth rate slumped drastically soon after and is now at around 5 per cent. Even so, compared to other countries we are not doing that badly, or so we are told. That the numerical growth rate has different levels of significance between a rich and poor country is never quite explained. This is what makes for the entire package of denial that our policymakers propagate and which, sadly, too many of us have internalized. To get a full view of the state of our economy, let us take in the good with the not-so-good. That should tell us, in the round, how urgently we need an elite of calling so that our democracy actually delivers to its citizens.

Very often a mixture of national pride and economic belligerence forces intelligent people to deny that India's growth story is not yet convincing. By refusing to learn from the recent reversals of the economy, by believing steadfastly that the market will right itself, they are actually doing their nationalism injustice. What the contemporary picture of India compels us to take on board is that unless Indian enterprises, public and private, shake off their dependency on informal labour, we will never be truly world-class.

It is time then for a reality check!

A Tale of Two Growths: What Shines and What Does Not

First, the bright side.

The Indian Information Technology sector (IT) and Information Technology Enabled Services (ITES) have grown remarkably. From roughly 1 per cent of our GDP just twenty years ago, it now contributes as much as 7 per cent to it. Not just that, it also accounts for approximately 25 per cent of our exports. (*Economic Survey* 2005-6: 148). Let us not forget that this entire sector employs about two million people. That we imagine their numbers to be greater is because IT specialists behave 'just like us', are around us in our workspaces and live in our neighbourhoods. Sociologically, we know that what appears true from one angle of vision is often quite different from another perspective. Also, what should cause concern is that the service sector, contributes about 52 per cent of our GDP (*Statistical Outline of India* 2007: 7). Shankar Acharya, one-time economic advisor to the government, believes that this is not how a developing economy should function: manufacturing ought to play a stronger role (Acharya: 2006: 23-4).

No need to worry, the high savings rate in India will come to our rescue. How reliable is this projection? As a percentage of GDP, India's Gross National Saving today is about 35 per cent (http://ablog.typepad.com/keytrendsglobalisation/2010/01/savings-by-india-germany-japan-the US-and-China.html; accessed on 21.7.2012; see also http://www.economywatch.com/economics-statistics/economic-indicators/Gross_National_Savings_Percentage_Of_GDP; accessed on 21.7.2012). This is about the highest after China and way above Germany (at 11.7 per cent) or the US (at 2.8 per cent), which are much stronger economies (http://businessweek.com/magazine/content/10-25/b4183010451928.htm, accessed 21.7.2012). Whether we look at numbers relating to Gross Domestic Savings or Household Savings Rate (http://econ365.files.wordpress.com/2008/10/gross-saings-rate.pdf; accessed on 17.7 2012), India's figures are very impressive, in contrast to the most powerful economies in the world.

Now, the other side of the growth story.

Let us begin with the savings rates picture which is undoubtedly positive. This basically implies that there is money to be used as investments, but the question is whether that is the case in India. It appears that only about half of household investment in terms of savings is invested in financial instruments (Jagirdar 2011: 69. 71). This is why, in terms of Investible Finance, China has approximately 2,400 billion USD (in 2010), the United States about 1,800 billion USD, but India is way down with only 482 billion USD (http://ablog.typepad. com/keytrendsglobalisation/2012/01/savings-by-india-germany- japan-theUS-and-china.html; accessed 21-7-2012). Rather than being impressed by the savings figures alone we should really examine it in the context of of investible finance, or what is also called 'Financial Deepening' (Jagirdar 2011).[1]

Notwithstanding their rapid growth, the Foreign Direct Investment (FDI) absorbing industries, including of course the IT sector, employ very few people. According to the National Skill Development Council, the number working in ITES in 2009 amounts to only 1,736,615 and their employment potentialities will always remain that way (http://www.nsdcindia.org/pdf/IT- ITES-Industry.pdf; accessed 21.7.2012). This is why the huge presence of informal labour in the unorganized sector should gain priority in any long-term planning. Staying within this mould and maximizing the given is just not good enough—we have to devise ways of encouraging instead the growth of the organized workforce. It is a tough call, no doubt, but one that has to be taken before long.

In practice, most of the small-scale industries, and not just the household units, fall in the unorganized sector. The most important reason why it is difficult to separate small-scale enterprises from unorganized ones is because they all use informal labour. Not surprising then that 93 per cent of our workforce should belong to this category (Jhabvala 2005: 154). We just have to face this truth: looking the other way will not make this unhappy fact go away.

The textile sector seems like an obvious place to begin. Though it does not employ highly skilled workers, it engages

---

[1] A high debt burden is not always bad news as long as investment is happening. This is why it is wrong to judge the financial health of a country in terms of what counts for a healthy household economy. Japan and the US have high debt compared to their GDP, but also have a higher credit rating. On the other hand, Estonia, Nigeria, Kazhakistan, Bulgaria, Russia and Peru have a much lower debt compared to their GDP (so a high GDP to debt ratio), but with much lower credit ratings. This basically means that one would rather invest in America than in Kazhakistan or Nigeria.

about 35 million people officially (http://business.mapsofindia.
com/india-industry/textile.html; accessed 14 July, 2012). The
real figure is much greater if we take the many millions of
unregistered workers in organized and unorganized units whose
existence is almost always unrecorded. The numbers of such
informal labourers dwarf the employment figures in the ITES
as a whole, yet their efforts remain unsung. Like the IT sector,
textile production has also grown over the years. In 1980-81,
six billion square metres of cloth were produced but by 2006
the number crossed 25 billion square metres (*Economic Survey*
2006-7: 141; see also Ramaswamy 2009: 617-8). This is a
remarkable achievement, but while lauding it we must not
forget that 85 per cent of this growth has happened in the loom
sector where informal labour predominates. As mentioned
earlier, when discussing growth it is necessary to go to the shop
floor, to the villages and household industrial units, to get a
fuller picture.

The Informal Sector: A Neglected Dimension

In fact, the National Commission for Enterprises in the
Unorganized Sector, headed by the late Arjun Sengupta,
also came out with the startling fact that the percentage of
informal labour had gone up dramatically from 37.8 per cent
in 1999-2000 to 46.6 per cent in 2004-05 in the heart of the
organized sector (*Report on Conditions of Work...*2007: 4).
Maity and Mitra support this conclusion and show how
informal labour in the manufacturing sector has increased in
the same period from 77.9 per cent to 84.54 per cent (Maity
and Mitra 2010: 8-9). Interestingly, but along the same lines,
non-agricultural units employing less that ten people have
increased by 110.8 per cent between 1980 and 2005 (*Five Year
Plan* 2002-7, vol.1 Annexure 5.3; see also *Statistical Outline of
India* 2006-7: 35).

So, in the high noon of liberalization and the 'fast growth'
period, the informalization of labour is not just going full steam

ahead, but invading 'organized' industries too. It is not as if sectors, such as those producing automobiles, are exceptions; in fact, they subscribe most robustly to the rule (see Annavajhula and Pratap 2012 for an excellent treatment). The informal sector may look ragged and untidy, but it contributed as much as 59 per cent of India's Net Domestic Product in the days when India's economy was growing at about 9 per cent per annum (*The Economist*, 11 October 2007: 163). The unorganized manufacturing units in India are upwards of 17 million (*Hindustan Times*, Business Section, 29 December 2007)—surely, a staggering number.

India's 'growth story' has the small-scale sector to thank for boosting export earnings as well. This fact is usually expunged by those who magnify our growth performances. From textiles to gems and jewellery to carpets, the small-scale sector, with its complement of informal labour, adds enormously to our export revenues, to the tune of roughly 32 per cent (*Handbook of Statistics on the Indian Economy 2010-11*: 212). About 10-11 per cent of world trade in carpets, silks and cotton originates in India (*Economic Survey 2011-12*: 160).

That is good news, but wait! If we look at the conditions under which those who help us earn foreign exchange work, it is quite shocking. For example, the weavers in the carpet belt of India around Varanasi in Bhadoi, Jaunpur and Mirzapur, are about the poorest craftsmen in this country. They all labour under informal conditions of employment, which can often be ruthless.

The fact that there are so many workers willing to toil under such difficult terms is primarily because the rural sector is incapable of absorbing labour any more. We shall come to that in a while when we discuss migration.

Nevertheless, it is worth noting now that the compulsions to move from village to city are very economic in character. Agriculture is clearly an exhausted sector today. This explains why the major reason for migration other than for marriage is the search for better jobs (Kundu and Saraswati 2012: 222; see also *Manpower Profile of India* 2005: 303).

It is not surprising then that a large number of household industries are in villages, a fact that can be gauged from the presence of workshops/worksheds in rural and urban India. Interestingly, 'backward' states like Assam, Chhattisgarh, Himachal Pradesh, Jharkhand, Madhya Pradesh, Odisha and Uttar Pradesh have more houses put to use as workshops or worksheds in rural areas than in urban settings. The reverse applies to the developed states, with the exception of Rajasthan, which cannot be easily explained (see http://censusindia.gov.in/2011/hlo/District_Tables/HLO_District_Tables.html). Using data from the Economic Census of 2005, the *Manpower Profile of India* confirms that rural India is quite active when it comes to non-agricultural establishments. If we take units that employ less than ten workers (and these far outnumber the figure of those that employ more than ten), then rural India follows close on the heels of urban India (see *Manpower Profile of India* 2009: 167). It should also be noted that it is not as if only women work in such units; in states like Himachal Pradesh and Rajasthan, the census records that more men than women are employed in household industries (http://www.censusindia.gov.in/Tables_publised/A-Series/A-Series_links/t_00_009.aspx).

Also, and this is significant, the more backward the region, the higher the proportion of men in household industries. In UP, for example, six times more men than women work in these manufactories. In Rajasthan the figure jumps to an unbelievable ten (ibid.: Part [II] B [9i] Primary Census Abstract: General Population). This shows that working in household units is most often the major source of livelihood for these families and many of them are located in rural India. It must also be remembered that migration of male workers from rural to urban India has gone up from 36.5 per cent in 1999-2000 to 41.6 per cent in 2007-08 (see Kundu and Saraswati 2012: 221; see also *Census of India*, 1991: Part ii, B I; Primary Census Abstract, General Population)

Given the predominance of the unorganized sector, it is to be expected that the majority of workers are either semi-skilled or unskilled. This is reflected in two sets of very interesting figures. On the one hand, we find that the percentage of workers with middle and high school degrees has fallen between 1999-2000 and 2005-06 (*Manpower Profile of India* 2009: 171), indicating that the demand for skilled labour is low. It is true that the percentage of graduates in the urban workforce did rise till 2004-05 but fell again in 2005-06 (ibid.). This was a surprising decline as it was growing steadily, though not remarkably, between 1993-94 and 2004-05. Uma Rani's field study confirms this trend for it shows that among the unskilled labour force roughly 58 per cent have a secondary or a higher secondary school degree (Rani 2008: 698). So a school education, which is hard fought for, does not take the poor very far.

Together, these figures tell us that the demand for skilled labour is really quite low. Not only is the percentage of such workers going down in general, but that of workers with school degrees is going up among the unskilled labour force. Their education is not reflected in the kind of jobs they eventually find. Finally, only 14 per cent of the registered workforce, and a mere 5 per cent of the total workforce, in India has had the benefit of a vocational training. The figure for South Korea is close to 95 per cent (see Gupta 2002: 49-50).

India's growth story thus requires a full acknowledgment of the contributions of the small-scale sector and informal labour. From textiles to gems and jewellery to shelling cashew nuts, workers in these industries contribute enormously to our foreign earnings. In 2005-2006, gems and jewellery exports from India constituted 15 per cent of India's total merchandise export, but also 8 per cent of the world trade. Lowly carpet weaving, which happens in little mud huts in east Uttar Pradesh districts like Jaunpur and Mirzapur, actually accounts for as much as 11 per cent of the world's market in floor coverings (*Economic Survey* 2006-07: p-S 118, table 6.8). Poor as these weavers are, they are connected to the world market. Perhaps it is because they are poor that the world market is interested in what they produce. Employing cheap labour is the Indian way of edging out international competition. In this process, as we have noted, several good (read formal) industries have gone bad (read, employment of informal/contract labour—see *Report on Conditions of Work*...2007).

Sources of Informal Labour: The Hollowed Out Village

Where does the informal sector get its labour from? A look at India's villages will give us an answer to that.

India was long considered to be an agricultural society, but not any more. When India became a free country, almost 50 per cent of the economy was dependent on agriculture; today it barely contributes 13.9 per cent to our national economy. The rate of growth in agriculture also hovers around 2 per cent per annum, very different from the picture in the industrial sectors (where, again, informal labour dominates). It would therefore not be incorrect to conclude that in recent years, during India's growth phase, the poor were pushed from one kind of informal labour to another. The fact that even in the organized sector nearly half the workers can be categorized as informal is supported by the census figures that record a huge jump, as mentioned earlier, of marginal workers.

Ironically, what land reforms did haltingly through the 1950s to the end of the 1970s, demography and population increase managed to accomplish easily with rather interesting results. Roughly 80 per cent of landholdings in India today are below five acres and about 66 per cent are below three acres. Most farms then are family farms with very little scope for hiring labour, except perhaps during the peak harvesting season. Large and medium farms are finding it hard to hang in, consequently the ranks of small farmers keep growing (Ministry of Agriculture 2003; see also http://dacnet.nic.in; accessed on 4 March 2011). The increase in the number of marginal farm holdings, that is those that are below one hectare, has also gone up, from 51 per cent of total holdings in 1970-71 to 65 per cent in 2005-06 (Chand, Prasanna and Singh 2011: 7). The average landholding was 2.63 hectares in 1959-60 and it has now come down to about 1.06 hectares (www.im4chage.org/farm-crisis/rural-distress-70/print; accessed on 29 October 2012). These figures indicate that those who were medium farmers and above are being pushed down to lower ranks on account of sub-division of holdings, or perhaps on account of distress sales.

One also gets a glimpse of this from the fact that the total number of large farms has fallen significantly, by about 38 per cent (ibid.). In Punjab too, landholdings have gone down in terms of ownership, though in some districts operational holdings are up. But the impact of this is rather marginal and does not substantially change the all-India picture. In Rajasthan and Punjab only 8.24 per cent and 7.2 per cent of farms can be designated as large. In more populous regions like Bihar and Bengal the number shrinks to 0.07 per cent and 0.01 per cent respectively (http://dacnet.nic.in). The total amount of land operated by big farmers has decreased by roughly 38 per cent, accompanied by a very substantial jump in the area under small and very small operational holdings (Ministry of Agriculture 2003).

The shrinking size of landholdings has resulted in low crop productivity and declining rural investment. This condition does not afflict big farmers alone, but the entire agricultural sector. Though population has grown steadily, there has been a decline in the total land area operated by about 2.5 per cent between the years 1960-61 and 2002-03. This should be seen alongside the fact that the area leased has also fallen, according to the 59th round of the National Sample Survey (2006: table 3.2). Sharecropping then is more or less a thing of the past. The area under food crops has also come down between 1950-51 and 2011-2012, by as much as 7.0 per cent (www.indiaagristat.com/agriculturalarealanduse/152/areaunderdrops19501951to20112012/stats.aspx; accessed on February 22, 2013; see also *India: Key Data 2007: 2008* 2007:

35). Naturally, and it is almost predictable, between 1994 and 2001 real investment in agriculture has declined by as much as 20 per cent (Acharya, Cassen, McNay 2004: 216). That this has been happening steadily over the years does not lessen the effect of its cumulative impact on agriculture.

Against this background it is not surprising that Rural Non-Farm Employment (RNFE) should go up in the country. According to the National Sample Survey (66th Round) the percentage of non-agricultural households has increased from a pre-existing high of 31.9 per cent in 1993-94 to 42.5 per cent in 2009-10 (*National Sample Survey* 2009-10; see also http:// www.indiastat.com/india/showdata.asp?secid=324; accessed 7 August 2007). Relying on the 50th and 57th Rounds of the National Sample Survey, Omkar Goswami estimates that 35.2 per cent of rural households are non-agricultural (Goswami n.d., see also Lee, Dias and Jackson 2005: 28). What is yet more noteworthy is that the rural non-farm sector contributes as much as 45.5 per cent of rural net domestic product (http://www.indiastat.com: 58; see also Chaddha 2003: 55). This is why the percentage distribution of employment for men in the agricultural sector has declined from 67.8 per cent to 50.8 per cent between 1977-78 and 2004-05 (*Manpower Profile* 2008: 185).

All these factors put together explain why a large number of villagers seek non-agricultural employment. It also fleshes out the earlier observation regarding the phenomenal growth of non-agricultural units employing less than ten workers. Moreover, as urban households earn on an average about double of what the rural households do, the urge to move to the towns and cities is that much greater.

When there exists such a vast reserve of an underskilled and underpaid workforce, it would be foolish for any entrepreneur not to take advantage of it. If this has to be corrected, if the labour regime has to be altered, it cannot be on the basis of individual rationality. It must be done from above, for society as a whole.

Horizontal Mobility: Moving from Poverty to Poverty

Migration figures suggest that in just one year, between 1999 and 2000, the proportion of people migrating for jobs has jumped by as much as 15 per cent (*Manpower Profile of India* 2005: 303, table 6.12). The bulk of this migration is from poorer regions like Uttar Pradesh and Bihar (ibid.: 25, table 1.1.17). It should not be surprising then that over five billion railway tickets are sold every year in India. As anyone who knows this country will vouch, a very large number of travellers also journey ticketless. In which case, the number of people using Indian Railways is bound to be much higher.

The fact that the proportion of men engaged in agriculture has fallen between the years 1997 and 2005 is another indication of why people are so willing to up and migrate from the village (*Manpower Profile of India* 2008: 186). Men are leaving their farms in the care of their wives and parents and migrating in large numbers in search of jobs anywhere. This is why the number of female cultivators has gone up, and so has the percentage of cultivators who are above sixty years of age. Thus while the percentage of cultivators in general is at about 44 per cent, when it comes to those who are aged over sixty, the number goes up to 63.36 per cent (*Manpower Profile of India* 2009: 233).

These migrants, poorly trained and desperate for work, will do anything for a living. Thus while there is little vertical mobility—though there is some—there is a huge tide of horizontal mobility. Urban areas, big and small, are where illiterate and poorly educated workers go to in equal numbers (Kundu and Mohanan 2010). The movement of people from village to town and from mud huts to urban slums is most impressive. Given the low level of skills in the industrial workforce, it would not be unfair to say that rich entrepreneurs get wealthy because there are so many poor who are willing to work at very low wages.

The informal and small-scale industrial sectors are also—and predictably—places where legal norms are hardly ever enforced (Gupta 2010: 49-67). That the organized industry is increasingly farming out work to the informal and unorganized sectors further illustrates where the poor find jobs once they leave the village. This is in tandem with the telling fact that the rate of urban growth in poorer states is keeping up with the better-off ones, and often higher than the national average (see also Kundu 2009). We should also remember that in a large number of instances, rural migrants do not leave the village for an urban workplace; they may go to another village and find a job in a household industrial unit there.

It is not unwise to conclude this from the figures that we have from the National Sample Survey (64th Round, 2007-2008), which shows that employment-related reasons account for the majority of households that have migrated from rural to rural areas (NSS 2010: 19). Given the patriarchal and virilocal nature (where the bride moves to the husband's parental home) of our family structure, a household would migrate only if the men find it lucrative to do so. When we take into account individual migrants we find that the majority of men migrate from rural to rural areas for employment-related reasons (ibid.: 19, 20, 31, 32). Thus when seen in conjunction with the migration of households, one should very seriously take the idea that many leave their rural homes for rural workplaces. Apart from marriage, which takes most women out of the village to another village, the movement of men in the same direction is quite noteworthy as well (see also Marius-Gnanou and Morican Ebrard, n.d.). This could only happen if we accept the earlier observation that the number of household industries in rural India is almost as high as those in the towns and cities.

As employment in the lowly skilled, unorganized sector is the only kind of work these migrants—lacking the benefit of vocational training—can do, and as this is usually the kind of job that is available, it is here that we find the largest concentration of workforce outside agriculture. It is not surprising then that there should be so many leaving their villages for work wherever they can find it. While discussing this, let us not forget the contribution of these informal units to India's overall growth picture as well as to her export performance. We ought to keep in mind that the long arm of globalization goes right down to the rudest hut in the poorest parts of India where a lonely weaver is making a tufted carpet or a craftsman is fashioning a shiny piece of brass.

However, it is this horizontal mobility that helps the poor to survive. They move from one kind of poverty to another, and with each move, hope bubbles up within them. Perhaps tomorrow will be a better day. As we shall see a little later, migration to urban slums is, under the circumstances, not such a bad idea at all.

The Trickle-Down Theory: Can it Deliver?

The Indian Information Technology (IT) Sector and Information Technology Enabled Services (ITES) have grown remarkably. This is widely commented upon and we too have registered this fact in the opening pages of this chapter. From roughly 1 per cent of our GDP just twenty years ago, it now contributes as much as 7 per cent to it. It also accounts for approximately 25 per cent of our exports. Let us remind ourselves again that this sector employs but less than 2 million people. As the IT specialists are around us, in our neighbourhoods, choking us with their petrol exhausts (we're choking them too with our exhaust fumes) we tend to believe that their numbers are huge. Engineering students too tend to opt for specialization in electronics, but not all will succeed.

We need some perspective again:

The flourishing ITES employ a little fewer than 2 million people, but the textile sector that is unsung engages about 35 million workers, yet in per capita earnings the textile sector is way behind. It would not be unreasonable to assume, given the preponderance of informal labour, that the numbers actually working in textile and textile-related industries are much higher. That we do not have clear figures on the workforce in a number of economic units leads us to underestimate the significance of informal labour to our economic health and growth. Nor is it that the financiers have overlooked this all important aspect, in fact they may have just deepened it.

Till about 2005, roughly 40 per cent of Foreign Direct Investment lodged itself in ITES, telecom industries, consultancies of various kinds, electronic equipment manufacture and financial services (*The Economist* 2007). Today, FDI has smelt blood and moved instead to the informal sector, primarily construction and real estate where there is quick money. Whereas in 2001, only 3.12 per cent of FDI went into real estate and construction, by 2009 the figure rose to as much as 20.82 per cent, showing a clear shift away from the ITES. Neither is it good news for the economy, that the proportion of FDI halved in manufacturing to almost 21.41 per cent by 2008 (Chalapathi Rao and Dhar 2011: 27, 28).

Clearly, FDI is going with the trend and betting on informal and contractual labour, which dominates real estate and construction. When 93 per cent of the workforce belongs to this category, it is not surprising that investors are drawn to placing their funds where labour of this sort can be easily put to use. This is a stark truth and we cannot turn our eyes away from this fact. Moreover, as we had noted earlier with the Arjun Sengupta Report, even the organized sector enterprises are increasingly relying on informal and casual workers. R.C. Bhargava, Chairman of Maruti Limited, made a candid confession in a television interview soon after the Maruti car factory saw one of its fiercest round of unrest in 2012. He said that it was about time that the company mends its current ways and gets back to hiring more formal labour, the way it used to be at the start.

As informal labour is cheap and plentiful, employment in the organized sector is stubbornly stuck at about 24 million. So much for the trickle-down theory! There has been a recent growth of 1.8 million or so, and that is largely because a large number of women have been employed in this category. The fact that the percentage of workers in the organized sector has stayed rigid can also be gauged from the census figures where the proportion of 'main workers' (when a person is employed for six months in a year) has actually dropped over the last decade. It was only by 1.1 per cent no doubt, but the number still fell, instead of going up or even remaining stable. Yet, in the same period, there has been a significant increase of roughly 11 per cent among those who did not have a job for more than six months in a year (see Gupta 2010: 43). The census classifies such people as marginal workers. Thus while the figure for main workers is stable to decreasing, the figure for marginal workers is going up. This ties in with our earlier discussion on the domination of informal labour and its growing presence in the Indian economy. So if anything is growing and trickling down, let us not forget that it is the informalization of labour!

The issue that comes to mind if one wants to give the trickle-down theory a positive gloss is that over time the workers should get better educated and move up the skill ladder. Till now, that remains a distant goal. While the percentage of literates has increased among the working class, sadly the proportion of those with middle to senior school degrees has fallen.

As one goes down this road a few other facts come up at every corner. Let us recall what was said a while back when we pointed out that about 57.5 per cent of unskilled workers today have a secondary or higher secondary qualification (Rani 2008: 678). Under these circumstances, what incentive would a person have for education if this is the flickering light at the end of the tunnel? Even so, the demand for education is growing, though the quality is still very low. We will attend to this issue a little later but if about 17 lakh students pass out of vocational institutes every year (Gupta 2002: 50), where are the skilled jobs for them?

So far the trickle-down theory has not done well, nor the various targeted approaches that have been sponsored with that perspective in mind. If anything most of these interventions have not removed poverty, but merely kept the poor alive. As we had said earlier, the Antyodaya of yesterday and the MGNREGA of today belong to that genre of goodwill.

Corporate Corruption: Flogging Informal Labour

There is always that fond hope among a section that the private sector will come to the rescue. Apart from the fact that many (but not all) of India's corporations are deeply mired in corruption—for instance, the revelations of the infamous Radia tapes—it must also be noted that they operate in conditions that encourage dodging the law. Once again, this arises from the pragmatics of taking advantage of what is 'given'.

For a time it was hoped that a simple, no-pain solution could be found if bribe-giving were to be legalized, then it would lead to a higher degree of reporting for now only the bribe taker would have to face the law. This suggestion was made recently by Kaushik Basu, then the prime minister's economic advisor. Sadly, such low-cost, budget one-liners invariably fail to fly. Eager to clean up the corporate sector, Narayana Murthy of Infosys, initially endorsed this suggestion, but later found fault with it. The bribe-giver could rat on the bribe-taker, but it would not be worth the halo. Word would go around and that person would be singled out forever in the real world of give and take. Besides, if the bribe-giver is never to be penalized, what stops the person from dangling a bait and complaining only if the authority does not bite?

Under current conditions, except for a handful of companies in IT, telecom and financial services, it is hard for business to play clean and be above board. When 93 per cent of the work force is unorganized and informal, it would require enormous will power and a dogged determination for the investor to do the right thing and not to tap into this gold mine. Not only is cheap labour pouring out of every vein, but there is no pressure either to maintain proper records. We are now in a zone where facts are concealed, less than proper wages are paid, not to mention the slurring over of provident fund, medical benefits and bonuses. If this means bribing the labour inspector, it is a minor expense.

This explains why, as we saw earlier, the dependence of the formal sector on the informal or unorganized workers has grown over time in India. When labour is ready to be hired for a song, it is tempting for business houses to rely on the informal sector. Besides, as everybody else is doing just that, it would be ruinous to play fair. The unseen hand of the market would give all such clean efforts a tight wallop behind the ears. That would straighten out any law-abiding entrepreneur.

In practice, it is difficult to separate the unorganized from the informal labour force, especially in India. This is probably why the National Commission for Enterprises in the Unorganized Sector underplayed both size and skill in defining the unorganized workers. Instead, it considered all those who were not covered by formal arrangements regarding employment conditions and social security benefits to belong to this category. The International Labour Conference of 2002 also held a similar position. Whether labour is organized or unorganized, formal or informal, depends ultimately on worker-management relations.

This has some unexpected consequences. If you think your swanky car is a product of the organized sector, think again. Reports suggest that even in a major enterprise like Maruti automobiles, 85 per cent of the workforce is made up of contract labour (see Annavajhula and Pratap 2012). Things have come to such a pass that garment-manufacturing units too resort to outsourcing. Shirts made in the main factory have their buttons sewn somewhere else. Suppliers of simple carpets, throw rugs and mats destined for children's nurseries in the west, have a long supply chain too. Relying on cheap, informal labour has become such a habit! Not only do such practices make our corporate sector corruption-prone, they also inhibit it from being world-class. Not surprising then that the vocationally trained labour force is such a miniscule proportion of the working class in India.

But why should any of that be worrisome? After all, on the back of informal labour, a third of our foreign exchange earnings come from exports of textiles, leather, carpets, gems and jewellery (Reserve Bank of India 2010-11: 212). In addition, if we take into account the contribution of the informal sector in the formal sector, the figure is much higher—nobody can tell by exactly how much. As the link between globalization and the humble cottage industry is doing well, the established entrepreneurs who profit from this chain see no reason to rock the boat. Even if one were to entertain good intentions, it is unwise to turn down easy money.

Corporate spokespeople may, however, explain this situation somewhat differently. In fairness, they are not always unconvincing. They would argue that the reason for their over-reliance on the informal sector is because government laws are so unreasonable. In their rendition, the Industrial Disputes Act makes it impossible to fire recalcitrant and non-performing workers once the unit employs more than a hundred people.

This is not entirely accurate but, unfortunately, that is how the law pans out in practice. True, the law specifies that neither factory-owners nor workers can declare a lockout or a strike without notice, but that is not unique to our country. In America too, the Worker Adjustment and Restraining Notification (WARN) Act requires a sixty-day period before layoffs and closures can be effected. Yes, there are stipulated laws regarding minimum wages and overtime in India, but so is the case in America as well. The Fair Labour Standards Act in the United States regulates both labour emoluments and maximum hours of work per week.

Therefore, for Indian corporations to demand that they should be able to freely hire and fire workers, or that wages should be determined by the market, is unfair. What, however, rings true is that it takes forever for an industrial strike to be settled in India. According to our law, during the pendency period, when the dispute is supposedly being sorted out, nobody can be dismissed. Yet, as there is no stipulated time limit within which decisions on such matters must be reached, the issue may hang fire interminably.

Business houses have found a way out of this. They try and make sure, to the extent they can, to employ less than 100 workers. This way they can get under the radar and not have to go through the legal rigmarole to fire a worker. That part is understood and it is silly of the Industrial Disputes Act not to take this matter under consideration. Even so, the fear of strikes is largely imaginary. In 1990 there were 1825 strikes nation-wide, but by 2006 the number had dwindled to 192. Why then should entrepreneurs fear strikes today?

Moreover, nothing stops the employer of a unit with less than 100 employees from providing social security benefits and wage guarantees to its workers. Labour becomes unorganized, or informal, not because it is unskilled, or because factories are small, but because of the manner in which it has been employed. Regardless of size, why should employers not register their employees on the company's muster and make them members of a 'formal' labour force? This would limit the contractor's role and make the delivery of wages and security benefits transparent.

The arguments then for encouraging the existence of unorganized labour are not really convincing. Entrepreneurs of even gigantic companies have learnt to live and function with segregated units with less than 100 employees in each. They may all be housed under one roof, or dispersed across the country, but the trick is to keep them small. Though this is not the best scenario, but what prevents management from making sure that those 99 who work for them do so under proper, 'formal' labour conditions.

If the corporate sector routinely lapses into corrupt practices, blame it on the easy pickings strewn in its path. Once you go down the road of informal labour, other malpractices soon follow as natural accompaniments. Records are concealed, payments docked for no good reason, and a little bribe on the side helps grease the wheels. As our low-wage products make us internationally competitive, there is little reason to change the rules. The law-enforcers and entrepreneurs are not just on the same page, but often on the same balance sheet too.

When it comes to the corporate sector, small may not always be beautiful, but it need not be informal either.

CHAPTER VII

It Is Not About Money: Fraternity and Universal Health

Universal health and universal education are both concepts that should be understood clearly. The term 'universal' in this case refers to the delivery of public goods at quality levels to all. Therefore, the term 'universal' is against policies that are targeted. Failing that, health for the poor and education for the poor end up as 'poor health' and 'poor education'. Universal health and education are put aside on the ground that we do not have the necessary money to make it work in India. To answer this concern we need to note that when Europe and Canada introduced universal health they were not the rich societies they are today, but were actually very poor. Also, those who initiated universal health and education were the 'citizen elite' and they were not necessarily forced into this by popular uprisings. A comparative picture is also presented to show how the European model of universal health is better suited to India than the American model of health insurance.

To further the arguments in the previous chapter, we shall now turn to two specific areas, health and education, and explain why targeted approaches are futile. While reading this section it is necessary to recall 'the iron law of dystopia' that we had mentioned earlier. When it comes to programmes such as universal health and education, utopian visions and drive must be uppermost. The natural tendency of the 'politicians of the given' is to assert that either we are too many, or too poor to afford such fraternity-oriented schemes.

To be aware of the magnitude of the problem facing India, a piecemeal analysis will not do. When over 70 per cent of the population is poor, with earnings below USD 2 per day (*Report on Conditions of Work...*2007: 6), how can one have special programmes? Targeted policies make sense only when the population concerned is but a fragment of the total. It is impossible to think in these terms when the target one is aiming at constitutes the overwhelming section of the population. Would it not be more appropriate to consider the possibilities of a revolution instead?

If revolution is not on the agenda, then the way out is to devise universal programmes on health and education. Universal here does not mean public sector or private sector. It does not matter who delivers these goods—they must be universally accessible in exactly the same way. In Canada, for example, one goes to a private doctor for treatment and consultation, but it is the government that pays the professional. In some other countries, the reliance is almost entirely on the public sphere, such as in France or Spain or Sweden. Much of this depends upon the situation, and on which mix is best for each country. What really matters is that the delivery should be universal: rich and poor can avail of these services in the same way.

Forget the Poor: Think Society, Think Welfare

The best way to fight poverty is to forget the poor and not plan for them. If one were to learn from the experience of today's developed world, the poor are served best when the delivery of public goods is at quality levels, such that all classes benefit from them. If one targets the poor alone, then the planners and those who can make a difference to a society's future are not quite as committed: after all, such measures have no real meaning to their own lives. As a result, targeted approaches attract corrupt officials and very little is actually delivered on the ground. This is why it is important not to be attentive solely to how much money is being spent on public goods; the emphasis must rather be on delivery.

In Chapter II we had discussed how the 'citizen elite' in Western Europe in the nineteenth century made a difference and created a more equitable society. It is time now to update this account with more contemporary instances from the twentieth century.

To begin with we must note that the welfare systems in Europe and Canada, as well as in East Asia, were set in place not when these countries were rich, but when they were poor. Sweden was not always rich, clean, healthy, and corruption-free. Chronic food shortages and venal practices characterized this country till well into the first decades of the twentieth century. Hunger and starvation drove over a million people from Sweden to the US in the years following World War I. Britain introduced the National Health Service in a full-fledged way after World War II when it was desperately resource-struck and even found India too expensive to afford. Health care in the Austria of today draws from the Red Vienna period between 1918 and 1934. At that time, Vienna was devastated, not just by World War I, but by refugees streaming in from West Ukraine (then part of Austrian Galicia). As if that were not enough, the middle classes found themselves in penury because they had bought war bonds which were now useless. On top of all that tuberculosis and Spanish flu were rampant, making Vienna the most besieged city of Europe. In this atmosphere, Vienna did the unthinkable: it introduced the eight-hour working day as well as unemployment insurance. Once again, an individual rose to champion health care in Vienna during those troubled times, and that man was Julius Tandler (see Gruber 1991).

There were other heroes with Tandler, many of them leading intellectuals of twentieth-century Europe. The Red Vienna period attracted scholars like Sigmund Freud, Ludwig Wittgenstein, Alfred Adler and Karl Krauss among many others. From 1921 to 1934, Otto Neurath lent his immense intellectual strength and energy to devising programmes that improve the quality of social life. For him, theorizing about society is theorizing from within it (see Cartright, Cat, Fleck and Uebele 1996). These individuals made Red Vienna the precursor of Austria's robust health policy today. As much as 76 per cent of health expenditure in this country is public and health care gets as much as 10 per cent of Austria's GDP.

Canada, France, Germany, Japan and Singapore all subscribed to universal health and education when they were far from being the prosperous countries that they now are. What is the harm in learning from these countries? Remember Lloyd George who said that Britain should 'emulate' Germany in social welfare schemes and 'not only in armaments' (http://en.wikipedia.org/National-Insurance-Act-1911: accessed on 8 July 2012). If emulation leads to learning, it should not offend our sense of national pride.

The usual response to universal health, education, and other public goods is that there is no money. Though this sounds like a legitimate excuse, a closer look will tell us how unconvincing it actually is. When the growth rate is about 8 per cent, there is a lot of money around. It is just that the political will in India does not incline towards the universal delivery of public goods at quality levels. Nor is there adequate pressure put on the system by the elite of the country. They too believe that such universal delivery of public goods is a luxury India cannot afford. This does not worry them too much as they can access private dispensers of health and education, but they do not know what they are missing. When public hospitals serve up bad medicine, it takes little for the private sector to trump it. This is why the overall quality of private health delivery too is so unsatisfactory.

Further, money is not the issue and never was.

Sweden's unemployment rate was around 25 per cent in 1932 when it established the *folkhemmet* ('home of the people') programme guaranteeing universal welfare. This gradually grew to become a model for the world. Today, when we talk of universal health and education, we think of Sweden first. It is this commitment to a strong public health and educational system that made Sweden the prosperous state it is today. It is not as if genetic features like being blonde and blue-eyed did the trick! Broad-based social welfare policies were deliberately devised by several European governments from the 1930s onwards (as in Sweden) to bring quality public goods to the public, and not just for the poor. Should we not also do the same?

Basque Spain introduced Osakidetza in 1982 when its economy was still recovering from the depredations of the Franco era. It did not take long for this region to prosper and now it has the best health service in Spain with a ratio of 4.5 doctors for every 1000 patients.

The Canadian province of Saskatchewan introduced health care in 1947 though it fared badly during the World War II years. This was the poorest region of Canada, but that did not deter it from doing remarkable things on the medical front. Under Tommy Douglas, Saskatchewan also included the 'cobalt bomb' for cancer treatment for the first time in North America. It was costly, but for Douglas, expenses be damned: people mattered.

Britain, likewise, implemented the National Health Scheme in 1948 when it was reeling under the burden of war expenses and needed food parcels from America to survive. It was so poor that it could not even hold on to India. Today, Britain is at the forefront in terms of universal health coverage the world over.

In nearly every case, certain members of the political elite led from the front to make this happen. It was Britain's National Insurance Act of 1911 which evolved into the National Health Scheme over the years. David Lloyd George, as chancellor of the Exchequer of the Liberal Government of the day, piloted this bill then, which became an Act about three years later. Introducing the subject in his budget speech of 1908, David Lloyd George made the famous statement that we commented upon earlier. He firmly recommended that 'we should be putting ourselves in the field on a level with Germany. We should emulate them not only in armaments' (http://en.wikipedia.org/ National-Insurance-Act-1911, accessed on 8 July 2012). When referring to Germany, Lloyd George was obviously thinking of Baron von Bismarck who is considered to be the father of social insurance in the modern world. In rapid-fire succession Bismarck introduced health insurance in 1883, accident health insurance in 1884, and old age and disability insurance in 1889.

Universal health care in Canada is much closer to European-style coverage than to that of its powerful neighbour to the south. Our investment in health is still below 1 per cent of GDP, which is inexcusable. In Upper Middle Income Countries—note, not just the developed western world—the figure is about 3.4 per cent (Gupta 2002: 54). In the US, where the private health sector is extensive, the public expenditure on health is roughly 6.8% of its GDP, but in Germany where health care is almost entirely public, the expenditure on this score is above 8%.

For the record, it needs to be mentioned that even in the US, the 1946 Hill-Burton Act, along with the Commission on Hospital Care, was put in place so that the country could gradually move to a more comprehensive system of medical care. When John F. Kennedy visited the Appalachian region, from Virginia to Kentucky, he was moved by the plight of the poor farmers there. He then promised health and unemployment insurance on a scale that would be unimaginable to a freemarket thinker anywhere in the world. Though Kennedy was assassinated soon after, his successor Lyndon B. Johnson took on this responsibility and the economic landscape of that region has changed ever since.

We can get there too—but we need political resolve of this order. We have to set our sights at the best possible model

and not be sidetracked by the more convenient ones. Our
poverty should not be used as an excuse for scaling down our
preferences and aspirations.

Europe versus the US: In Search of a Model

Europe has done extremely well by all health parameters but
it has not been able to broadcast its model effectively. In fact,
every time medical expenses as proportion of Gross Domestic
Product (or GDP) goes up by even a tiny bit, either in Sweden,
Italy, France or Luxembourg, influential policymakers in
America, as well as in India, use it to discredit the European
medical system.

Notwithstanding nips and tucks, the bare fact that Europeans
live longer than Americans should have settled the contest long
ago. In America only 12.6 per cent cross the age of 65 whereas
the figure is 16.7 per cent and 21.5 per cent in Europe and
Japan respectively. What is more, the European model is also
cost-effective. The United States spends about 16 per cent of
its Gross Domestic Product (GDP) on health—most of it in the
private sector—whereas the European average is around 9 per
cent, almost all in the public sector. But Europeans live longer
than Americans do. In the OECD (Organization for Economic
Co-operation and Development) countries[1] the average life span
is 79.1 but for the US the figure is 78.1. Even on the Infant
Mortality Rate the US performs much worse than Europe
does (see Anderson and Frogner 2008: 1718-1727; see also
Thompson, Gavin 2009).

Interestingly, while the OECD average health expenditure
is about 8.9 per cent of GDP, in the US it is over 16 per cent
(http://www.irdes.fr/EcoSante/Download/OECDHealthData_
FrequentlyRequestedData.xls#TotalExpenditure; accessed on

---

[1] The OECD includes all the major European countries and a few
others like the US, Japan, Turkey, Mexico, South Korea and Chile. It is
basically a club of the developed economies.

30 May 2011). The per capita cost for health in the US is about $ 6000, which is almost double of what it is in Canada next door. It is even lower in Sweden, Japan, Ireland and Germany. Health Administration cost in the US is $516 per person but only $247 in France and $191 in Germany. Administration cost constitutes 7 per cent of total health spending in the US, double that of OECD countries. Surprisingly, the fault to a large extent lies in the fact that the US has not invested enough in Information Communication and Technology (or ICT) in its health care administration system (see Shiva Kumar, Lincoln C. Chen, Mita Choudhury, Shibani Ganju, Vijay Mahajan, Amarjeet Sinha, Abhijit Sen 2011). Even drugs cost a lot more in the US than in Europe and, according to the McKinsey Global Institute, the difference can be as much as 50 per cent (ibid.). This prompted Victor Fuchs, Professor of Economics at Stanford, to comment: 'If we solve our health care spending, practically all of our fiscal problems will go away' (quoted in Kolata 2012).

Has state-sponsored universal health delivery undermined medical care in Europe? No. The tale of the tape does not flatter the US when we compare its health statistics with Europe. In Europe there are as many as 3.7 hospital beds per thousand population, whereas in America it is just 2.8. On this parameter alone, the US would rank a lowly 23rd amongst other European countries. It might seem paradoxical then that there are proportionately higher numbers of surgical interventions in the US compared to Europe. Far more knee replacements and tonsillectomies, for example, are performed in America than they would be in OECD countries (Shiva Kumar et al., op.cit.). In the US the ratio of specialists to primary care physicians is 2:1 whereas in other developed countries it is 1:1. Again, in the US, MRI scanners are used 4.2 times more often than in Canada (Kolata 2012). Puzzling as this may appear, it can be explained by the fact that using the knife pays hugely to private interests in the health field.

The status of the US falls further when we consider infant mortality rates (IMR)—an important public health index. With an IMR of 6.75 per 1000 live births the US occupies a position below the average for the European Union countries and much below Sweden, France, Spain and Germany. Even Macao, South Korea as well as Cuba do better on this account! Infrastructure-wise, there are other bits of bad news from the US. In terms of practising physicians, for example, Europe easily outdoes the US. Whereas there are 2.4 such professionals for every 1000 people in America, the number rises to 3.1 when we look at OECD countries. This is why, compared to Europe, on an average, fewer people are admitted to hospital in the US and their length of stay in hospital is also much shorter.

To get to the bottom of the irrationality of the American model we need to know why health costs are so high in that country? There are several reasons for this: some are frivolous and stupid, but others border on the unforgivable. Let us take this last aspect first.

As many as 181 essential prescription drugs cost about 30 per cent more in the US than they do in Europe. According to the 2008 study of the McKinsey Global Institute, the price difference actually hovers around 50 per cent. As pharmaceutical products constitute around 20 per cent of all health expenses, it takes a fat wallet to stay healthy in America. Some of these drugs perhaps cost more because they are born in the US and carry a designer label. That, however, does not change their essential composition. A pill is a pill is a pill, and at any other price it works just as well.

Not just the high costs of medical administration, but consider some other strange features of the American model. The rate of tonsillectomy is four times higher in the United States than it is in Europe. It is no surprise then that the proportion of caesarean births in the US should also be greater than anywhere else in the world. Knee replacements in the US also outnumber such procedures in Europe. Interestingly, the *Dartmouth Atlas of Health Care* shows that the rate of knee surgeries also differs from state to state within America.

Quite obviously, it is hard to explain such variations on the basis of patient need alone. Given the fact that the average

European is healthier than the average American it makes one wonder what these surgeries were all about. As elective medical interventions usually take place in the private sector, American medical entrepreneurs have a lot to gain. All of this naturally raises health costs in the US well above that of Europe.

The American-sponsored view that the European health care system is unnecessarily profligate and a tremendous burden on the state exchequer needs perspective. Except for the curious case of Belgium, nowhere else in Europe have medical costs increased by more than 1.6 per cent of its GDP between 1995 and 2009. In several instances, the rise in health expenditure, as a proportion of GDP, has gone up by less than 1 per cent in these fifteen years. This is true of major European countries like France, Germany, Iceland and Norway. In Germany, believe it or not, the increase during this fairly long period was only 0.4 per cent (http://www.irdes.fr/EcoSante/Download/ OECDHealthData_FrequentlyRequestedData.xls#Total Expenditure; accessed on 30 May 2011).

Interestingly, wherever in Europe the private sector has a fairly visible presence, the increases in health costs also tend to be high. One can point to Spain and the Netherlands as examples of this phenomenon. On the other hand, in those countries in Europe, like Norway, Sweden and Italy, where private players are negligible, medical expenses go up more slowly. Obviously, the private sector inflates doctor and hospital bills everywhere, even in Europe. Yet it is not as if its presence improves the quality of medical care. The difference in the health status of Europeans and Americans demonstrates this truth better than anything else.

Which route then should India take? Should we look to the US or to Europe when designing our health care services? Undoubtedly, the verdict should favour Europe but for that decision-makers must rise above cost-benefit calculations that so suit those who work to maximize the given.

For Universal Health: Health for the Poor—or Poor Health

We must always keep in mind the all-important statistic that the overwhelming chunk of India's health expenditure in our country is out of pocket, borne by individuals from their own meagre resources. A fact like this can bear a thousand repetitions. *The Lancet* reports that in India, out of pocket expenses for health are around 78 per cent, the second highest in the world (see Shiva Kumar, et al. 2010). There is only one other place where it is worse than ours and that is, you have guessed it, Pakistan. Such a high figure is hard to match and aren't we lucky, there is always Iraq and Pakistan that fare poorer than we do!

Even in America, the Disneyland of private enterprise, the state picks up 45 per cent of health expenses. It is bound to get much more once the recent Obama-led health bill kicks in. In European countries, on the contrary, the figure touches anywhere between 75 and 90 per cent; in Britain, the state spends 86.3 per cent of all health expenses. We in India have borrowed the Westminster model of parliamentary democracy but here our health expenses are paid out of individual pockets.

Such a burden obviously drives a large number of people into indebtedness as only 10 per cent of Indians have some kind of health insurance. Hospital costs are anything but cheap. Basing her study on the 60th Round of the National Sample Survey, Indrani Gupta finds that among those who reported going to hospitals the cost of treatment was on an average, per capita, ₹6332 for rural India and ₹9806 in urban India. The share of drugs is as high as 63 per cent of all medical expenses and this raises poverty rates by 3.6 per cent in rural India and 2.9 per cent in urban India (Gupta 2009). From the earlier S.P. Gupta Report to the Planning Commission we learn that only 35 per cent of Indians have access to essential drugs. This fact sounds even worse when we compare India on this axis with other Upper Middle Income countries where such drugs are available to about 82 per cent of the population (Gupta 2002: 54).

Given the high levels of private spending on health in India, what is it that a typical rural patient is getting in return? Surely they must hope and expect a lot more when they are paying for it from their own pocket or cashing in an invisible credit card with the local money-lender. It is an established fact that after agricultural inputs, the next big reason for the rural population to go into debt is for medical reasons.

The evidence from *The Human Development Report* (Desai, et al., 2010) on the state of private health providers is very discouraging. Most private clinics in India fare poorly on several indicators when compared to public health facilities. This must be quite hard to accomplish, given the abysmal services that government hospitals and health centres provide.

Even so, compared to public health facilities, private clinics and hospitals have fewer toilets, examination tables and sterilization equipment. Clearly, there is a whole world out there which medical tourists do not care to know about. The most numbing fact is yet to come. The percentage of doctors with a regular MBBS degree is much higher in public health facilities than in private ones. In fact, 24 per cent of private health professionals have no medical training at all; in other words, every fourth village doctor is a certifiable quack. For the time being we are not counting those whose qualifications read like a line out of an optician's chart.

In spite of this, there is a great distrust towards government hospitals and dispensaries, where the facilities are seemingly way better. About 86 per cent of government doctors are qualified with a proper degree, while only 60 per cent in the private sector have legitimate credentials (ibid.: 116). Yet, because government doctors pay less attention to their poor patients and are difficult to get to, private medical practitioners are usually preferred. As many as 71 per cent of the sick regularly go to private doctors in contrast to just 17 per cent who still depend on state institutions for medical care (ibid.: 107). The *India Human Development Report* (2011: 169) comes up with somewhat similar figures when it records that in '2005-06, almost two thirds of the houeholds sough health care from the private sector...' Consequently, a significant number of people fall into chronic debt every year on account of medical expenses. The *Human Development in India* estimates doctors' fees, tests and medicine drives about 16 per cent of the population to this penurious condition (Desai, et al., 2010: 111). According to Koutelya Sinha about 39 million people are pushed to poverty yearly on account of ill health (*Times of India* 2011; see also Srinath Reddy, et al., see also, Shiva Kumar, et al., 2011).

Universal health does not mean average health, or only health for the poor. Sometimes we feel that private health care would be the best, but that is an illusion. Ask any number of people who belong to India's privileged class and have sought private medical care and their responses will be sobering. Nearly all have negative stories to tell. Just because one is being charged more does not ensure quality health. Private health care can be responsible only when the state medical delivery is of a superior quality. This will force all private practitioners to try and better it. Even so, in almost all of Europe, such attempts by medical entrepreneurs have failed. If you have a serious ailment in France, you had better check in to a government hospital.

In India, as the public delivery of medicine is so poor, it takes nothing for private investors to flood this area and trump what the state offers. Thus while health and education belong to the realm of public goods, and should be seen as such, they have been extensively privatized in India. This is why health care and education for the rich and the poor remain highly compartmentalized. This enormously compromises the delivery of these public health goods to the citizens of our country.

The private sector works best in those societies where the public sector poses a challenge to it. One feels stupid to advocate public services in our country, but that is the best way to buck private enterprise and force it to excel. Or else, as in India, we will have a slothful public sector and a slightly less slothful private sector. This would compel the poor to be not just risk-takers, but gamblers too.

Yet it is not the amount of money that is put in, that is alone of significance. Wherever health services function best it is when they are universal in character. Their services should be of the kind that people of all classes would want to avail of. What are we doing about this in India? Not only is our health delivery system not universal in character, it also gets niggardly sums of money, barely scrambling to 1 per cent of our GDP. Not just that, these funds are often cut even further to meet some shortfall elsewhere. For example, the Strategic Eleventh Five-Year Plan reduced the budget for the National Rural Health Mission by a massive 30 per cent. Sadly, the 13th Finance Commission also yielded to orthodoxy and did little to raise human capital in any of its recommendations. Instead, this Commission actually advises the government to cut funds for National Disease Control programmes by ₹577 crore and to super-specialty government hospitals, AIIMS included, by as much as ₹700 crore. This would drive more patients to private hospitals and raise levels of indebtedness. As it is, over 70 per cent of all health expenditure in our country is in the private sector. This is some kind of an international record, but it comes at such a price when we look at the numbers of the poor in our country.

Our leaders just do not seem to be interested.

As we have noted, the second-largest cause for chronic indebtedness in our country is on account of health (see Desai, et al., 2010; Chowdhury 2011: 60). Recall the Planning Commission-sponsored study found that only 35 per cent of Indians have access to essential drugs. In Upper Middle Income Countries the figure is about 82 per cent (Gupta 2002 54). In terms of doctor-patient ratio we rank 96th in the world, behind Belize, Ecuador, Tunisia and even Pakistan (there goes our fig leaf!) (http://www.globalhealthfacts.org/data/topic/map. aspx?ind=74: accessed on 14 July 2012). When it comes to the ratio of hospital beds to patients the picture is again depressing. India has only 0.9 hospital beds per 1000 population and an estimate suggests that in rural areas the number may well be somewhere around 1 bed per 6000 people (http://ehealth. eletsonline.com/2011/09/india-with-low-hospital-bed-density-and-poor-doctor-patient-ratio-says-report.htm; accessed on

14 July 2012). India is 64th on a scale of seventy-two countries whose data on this score is available, and ranks below Samoa, Guinea-Bissau, Gambia, Malawi, Haiti, Djibouti, Congo and several other poor countries. Fortunately, Pakistan is below us on this measure (http://wwwglobalhealthfacts.org; accessed 14 July 2012).

Morbidity and Death Rates: Demographic Dividend Re-examined

The discussion so far brings up a related issue, namely that of 'demographic dividend'. We are congratulating ourselves that we have a very youthful population but that can only be good news if the young are healthy and educated.

Better drugs, principally antibiotics, is the main reason for the fall in Infant Mortality Rate (IMR), which is why the percentage of Indians living upto the age of sixty is increasing. Even though IMR in India is 46.07 per 1000, much too high by civilized standards, it has dropped significantly over the last fifty years. On the other hand, a falling IMR has other consequences.

Societies with low Infant Mortality Rates do not keep churning out babies. Over a period of time couples realize that they now have more children than they want, or need. This depresses fertility, resulting in fewer births. The time then to take advantage of an overwhelmingly young population is very short, just about a generation or so.

It is that fleeting period between falling IMR and a high fertility rate when the iron is really hot. If at this time the youth are exposed to better health, quality education and innovative industrial practices, then the demographic dividend is like cash in the bank. This window does not stay open for too long. Consistently low IMR will soon prompt rational parents to limit their family size (see for a fuller treatment, Carvalho and Wong 1998: 208-240).

An initial fall in morbidity, such as with a drop in Infant Mortality Rates, causes a 'boom generation' of the young. Now what happens with this group of young people is a matter of policy and not of nature. For a long time it was believed that high population slowed down economic growth. It has now been concluded that rising numbers do not necessarily lead to lower per capita incomes. Even the United Nations, which is a notoriously slow learner, has woken up to this reality. It has now curbed grants for purely population control interventions.

The emphasis among demographers today is to look at the age structure and not just at numbers, especially when linking population with development. This draws our attention to the difference between demographic crowding on account of a birth boom, and a true demographic dividend. It is only in the latter case that a society can stick out its chest with pride and say that its young are usefully contributing to it.

It is not just a falling Infant Mortality Rate that raises the proportion of those in the working age group. This figure can also go up if the elderly population does not live very long. The number of people over eighty years of age in India is about six million in a country of over a billion. In the United States more than 9 million people cross that age and it has only a quarter of our population.

Sweden did not always have a low birth and death rate. Before 1800 life expectancy in Sweden was similar to the rest of the world, somewhere between twenty and thirty years of age. From 1918 onwards the situation began to change in that country. Health care facilities are now so good in Sweden that today almost 5 per cent of its population is over eighty years old.

Japan has an old-age profile similar to that of Sweden and it achieved this transition in less than twenty-five years supported by strong social insurance and health policies. Even China, whose numbers are closer to India's than of any other country, has more than 12 million people aged above eighty. Our old-age care is clearly not up to the mark. This factor cannot be overlooked when discussing the demographic dividend. If they don't watch out, the sins of the young will soon visit them when they grow old.

Demographers such as Ronald Lee, Andrew Mason and Steven Sindig (Lee, Mason and Sindig 2001: 137-162) have found that the health of the elderly does not depend so much on family care. If they are living longer it is because of savings resulting from pension wealth accumulation (see also Lee and Mason 2011). But for most of India's aging population, there is no pension. If 93 per cent of the population works in the unorganized sector, such benefits cannot be imagined. This forces many to function beyond what would be considered the proper age of retirement. It is hard to stay alive when young, but that is not all; there is no rest for the aged either.

Only social policies can convert a proportionately large working-age population into a demographic dividend. This has been the universal experience. India too needs a very visible and determined effort for candles to light up in its coming-of-age party. No natural law or unseen hand can strike the match on its own. This is equally true when it comes to the delivery of universal health as well.

Universal Health: Realizing Utopia in One Fell Swoop

Given the poverty and want in India it is tempting to argue that universal health must wait till we are ready for it. As a first step, some would suggest, let us begin on a modest and more realistic fashion. Yes, we do have a problem with delivering health, so let us first start by producing more doctors. As this immediately runs up against the resource constraint, such people advise a slow and gradual implementation of this proposal over a long period of time. Concomitantly, in their view, we should also upgrade the current doctors, many of whom are all manners of quacks. The hard fact, however, is that measures like Universal Health cannot wait but must begin now and all its various aspects be inaugurated in one fell swoop. Tinkering with the system, producing more doctors or running quacks through a quick medical training will not work. We are only postponing the taking of tough decisions, so even by book-keeping standards, we are wasting money in the long run. If this sounds unreasonable, consider the following issues.

Money, as we have argued, was never a problem wherever universal health was put in place anywhere in the world, so why not here? Once we dismiss these short-term ledger calculations we need to address universal health by first changing the way the current public hospitals work. Before we get more doctors on board, let us make medicine an honourable profession again. The All India Institute of Medical Sciences (AIIMS) was a great place not too long ago. Then it became a tool for political manipulation, which forced many of the doctors out into private hospitals. But ask the question: if the conditions of work were good in the AIIMS, would these doctors have left? Ask another question: even though the conditions are deplorable in the AIIMS, why do many of the best doctors still stay on there?

The fact is that doctors are not always looking for money but for better conditions of work. Once that happens, not only will their performance levels go up but also patients from all backgrounds will seek them out in public hospitals: as was the case with AIIMS till recently. This would put pressure on the system to deliver better and more efficiently. So for all of this to start ticking, universal health demands a public investment of about 5 per cent of our GDP—way above the current 1 per cent, which has lingered on for years. Even at 5 per cent we would still be low by European standards.

Money does not solve every problem. It all depends on how it is spent. The added resources should now be made available to patients, regardless of their background, so that they can buy the medicines they require and get the pathology tests as the doctors have ordered. Today, so many poor people go to private laboratories for tests and to pharmacy stores for medicines. These expenses eat up what little they have with no money left for anything else. Not surprising then, as we noted earlier, that about 16 per cent of the sick get into debt and 9 per cent of those who should seek medical help do not do so at all because they do not have the resources for it (Desai, et al., 2010: 108-09). This, therefore, clearly demonstrates that public hospitals need a full complement of services and cannot just offer medical advice without the necessary back-ups. Once again, let us start with what we have and rework the available infrastructure and facilities on a completely different format.

Alongside with making drugs and tests available to people, research facilities in existing hospitals must be ramped up. What is often overlooked is that when the conditions of work are sub-standard only the sub-standard will seek jobs there. As the old corporate adage goes: 'If you pay peanuts, you can only hire monkeys.' If in spite of these constraints, there are still so many committed doctors in public health institutions it only goes to show that not everybody in this profession is looking for money. For some, medicine continues to be a truly pastoral occupation. This, however, does not mean we must take advantage of them. By improving their conditions of work these hospitals and medical teaching institutions would attract better talent who would happily stay on (see Srinath Reddy, et al., 2011: 765). This is a key consideration that is always buried.

The policy approach experts would not like to rock the boat this seriously, which is why their plans on universal health are long-drawn-out and extend into the distant future. Before we begin, they argue, we must start more medical colleges. This is not a bad idea by itself, but if the conditions of work and of medical care are left unattended, all this money and effort will not yield the benefits we are looking for. If doctors get, once they are trained and ready, the same ill-equipped hospital with poor pay and worse working environment, then they too will move on and go elsewhere. What stops them? Or rather, how can you stop them?

Let us step back a bit and do a thought experiment. If laboratory and pathology equipment goes missing or is left unused, if research programmes are not on the agenda, if salaries are not adequate, if professionalism is not respected, why then should a good student want to be a doctor? Besides, where will one get good medical instructors from either? The answers to both these questions are plainly in the negative. Try this question alongside the previous one: though 86 per cent of households have a sub-health centre within three kilometres of where they live, why do they not use those instead of going to a private doctor, very often a quack? The reason, very simply, is that these health centres are not equipped, which is why patients are driven to private practitioners (Desai, et al., 2010: 105, 107; see also *India Human Development Report* 2011: 169). If these conditions remain unchanged, what is the point of opening new medical colleges and producing more medical graduates? We will either have a surfeit of mediocre doctors or a bulge in the numbers of those who start work in the private health sector. Neither of these two will alter the health status of us as citizens. It will end up as more of the same.

Producing more doctors is not going to help unless the framework of universal health is already in place and we can begin with what we have and change the conditions of the institutions that are around. Failing that, these new doctors will be either of poor quality or will take the road to private practice as so many others have done before them. At the end of the day, we have lost all this money. A realistic utopia is one that begins from what exists and then strains at every level to change it.

All utopian programmes begin with what is immediate, but instead of tinkering with it with low-pain alternatives, they go for the larger goal at once. While they do consider the limitations of the existing conditions, they do so in broad daylight without looking for excuses or for other prevarication-inspired clauses. This is equally true in the case of universal health; the same method applies. The factors that come in the way of realizing this realizable utopia are several.

First, the administrative mind-set is most comfortable with the given. Second, politicians do not want to lose control over the running of health institutions, for they benefit from patron-client networks which are so effective when it comes to health (education is a close second). Finally, not everybody is able to dream a future if they might have to endure some uncertainties in the present.

Only the citizen elite can change this, for a shake-up in the direction of greater fraternity will not come about in the ordinary course of events. If working conditions in medical institutions are poor, not only will doctors seek other pastures in the private sector, but also the best may not enrol for medical training. To change all of this requires a determined push from the citizen elite, as was the case elsewhere, for our ordinary politicians are not interested in such matters. When they fall sick they go abroad, and very often to countries that have universal health.

If universal health is to be realized, its various components must be in place in one fell swoop and not in dribs and drabs.

CHAPTER VIII

It Still Is Not About Money: Call for Universal Education

The position taken in this chapter is a continuation of the previous one on universal health. Without universal education, which again is not education for the poor, we cannot create conditions where everybody as citizens has equal access to gaining socially valuable skills. As in the previous chapter, the criticism of the targeted approach continues. It is also clarified that it often takes decades before the positive effects of the investments made in education can be measured in pure economic terms. This is another reason why talking money cannot take democracy forward. To make that advance, one has to go against the given and think fraternity instead.

'Universal education' does not mean 'average education' nor does it mean 'education for the poor'. Much of what has been said regarding health works for education too. Nevertheless, as education is so important, this chapter is devoted to it, albeit in a less detailed fashion. As the fundamental points regarding the inadequacies of the targeted approach and the need for fraternity-driven universal public welfare programmes have already been made, we can now be brief.

In education again, we are falling behind. In India, about 48 per cent of expenditure on education is state-funded, whereas in the US it is 75-80 per cent. In European countries it is often above 90 per cent. Once again, investment in education in India as a percentage of our GDP is struggling to reach 3 per cent—which is abysmal by international standards. We do not have to look only at Europe for inspiration in this matter. In 1949, 85 per cent of Chinese were illiterate. Today there are a billion literates, and this advance has happened in the last thirty years. In Japan the tradition is longer and can be traced back to the Meiji Restoration. Though South Korea was a very poor nation in 1953, it backed universal education and today 93 per cent of its population is literate.

Education and Skill Development: the Need for Quality Manpower

Our shortfalls in education can be felt at various levels. Not only is our skilled workforce very small, but even where it exists, the standards are very low. Even in the ITES sector, just a third of its engineers have a proper technical degree. On a per million basis the number of degree-holding engineers in India is six times lower than the Philippines and ten times lower than what prevails in Germany (see Gupta 2010: 71). This is on account of very low investment in India on Research and Development. In fact, Sengupta and Basu argue that Indian firms find no need to hire those with advanced degrees in science for they have no need for such qualified people on their rolls (Sengupta and Basu 2012). Indian businesses are just not interested in cutting-edge research.

Even in our famed IT sector, only 3 per cent of its sales go into R & D. The comparable figure in other countries is 14-15 per cent (Gupta 2002: 48). Our R & D is 1/60th of Korea; 1/250th of the US and 1/340th of Japan (ibid.). No wonder Delhi's famed Jawaharlal Nehru University (JNU) ranks at 170 in the international arena among institutions of higher learning. Even Fudan University in China is about a hundred places ahead of India's prestigious JNU! When we talk about our huge human resource potential we should be a little more realistic and humble.

The local private school which an indigent village boy might attend could cost as little as ₹50 per month. But that is a lot of money for a family hovering around the poverty line. Yet such a household would often invest that sum in the hope that this would be a ticket to a brighter future for their young. Panchmukhi and Mehrotra noted this trend as far back as 1999. Quoting a study by PROBE, the authors argue that it is not just the well-off who send their children to private schools, but also members of the Scheduled Caste and Other Backward Class groups (Panchmukhi and Mehrotra 2005: 239). Nor is it true that only prosperous states show a high incidence of enrolment in private schools. In regions where the educational services are generally poor, like Bihar and Uttar Pradesh, there are a large number of private schools to pick up the slack (ibid.: 237). Even so, after a small fortune is spent, a full 31 per cent of the children in these private schools cannot read a simple paragraph. The *Human Development in India* study which appeared recently tells us this story in graphic detail. That the figure soars to 50 per cent in government schools does not take away the fact that so many poor parents are actually gambling on private education (see Desai, et al. 2010: 83).

Clearly this trend continues, and is getting stronger. Not that long ago, in the 1980s, only 2 per cent of India's children, rural and urban combined, went to private schools. Since then the numbers have been steadily rising. By 2010, when *Human Development in India* was published, 21 per cent of rural children and 51 per cent of urban children were in private schools. In a poor state like Uttar Pradesh, 43 per cent attend private schools. Try supersizing this (ibid.: 82).

Of those enrolled, about 15 per cent drop out before completing Standard 5. But 50 per cent of those who cross this hurdle drop out before Standard 10, and another 43 per cent leave the school system before Class 12. With women, expectedly, the situation is worse—about 40 per cent do not enrol at all. Family backgrounds too matter. Poor children fare worse in school than the better-off (ibid.: 77). While 73 per cent of those from the highest quintile are able to read a short paragraph, the figure is about 44 to 46 per cent when it comes to poor Dalits and Muslim children (ibid.: 79-80). On top of this there are also rural-urban differences as children from villages fare poorly compared to their counterparts in cities and towns (ibid.).

Where Cost-Benefit Does Not Work: Investing in the Future

Just as we had observed when discussing health, the mere presence of trained professionals in government clinics is not enough to inspire patients; likewise, trained teachers do not always make for higher educational standards. On an average, 70 per cent of primary teachers have been properly trained in Bihar, Rajasthan and Uttar Pradesh (UP), but that does not quite show up in the educational standards of these states (Srivastava 2005: 98). Therefore, though the number of teachers (ibid.: 33) has increased over time, and many of them are qualified, we should be careful in concluding that their contributions have always been along desired lines.

Like health, education too does not do well when it is looked at in terms of immediate cost-benefit analysis. Studies, whether in France, the UK or Germany, have repeatedly demonstrated that 'high levels of GDP per capita are associated with high levels of primary school enrolment some 30 years earlier' (Steven and Weale 2007: 106). This is why private players in education will not want to go down this road, other than setting up schools for the well-to-do for immediate profit. Not for them to wait out three decades when they can exploit a niche market right now.

As it takes a long time for education to yield tangible GDP results, it is unwise to draw conclusions from numbers which have a shorter time span. This is why it is essential for the state to invest long term for generating this human capital without which no amount of economic resources will do much good. Far from being a passive spectator of democracy, education plays an active role in the development of citizenship. As Max

Adler once said the 'future of democracy does not lie in politics but in pedagogy' (see Cartright, Cat, Fleck, Thomas, Uebele 1996: 57).

Knowledge is a public good and an asset whose impact is not limited to any one zone of economic activity. Nor will just the setting up of schools do the job, unless we pay attention to 'quality' of schooling (Behrman and Birdsall 1983). A targeted approach to education that is happy to set up a classroom with indifferent teachers will hardly serve the purpose. Behrman and Birdsall persuasively argue that we are often seduced by quantity in assessing how education is progressing. The real test lies, however, in the quality of education. Sadly, the tendency in India is to emphasize quantity instead.

We are given figures on how many schools have been set up, the progress in teacher-student ratio, the proximity of primary and upper primary schools to habitation, and so on. Very little, however, is said about the quality of education imparted and even much less about attendance. It is satisfying from one point of view that 94.17 per cent of the rural population have a primary school within one kilometre; or that 93.33 per cent have an upper primary school within five kilometres (see Mehta 2011: xxxi-ii). Yet why do we have such a high drop-out rate? Why are our children unable to read, write or compute as they should, given the grades they are in?

There are many interesting issues on the way to answering these questions. For one, small schools (and most primary schools are of this kind) 'function unnoticed and perish ignored' (Diwan 2012: 37). Would it then be viable to consolidate primary schools with secondary schools, from Grade 1 to Grade 8, to achieve better results (ibid.: 39)? Not only would this allow for greater competition, supervision and attendance; it might also undermine the influence of village oligarchs over the school teachers (ibid.: 9).

Mukhopadhyay and Sahoo take this discussion further. They argue that when secondary education is easily accessible there is a lower drop-out rate at the primary level. The chances of continuation from the primary school stage increase when parents see a higher-level school in the vicinity. As secondary schools enjoy a better reputation, the primary school drop-out rate tends to fall. Parents begin to think that the investment they make in terms of time and money on their children's primary education now gets more worthwhile (Mukhopadhyay and Sahoo 2012).

The other interesting suggestion we find in the study by Mukhopadhyay and Sahoo is that a bus-stop in the village helps in shoring up continuation from primary to secondary school (ibid.: 31). Simply put, distance is not just a physical feature but one that is felt and experienced. If a bus-ride eats up the kilometres easily, it does not really matter that much if the school is at a slight distance. This reminds one of the great advances the US made when it introduced buses in the school system.

Quality over Quantity: It Is Never about Money

Neither for health nor for education have I emphasized how much money, in absolute terms, is spent by the state. True, health expenditure is less than 1 per cent of our GDP and education less than 3 per cent. By all standards, these sums are very low. In other Upper Middle Income countries, for example, 3.4 per cent of GDP is devoted to health (Gupta 2002: 54). The reason the quantum of money does not figure prominently in my analysis is because I would like to measure poverty not in terms of money spent, but in terms of actuals, and that includes the delivery of public goods like health, education and even energy. Consider this: 44 per cent of households with electricity lack power for over twelve hours a day (Desai, et al., 2010: 65). In the final analysis then, the delivery of public goods can act as an objective indicator of poverty. Money can be fudged, statistics on calorie requirements can also be fudged, but it is hard to disguise the poor delivery of public goods in the country.

This brings us back to where we started. Poverty is not just about numbers; it is about where the poor find work, what kinds of outlets are available to them, their health and education status, and the nature of the economy as a whole. If the trickle-down theory were working, we should by now have seen a growth in the number of skilled workers and a greater reliance on organized-sector industries, particularly in the manufacturing sector. We would also have seen greater agricultural production and productivity, and fewer farmers' suicides. But what would be immediately visible to all is that the average Indian would be healthier and better educated. When money goes from one's pocket to cover expenditure on health and education, it is never covered by a 'satisfaction guaranteed or your money back' scheme. Neither can one say that the cheque is in the mail when you go to a private hospital or school. You pay first and gripe later.

In terms of money invested in social welfare, India's performance, as we have already noticed, is very poor. If successive governments have not been mauled on these issues it is because public goods have been easily equated with the public sector in the popular mind. As state enterprises have a well-deserved bad reputation in India, it is easy to elide over the need for quality-level, universal delivery of public goods. At the same time, there is nothing inevitable about the poor quality of state-level services. Sweden and Denmark allocate over 30 per cent of their GDP to public goods delivery but that has not made the administrations in these countries inefficient. Even in the United States, the country that is most pilloried for its inadequate commitment to social welfare, as much as 17 per cent of its GDP is devoted to that purpose. In India, as we have already noticed, our spending on health is less than 1 per cent of our GDP and the expenditure on education around 3 per cent.

The reason why there is no pressure to increase the allocation of resources to public goods is because we are not thinking in terms of delivering them universally at quality levels. As long as we target the poor in our development projects we might succeed in keeping the poor alive, the economy growing, but we will be a long way from being a developed country.

Poor Scheduled Caste (SC) children, for example, are still not making the grade, because their schooling is so dreadful.

Further, this miserable condition does not afflict SCs alone, for, as we mentioned earlier, about half the children aged between eight and eleven have deficient literacy and numeracy abilities. In areas which are relatively better off, say Punjab, government-run schools cater disproportionately to SC children as they are generally the poorest. Given this reality, how can the state administration concentrate its attention around reservations alone?

Any family with some economic cushion sends its children to private schools. Therefore, reservations notwithstanding, we are not taking our young and poor SC population out of poverty and into the kind of lives that they deserve to live with the rest of humankind. I have, however, rarely come across reservation activists who campaign for quality delivery of education for SC children. We could take it further: they seem to be averse to the notion of 'quality' itself. They are usually content in asking for more and more reservations in more and more areas without paying attention to the content of services or to the needs and well-being of different public institutions (Beteille 2005: 414-436).

What all this tells us is that ideologies have distracted us in the past, and so has geography. Good things can happen anywhere; what we need is the determination to get it right. Most commentators on this subject will probably accept the need for quality health and education, once this proposition is placed in front of them. They will, nevertheless, demur at adopting these propositions because there is paucity of money or expertise, or both. In their considered view, these are issues of the kind that cannot be hurried; they grow gradually as they need patience and not a shot-gun approach. In the meanwhile, to tide over pressing exigencies, let us have targeted approaches that address the 'given'. Naturally, we are always postponing taking tough decisions and muddling through at every stage on the pretext of being 'realistic'. The only way forward is to take the plunge, as Europe did less than a century ago when it was not affluent, and adopt measures for universal health care and education.

CHAPTER IX

Planning Urbanization:
The Neglected City and Popular Aspirations

The urbanization process is not simply about migration from country to town, for it tells us a lot about the quality of migrants, their skill levels, and where they find work. Demography then reveals, most importantly, information about the kind of society we are living in and the direction it is taking. In which case, urbanization cannot be left to happen spontaneously and sporadically, but needs to be engineered keeping in mind the welfare of citizens. Further, urbanization should not take our eyes away from the village for that is where a lot of migrants begin their journey. We need to know what drives villagers to cities and small towns—indeed, to investigate how non-metropolitan settings contribute to the overall urbanization and growth process. Once again, as in Chapter VI, the economic nexus between town and country becomes very salient. The magnitude of this relationship is complex enough to merit special attention. What is also striking is that urbanization in India has not attended to the fact that migrants have aspirations and not just needs. Further, it is by advancing a strategy of planned urbanization that the exodus from the village and the transformation of the rural can be accomplished without giving into squalor.

It is a big talking point that India's urban population has continued to grow steadily, though at a slower rate in the metropolises. This should draw our attention to the further fact that over 70 per cent of urban Indians live in small towns with a population of 100,000 and above. The share of urban population in India that lived in the million-plus cities stood at 68.7 per cent in 2001 but by 2011 this figure came down by 26 per cent to stand at 42.6 per cent. This gives us an indication of where urban growth is taking place, and consistently so.

When studying India's population statistics one cannot help but be surprised by certain facts. The first is that the fastest-growing towns are not the metropolises of Delhi, Mumbai, Chennai or Kolkata. Much of the action in recent years is taking place in smaller urban areas. The speed at which Class I towns (with over 100,000 people) and some new million plus cities are expanding is way faster that the old mega-cities of India, like Mumbai, Delhi or Kolkata. The second startling fact is that, contrary to the popular impression one gets in big cities, the all-India rate of urbanization has actually been decreasing since the 1980s. There is a definite slowing down in the tempo of urbanization in general, though certain towns and cities continue to expand quite rapidly. Between 1961 and 1971, urbanization grew at 3.2 per cent, but has been declining ever since. The latest census of 2011 puts the number further down, at 1.6 per cent.

In the Greater Mumbai Urban Agglomeration (UA) the 2001 census recorded a population increase of 30.47 per cent, but it is down now to 12.05 per cent in 2011. Likewise, growth in Delhi UA has slowed from 52.4 to 26.69 per cent (the lowest since 1931), while that of Kolkata UA has decreased from 19.6 to 6.87 per cent in the same period. But, interestingly enough, the number of census towns has increased from 5161 in 2001 to 7935 in 2011. Likewise the number of Class-I cities (with over one lakh population) has gone up from 394 to 468 and cities with a million-plus population have increased from 35 to 53 in the same inter-census period.

The census also confirms a long-held and rather unsettling truth about India. Urbanization has not led to an urban, metropolitan value system. The past lingers in India's present, and yet India is changing. The imbalance in the sex ratio exemplifies this most of all. Shamefully, the 2011 census tell us, the gender imbalance is very pronounced in India's capital as well: there are only 868 females to every 1000 males in Delhi.

A closer look at this phenomenon reveals other interesting details as well. First, long-distance migrants to big cities (like Delhi and Mumbai) are mostly men who are not only unskilled and barely literate, but they also come alone. This contributes to the skewed gender ratio in almost every Indian city. Once again, when it comes to sex ratios, big cities fare worse than smaller ones.

Big, Bad Cities: The Many Faces of Urbanization

If investments come to big cities, then so should skilled manpower. But, surprisingly, better-educated rural migrants tend to avoid metros and head to small and medium towns instead. Even places like Mumbai and Delhi do not attract as many skilled migrants as they should. Here too entrepreneurs depend largely on mule packs of semi-qualified and half-literate workers. True, these metros are not quite as bad as Jaunpur or Moradabad, but they ought to be much better.

A recent *The Times of India* (21 October 2011) report on the 2011 census shows that when it comes to literacy, fast-growing cities have a lower literacy rate than smaller ones. Hyderabad is behind Raipur; Chennai ranks after Nagpur and Ahmedabad; while Surat, Pune and Aurangabad, to name a few, have better literacy figures than Delhi. This is interesting, as the fastest-growing urban agglomeration in recent years has been the area around the capital.

This trend was noticed some time ago but now that the latest census has confirmed it and leading Indian dailies have headlined it, this fact has attracted public attention. The one big conclusion that stands out is that a decade and more of high economic growth does not seem to have made much of a difference to the quality of our workforce. Should we now be paying greater attention to the quality of economic growth and not just to quantitative figures?

Is our liberalized economy then being powered by low-wage and low-skilled labour? Using the material from National Sample Surveys collected through the 1990s, D.P. Singh noted in a Ministry of Housing and Urban Poverty Alleviation Report (Singh 2009) that the proportion of illiterate migrants in million-plus cities was 37.08 per cent, whereas it was 26.73 in smaller towns.

Shekhar Mukherji, a noted demographer, too pointed out in a 2006 publication that Delhi attracts more than the usual share of lowly skilled and poorly educated migrants. According to him, almost 65 per cent of male inter-state migrants to this megacity are either illiterate or semi-literate (Mukherji 2006: 125). In Kolkata the figure is lower, at 30 per cent (ibid.: 93), but in general the numbers of lowly skilled and lowly educated migrants to big cities is quite large. This is significant as the search for jobs is the most important reason for male migration, and shows up in the high interstate migration for men in the 1991-2001 census (see Kundu and Saraswati 2011).

While the national sex ratio is bad enough, at 914 females for 1000 males (in the age group 0-6 years), it is 898 women per 1000 males in million-plus cities (only 868 in the case of Delhi) and a slightly better ratio of 902 per 1000 males in smaller-sized towns. This is true in most places, but Chennai is certainly a rare exception to the rule. The *National Family Health Survey-3* found that in Chennai the sex ratio is 1109 women to 1000 men in slums. This is because in Chennai, unlike much of North India, there is a large number of women migrants (*National Family Health Survey-3*; International Institute of Population Studies 2005-06: 23) as well.

Further, with the increase in migrant population, the gap between the rich and the poor in urban India also gets aggravated. This by itself is unremarkable as inequality is a ubiquitous feature in this country. But there is something else which is going on simultaneously that is worrying.

Quoting *The National Family and Health Surveys*, Sonia Hammam and Richard L. Clifford (2007) noted in a World Bank presentation, *India's Urban Poor*, that the quality of health services for the poor falls as the cities they migrate to get larger. For example, Infant Mortality Rate (IMR) is 77 per 1000 among the poor in large cities but 66 per 1000 for the same class of people in a small or medium town. This trend also holds for neo-natal and post-natal mortality, as it does for childhood anaemia.

Rural-Urban Relations: From Continuity to Nexus

While 70 per cent of urban Indians live in towns with a population of 100,000 and above, that is far from being the full story. As small towns are growing faster than million plus cities it is clear where India's urban growth is primarily taking place. At this stage it would be worth recalling our earlier examination of how the countryside has changed and contributed to the movement away from agriculture. This is probably the first step towards a more generalized urban trend, but is not always recognized as such. To quickly refresh our memory, let us recall the startling fact that 45.5 per cent of rural Net Domestic Product in India is non-agricultural (Chaddha 2003: 55; see also Goswami, n.d.). This is another reason there are so many workshops and household industries all over rural India (*Five-Year Plan 2002-07*, vol. 1, Annexure 5.3; see also *Statistical Outline of India 2006-7*: 35). In other words, people are staying in the village but not necessarily working on the land—at least, not for a lot of their time. This rise in commerce in rural India is a symptom of how urban areas in the vicinity of the village are also changing. This is why small towns, and not large ones, are showing a lot of dynamism.

Notwithstanding the increasing urban population, the population in rural India is still very high. The most recent figures show that roughly 69 per cent of our people still live in India's 641,000 villages (*Census of India 2011*; see also Bhagat 2011: 12). Thus, while the ambition to be urban still beats in many rural breasts, the numbers tell us something different. Why are there still so many villagers in India?

Is it at all possible that people move back and forth with great rapidity, from country to town and back? But that cannot be very significant, as the movement from urban to rural is very slight. The 2001 census records that only 8.6 per cent of male intra-state migrants and an even lower 6.1 per cent of inter-state male migrants move from cities to villages. The alternative possible explanation centres on the rural location of household industries. This probably gives us a clue as to why the percentage of male migrants from village to village, both intra-state and inter-state, is so high, at 41.6 and 20.7 per cent respectively (see Deshingkar and Farrington 2009: 15; see also Kundu and Saraswati 2012: 220).

In other words, a migrant's destination need not always be a city, even though that is preponderantly the case, especially when the transition is from country to town. There are many who are staying in villages, often not their own, but engaged in non-farm occupations.

All of this should be read in conjunction with the way rural India itself is transforming and becoming proto-urban. One should not be deceived by the fact that villages, for the most part, look like they always did. Yet a little attention to detail immediately reveals that something very important has happened in the past few decades. Agriculture is no longer the mainstay of the economy of the countryside allowing for extensive non-farm activity in the villages.

Yet this should not be taken to imply that industrial activity has fallen in urban India as a whole. While Pune, Lucknow, Pondicherry, Jaipur are getting bigger in this regard, giants such as Mumbai and Delhi may show a declining trend. This is why there has been an increase in the number of Class-1 towns from 24 in 1901 to 393 in 2001 to 468 in 2011. While rural population growth between 2001 and 2011 has been 12.18 per cent, the corresponding urban population growth is 31.8 per cent. In terms of numbers, rural India grew by 90.47 million, while urban areas recorded a clear 91 million increase. Put all this together and we get a handle on why non-metro cities are growing so fast. Tirrupur in Tamil Nadu alone accounts for 23 per cent of India's garment exports (Government of Tamil Nadu).

Thus while Delhi may be growing faster than Mumbai, it is the towns around it that are showing a much higher rate of population increase. The National Capital Region comprising Ghaziabad, Faridabad, Gurgaon and NOIDA are experiencing much higher population growth than what Delhi by itself is. If Delhi's numbers have grown at the rate of about 26 per cent, it is nearly 110 per cent in NOIDA, 41.6 per cent in Ghaziabad, and 73.93 per cent in Gurgaon (see urbanindia.nic.in/theministry/subordinateoff/tepo/DMA_Report/CHAPTER_3.pdf; see also *The Times of India*, 20 October 2011). While Mumbai has grown by about 5.79 per cent in the decade 2001-2011, Thane's numbers grew by 35.9 per cent, followed closely by Nhavi Mumbai (censusofindia.gov./in/2011-prov-results/data_files/maharashtra/Census2011). Outside the periphery of metros, other towns too have grown rapidly: Agra, Vishakapatnam, Hissar, Nellore, Tirrupur, and the list goes on. Step out of the limits of a metropolis and be overwhelmed by the fast pace of the small urban agglomerations that accrete to it. According to the 2001 census, Pune's urban population grew at 50.08 per cent. Though the 2011 figures show that this number has since decreased to 30.34 per cent, it is still impressive. Surat shows a higher growth rate than Pune in the years 2001-2011; the figure stands at 42.19 per cent in the 2011 census. NOIDA, as we have already seen, has had an unbelievable urban growth rate of above a 100 per cent during the years 2001-2011.

Small-town Wonders: Not by Metropolises Alone

This is not a recent trend but it is getting more and more noticeable over time. In Agra, for example, there are at least 7200 small-scale industries (SSI) that produce leather garments, textiles, zari work, handicrafts and marble stone for construction. Bhiwani, a small town in Haryana, is also busy manufacturing all kinds of products for export and even has technical institutions for students who want to specialize in textile production. There are 2250 SSI units in this town, with names such as Chinar and S.K. Foils prominent among them. Such enterprises also attract graduates from rural areas, who tend to prefer non-metro settings (see Kundu and Mohanan n.d.: 13; see also Dutta 2010; Kundu 2006). Let us not forget that about 20 per cent of India's billionaires come from small towns.

It is important to know why smaller towns and not metropolises are growing so fast. What attracts entrepreneurs and workers to these places?

There are probably many reasons for this shift to small towns. The most widely acknowledged is the simple fact of lower real-estate costs. Executives of many large companies, like Domino's Pizza and Yum Foods (of Pepsi fame), complain that rental values in Delhi or Mumbai make it difficult to generate the kind of profits that would justify their salaries. Alongside we also need to recognize that the kind of skills required in Indian industry are not really cutting-edge, and never have been. We are generally in denial on this one, but it is stubbornly true.

It is also true that the smaller the urban area, the greater is the proportion of land given to industry and mercantile activities. Cities with a population of over 100,000 have about 1.8 per cent of their developed land devoted to commercial use, whereas in smaller urban areas the proportion is almost 3.2 per cent (Venkateswaralu 1998: 23). When we come to industrial use, we find once again that while 6.8 per cent of all land is devoted to that purpose in all states, it is but 5.1 per cent in metros and as high as 14 per cent in towns with populations between 500,000 (five lakh) and 10,00,000 (ten lakh) (ibid.).

Take again Tirrupur in Tamil Nadu as an illustration of how economically active non-metro urban centres are. This city is the hosiery capital of India. It contributes 40 per cent of all knit wear exports from India amounting to a mammoth

₹5000 crore annually (Government of Tamil Nadu: 12). Tirrupur's contribution to India's apparel exports has gone up from 10 per cent in 1987 to 23 per cent in 1996, and this trend has kept growing (ibid.: 13). However, we need to recognize the important detail that much of this economic growth is powered by the informal sector.

While, in general, metros lead in the number of new managerial jobs created, Pune, Lucknow, Puducherry, Ranchi and Mangalore are not lagging behind by much. A large number of firms are now beginning start-ups in small towns with local-level administrative and managerial expertise. A recent survey conducted jointly by India's two apex industry chambers, FICCI and CII, reveals that while white-collar private-sector jobs are being lost in premier cities like Chennai, Delhi and Mumbai, the story is different in smaller tier-2 cities. For example, such positions grew in Lucknow by 54.1 per cent, Patiala by 61.3 per cent, Hoshiarpur by 100 per cent and Meerut by a remarkable 133.3 per cent (see Nayyar and Jain 2012: 21).

Those who are employed in these capacities may look a little unsophisticated compared to the high-fliers in large urban corporations, but they have a job and it is not in the mega-cities any more. Besides start-ups, there are bigger companies too, like Reliance Life Insurance, that have also opted for the same strategy (see http://articles.economictimes.indiatimes.com/2012-08-31/news/33521296_1_owns_justin_sargent_promart; and also www. indiweb.in/insurance/rli-target-small-town-to-hire-wage-based-agent/- accessed on 3 September 2012). This also explains why several Class-II cities like Surat, Patna, Pune, Jaipur and Indore have growth rates exceeding that of Kolkata, or even Mumbai. To a significant extent this aspect is aided by the fact that the demand for highly qualified labour personnel is nowhere that strong, anyway. Ghari Detergents is a very popular brand, but how many metro consumers have even heard of it, and it is unlikely to have much need for professional skilled workers. Yet, from a factory a few miles away from Kanpur, it caters to a huge market, with a turnover higher than all the Godrej FMCG products (including Cinthol) put together. Only Hindustan Unilever does better than Ghari in terms of revenues.

Coming second to a front-runner like that is almost as good as winning the gold. Similarly, Sanjay Ghodawat runs a ₹1,000 crore conglomerate in Manakpur. To locate this nondescript place you may need to reach for the map. It doesn't help to know that it is a hundred miles or so from Kolhapur, another small town in Maharashtra. He made his big money selling gutkha, but now he has companies that manufacture such diverse products as wind energy turbines, mosquito coils and oxalic acid.

We have already been introduced to Tirrupur in Tamil Nadu (Tirrupur Municipality Report, Government of Tamil Nadu), so let us move on to other small towns. Hosur in Tamil Nadu is also very fast-growing, and so are slums in places like Parvathinagar. It has a strong manufacturing base, home to many automotive-part makers, a thriving IT sector, as well as granite mining and polishing companies. Betweeen 1991 and 2001, the population in this town grew from 41,739 to 84,394. Maduravayal, again in Tamil Nadu, has grown about three times in this period.

In Uttar Pradesh, Moradabad grew by about 51 per cent between 1991 and 2001 and 28.3 per cent between 2001 and 2011. Much of this population growth has happened courtesy the brassware units and factories in this town. Varanasi city too has grown 40.16 per cent between 1991 and 2001 because of the expansion of carpet and weaving industries. On the other hand, Gonda and Hardoi have not grown as much for they have not attracted small-scale, labour-intensive production as some of the other fast-growing towns have. Panipat, in Haryana, is a good illustration of a city that has shown a spurt in population and economic growth. Here are some of the features of this city, whose population topped one million in the 2011 census.

Panipat has three major public-sector projects: the Indian Oil Corporation oil refinery, the National Fertilizers Limited plant and the thermal power station. It is also the biggest centre in the country for producing shoddy (recycled) yarn, and a large consumer of rags for reprocessing and for producing low-priced blankets: a national supplier to the barracks of the armed forces. The bulk of the country's export of cotton durries, made-ups, and throw mats is also produced here. The economic growth of Panipat is primarily in areas of low-skilled production, and that has led to a spurt in its population figures as well.

Small-town Aspirations: Many Indias in One

Small towns all over India are lined with beauty parlours and gymnasiums. In the Doaba region of Punjab, it is not necessary to sport an urban status to avail of these facilities. Nearly every biggish village in these districts has beauty parlours and gymnasiums juxtaposed with typical village houses, mud walls notwithstanding. The lines outside ATMs in places like Darbhanga, in distant Mithila in Bihar, are much longer than one would expect. BPO is a huge business; not just Pune, but even Indore has become quite a hub for these activities, as have several small towns between Punjab and Haryana. Peerless Mutual Funds is opening thirty-one branches in tier-2 and tier-3 cities, while Karur, the 'textile capital' in Tamil Nadu, supplies to international companies like Wal-Mart, J.C. Penney and Target. The 7.7 trillion rupee fund industry (where entities pool their investments, particularly in mutual funds) has reached saturation point in the eight big cities of India, forcing it to move to smaller urban agglomerates.

Is it surprising then that nearly 20 per cent of India's billionaires live outside metros? Not too long ago, Azim Premji (of Wipro fame) started his upwardly mobile journey—from millionaire to billionaire—from a small town called Amalner in Maharashtra. There are others who are less famous but seriously wealthy, and are from non-metropolitan centres. Names such as that of Nafisa Radiatorwala of Vadodara's Nature's Glow (a herbal skincare company); and S. Susindran, the CEO of Sabare International, a garment manufacturing company, from Karur, come readily to mind, but there are scores of others. While these are not exactly household names, they have become wealthy even as they operate out of small towns.

When it comes to ostentatious splendour alone, it is hard to beat Sanjay Ghodawat, the quality gutkha manufacturer. He has 102 cars and is in a fix every morning as he has to choose which one to take to work. More often than not, he gets out of his misery by just flying to his office in his own helicopter. Not just money, but intellectually too we are witnessing a kind of turnaround in smaller urban centres. Patiala is known today not just for its princely past and its aggressive rich landowners. In the district headquarter of this state we now have the renowned Lakshya Institute which coaches eager young aspirants to technical colleges. Last year 116 of its students were selected for the IITs, and the bulk of the successful candidates came from Patiala.

These small towns are furiously establishing educational institutes and technical schools and colleges. Obviously, there is a great desire amongst those who live here to better their lives. Moradabad has many such institutions and among them are the Teerthankar Mahavir University, the Moradabad Institute of Technology, Wilson Degree College as well as English-medium schools such as Delhi Public School and St Jude.

Hanamkonda in Andhra Pradesh too has many colleges as well as institutes that specialize in pharmacy, technology and business. In Kazipet there is a Mary Convent School as well as the renowned National Institute of Technology. Kuppar, another small Andhra town, is a kind of educational hub with engineering and medical colleges. In the 1980s, Odisha had but three engineering colleges; today it has over ninety such institutions.

The above are only examples; almost every small town has an English-medium school as well as a technology and management institute of some kind. This is significant as it demonstrates a strong desire for upward mobility among small-town residents. The fact that the rate of literacy is increasing faster in rural India than in urban India indicates how motivated the villagers are about getting educated and leaving the village for an urban job. The census figures of 2001 show that the rate of literacy in rural India has gone up by 14.7 per cent compared to the 7.2 per cent increase in urban India.

According to Kundu and Mohanan, those migrants with higher secondary and college degrees tend to go to small towns and medium-sized cities. This is interesting, for when it comes to those who are illiterate or poorly educated, there does not seem to be any bias: they would go anywhere (see Kundu and Mohanan, n.d.). In other words, rural graduates find it easier to get a job in small towns rather than in big metropolitan centres. This must be seen alongside the fact that 30.3 per cent of rural migrants leave for economic reasons.

Further, as Biplab Dasgupta noted in the context of West Bengal, migrants begin to earn as soon as possible. They cannot afford to stay unemployed for too long. This also keeps many of them from returning after they make the move to urban centres from villages (Dasgupta 1988: 47). Obviously, once the ambition is formed to leave the village, its natural corollary is to limit the size of one's family to a small one. This also explains why so many children are today going to private schools. Only when the family is small can parents think of sending their children to more expensive educational institutions. Consequently, their dependence on government schools declines.

Illiteracy is definitely down among the rural labour force. If we take just males into account for the time being in the rural workforce, the number on this score has fallen from nearly 60 per cent in 1977-78 to about 31.0 per cent in 2005-06 and in urban India from around 23 per cent in 1977-78 to less than 11 per cent in 2005-06. At the same time, there is a big jump in the number of those in the rural labour force with graduate qualifications and above, from 1 per cent in 1977-78 to 10.1 per cent in 2005-06 (*Manpower Profile India* 2009: 102). This shows that more and more young people are staying on in schools and colleges, despite the still persistent high drop-out rates. This is also consistent with the fact that the number of those aged between fifteen and twenty-nine in the rural labour force has also gone down significantly (ibid.: 101).

Yet the demand for educated and skilled migrants is not very high. We are therefore forced to ask two questions. Is there a sufficient demand for skilled labour yet? Second, how good is the quality of these educational institutions?

Informal/Household Industries: Linkages Between Country and Town

Before we take on such questions directly, it is necessary to quickly examine the linkages between country and town.

If one looks at urbanization as a consequence of moving out of agriculture, and not just in terms of expansion of metropolises, then the results are very impressive. It is not necessary that the shift from rural occupations should only take place when big factories are set up with organized workers on their rolls. Much of India's non-agricultural output, including manufacture of various kinds, happens in small units.

While observing these trends, we must not lose sight of two significant facts that should be examined together. The first is the increase in literacy levels of migrants and, at the same time, the overwhelming numbers of unskilled labourers that come in large numbers to cities in search of jobs. Annapurna Shaw found both these features in the making of Navi Mumbai. What was most striking in her presentation is the sheer magnitude of unskilled labourers who were flooding into the city, increasing the density and incidence of unauthorized settlements (Shaw 2004: 122). This is significant, as the search for jobs is the most important reason for male migration and they generally end up in the unskilled labour force, much of it in the informal sector. Consequently, 51.7 per cent of Mumbai's population lives in slums and many of them are migrants from near and far. Delhi has a lower proportion in these shanty quarters, but the numbers are growing.

As Deshingkar and John Farrington write: '[M]asses of poor, landless, illiterate and unskilled agricultural labourers and petty farmers from backward states make quantum leaps toward large metropolises like Calcutta, Bombay, Delhi and Madras, often, but not always, bypassing local small towns and small cities. This leads to acute urban involution, congestion and decay' (2009: 13). So it is not as if small towns are being by-passed, as was the case earlier in the 1960s and 1970s. At that point it was believed that big cities attract people with higher skills (D'Souza 1975), but that, as we now know, is no longer true. Small towns, as was mentioned earlier, are growing at a much faster rate than established big cities. All of this basically condemns urban India, metros and non-metros alike to suffer slums on a large scale. From a little over 18 per cent a decade back the proportion of slum dwellers in India's capital today has crossed 20 per cent.

Moving with their Feet: How Migrants Contribute

In villages and town, east to west and north to south, migration plays an important role in urbanization. Consider the construction industry. Without cheap labour from Chhattisgarh, UP, Jharkhand and Bengal, real-estate development would grind to a halt. Or take the textile sector. Forget the mighty Jullundur; even without Panipat in Haryana and Jaipur in Rajasthan, the loom sector would face a serious crisis.

Carpets next. India, as we know, generates 11 per cent of the world's trade in carpets. Most of these floor coverings are produced in the UP districts of Jaunpur, Mirzapur and Bhadohi, with a lot of help from Latehar and Lohardaga in neighbouring Jharkhand. Moreover, factories in Vapi and Bardoli in Gujarat, as well as those in Maharashtra's Mumbai-Pune belt, depend heavily on cheap labour from the northern states.

Tirrupur, which is the hosiery capital of India, has workers from as far away as Jharkhand and Kishenganj in Bihar. The reason they are welcome in the heart of Coimbatore district is because they can be satisfied with poor wages. They may be low-skilled, but they are high risk-takers; they travel for miles on a prayer and a promise of work. Besides being low-cost, migrant workers are pliant, take less leave, and can be easily switched around by contractors from unit to unit. This strategy keeps local labour under control and nobody has yet found a better way yet of shutting trade unionism out. The contribution of migrants in small towns can be put in perspective if we keep in mind the fact that tertiary employment in the country is going up and primary employment going down (*Manpower Profile of India* 2008: 185).

The migration to big cities is indeed remarkable, but if we take a close look, then in terms of total migration, small towns have many more such people. It should also be kept in mind that migrants go where they have networks already in place. As S.C. Joshi has pointed out, as many as 78.9 per cent of his sample of migrants in Delhi already had prior contacts (Joshi 1994: 61). Migrant labourers to farms in Punjab are often contacted by phone by land-owners so that they come at the right time, in fact, even on the right dates (Gill 2005: 95).

Trends in urban population can, therefore, also be judged in terms of the kind of industrial activity that migrants usually find positions in. Industrial function dominates Kerala, Gujarat and Tamil Nadu. Seventy-five per cent of all urban Maharashtrians live in industrial towns, while the figure is 70 per cent for Gujarat and 57 per cent for Kerala. On the other hand, only 20 per cent of the urban population in Bihar, Himachal Pradesh and Odisha live in industrial towns (see Misra 1998).

This is probably why there is a high degree of migration from these states. If we study the relationship between urban to rural workers we find that in Gujarat it is almost even: 1.7 rural workers for every urban worker. In Punjab, Delhi, Karnataka and West Bengal the figure is two rural workers for every urban worker. But the proportion of rural worker jumps once we come to UP and Rajasthan where there are respectively 4.5 and 3.5 rural workers for every urban worker. The greatest number in this regard is Bihar and Assam where for every urban worker there are about eight rural workers. Migration is clearly promoted by this fact (*Census of India 2001*: Final Population Tables: 1-9).

As we have already remarked, registered small-scale industries are growing at a faster rate in less prosperous regions of India, such as in Uttar Pradesh, Odisha and Bihar. Though such enterprises are located in smaller towns with lower real-estate values and though they do not attract skilled workers, we should not dismiss their contribution to the Indian economy. It is worth repeating once again that the official SSI sector contributes roughly one-third of our foreign exchange earnings (see *Handbook of Statistics 2011*: 89, 207). It is hard to estimate the total number of workers in the SSI sector as so much of it is informal and unorganized in character. It is, therefore, not unreasonable to suggest that these units employ more informal labour than the figures that are officially recorded.

Slums as an Index of Urban Growth: Poverty and Hope

Slum settlements have had a rocky and uneven path. In Delhi, for example, till the 1960s the idea was to find alternate houses for slum-dwellers in the capital itself. This policy was favoured so that Delhi's residential areas would have a class mix. But after 1990 this pretence was dropped without a backward look. The earlier provision for *in situ* upgrading of shanty clusters was abandoned as well. The emphasis now is almost entirely on relocating slum-dwellers in distant suburbs so that prestigious and high-priced urban property in the city do not lose their shine and value.

This is a quick assessment, but there are at least eleven resettlement colonies that are between twenty and thirty-five kilometres outside the boundaries of Old Delhi and five which are clearly fifteen or twenty kilometres beyond New Delhi's perimeters. The rest are closer but not by much. Most of them are more than ten kilometres away from New Delhi or Old Delhi (see Dupont 2008).

It is an established fact that wages decline the further one goes from the city. Eventually, it is a toss-up. Should the worker come to Delhi and earn more money only to spend much of it on transport, or look for a lower-paying job closer home, but away from the metropolis? In most cases the latter option is a less remunerative one, which forces the poor to make the long trudge to Delhi on a daily basis. As that works well for 'us', we do not worry about the rest.

It is true that places that were once slums are now prime urban property. The land mafia, commercial agents and several politicians have made a killing out of this. Yet there are still many demolished sites which have not been developed for years. What purpose then did those evictions serve?

Of course, Delhi's slum-dwellers have grown hugely in number. In 1981 they comprised 8.6 per cent of the population, but the figure today is at around 18 per cent—a more than two-fold increase in less than thirty years! It would have been higher, by all accounts, if the re-settlement drive, discussed earlier, had not happened. Yet, it is never population but the manpower quality and social statuses of those other people that makes the numbers unbearable to 'people like us'. As slums offend our senses, we see them everywhere, though they occupy only 6 per cent of the land (Dupont 2008: 108).

At a national level, between 1981 and 2001 there has been a 45 per cent increase in the number of people who live in urban slums (Chandrashekhar n.d.). Thus while the population of India grew at 2 per cent per annum between 1991 and 2001, the population of slums grew at 3 per cent and that of megacities by 5 per cent (see Gupta, Arnold, Lhungdiu 2006). Much of this is on account of migration. In Lucknow, for example, migration alone accounts for a 36 per cent increase in urban population in the last decade (see *Master Plan of Lucknow*), but strangely, Lucknow's local body does not recognize slums (Gupta, Arnold, Lhungdiu 2009).

It is not as if slums are proliferating only in Maharashtra or in the Delhi National Capital region. The growth of slums in states like Haryana and Andhra Pradesh, which do not have a major megacity, is nearly equal to that of Maharashtra, famous for Mumbai, Pune and even Nagpur (http://mospi.nic./mospi_new/upload/sel_socio_eco_stats_ind_2001_28oct.pdf; accessed on

3 September 2012). Whether north or south, east or west, one can judge where economic activity is growing by the population in slums. Predictably, there is a huge rise of such squalid quarters in small and medium towns like Moradabad, Jaipur, Tirrupur and Surat where there is a lot of entrepreneurial activity. In all these places, once again, low-technology items, from diamond cutting to brassware to hosiery, are manufactured and much of it exported.

Interestingly, there are some non-metros which have a high slum population. In Pune the number of those living in slums grew by an astounding 176.4 per cent between 1991 and 2007 (http://articles.timesofindia.indiatimes.com/2007-04-24/27883809_1_slum_population_growth_rate_mashal; accessed on 3 September 2012; Chandrashekhar n.d., see also *Eastern India: The Complete Data Base* 1994: 6.10, 6.1; accessed on 12 July 2010). In Meerut 43 per cent of the population lives in slums, in Nagpur 33 per cent, and in Surat 20.89 per cent (between 1981 and 1991 the growth in the number of slum-dwellers doubled the growth rate of the city's population). This is higher than the figures in Delhi, Kolkata, Bangalore (www.measuredhs.com/pubs/pdf; accessed on 24 April 2011).

If between 1981 and 2001 there has been a 45 per cent increase in slum population in India as a whole, then this amounts to every seventh urban person being a slum-dweller (Chandrashekar n.d.). They are also among the poorest in the country.

This shows that a large number of migrants are probably coming to these places in search of jobs; because it is class-1 towns like these where the action is (Ministry of Health and Family Welfare 2005-6). In the opinion of Marias-Gnanou and Maricano-Ebrard (n.d.) manufacturing and transport towns grow faster than service and trade towns.

This may give us a perspective on why Ludhiana, a metaphor for a manufacturing industry town, should have a slum population that touches 50 per cent (*Eastern India: The Complete Data Base* 1993: 6.10). In Pune it is 40 per cent,

Meerut 44 per cent (Chandrashekhar, n.d.), Hapur 42.52 per cent, and in Hathras and Mainpuri, exceeding even 60 per cent. (http://www.rcueslko.org/states/Compendium per cent20of per centUrban per cent20Data per cent2(Uttar per cent20Pradesh)/13 per cent20Slum per cent20P; accessed 2 September 2012). We are accustomed to large slum populations in big metros like Mumbai but are unprepared for such high figures in smaller towns, whose slum figures, in percentage, exceed those of metropolises by substantial margins.

Not only is there an increase in employment in the informal sector and substantial growth in the tertiary sector; more poor women are in employment in slums than anywhere else. It must be underlined too that in Meerut, with a huge slum population, the working population aged between fifteen and fifty-five is as high as 59 per cent. That the figure in Kolkata is only 12 per cent tells us once again that small towns offer more employment opportunities than metros in general (Ministry of Health and Family Welfare 2005-6: 23).

Why do people leave the countryside for urban slums? Why abandon the clean air and open fields for squalid hutments in filthy alleyways? The simple answer, strange as it may sound, is: for a better life, of course. This may sound outrageous to many who believe that rural India is the ideal for the majority of Indians. If about a quarter of those who live in cities are slum-dwellers, then it is simply because they are much better-off here than back home in the village. Not only are literacy rates higher here than in villages but, surprisingly, people below the poverty line are proportionately fewer in urban slums than in all of rural India (see Gupta, Arnold and Lhungdiu 2009: 14). There is just no competition! In poorer states like Bihar, MP, Rajasthan, Odisha and UP, the literacy rate in slums is significantly higher than in the surrounding rural areas (Chandrashekhar n.d.). Additionally, according to Chandrashekhar, in 'states that do not rank high in terms of rural female literacy, the improvement in literacy in case of slum women is higher than for men residing in slums' (ibid.). This is an interesting observation worth investigating further.

Trends in Urban India: The Country in the City

In spite of growth why does India continue to be so rural? The latest 2011 census shows that our rural population is still a little above 69 per cent. This figure has changed by just about 2 per cent since 2001. Also, nearly half (47.5 per cent) the towns still list agriculture as their principal activity. This is particularly true of class-3 to class-5 towns (Misra 1998).

France was only 55 per cent urban in the 1940s; so were large parts of Europe. Today, France, Italy and Spain, not to mention Germany and the Scandinavian countries, are only 2 to 3 per cent rural. This is an indication of their prosperity. Latin America too has just driven into the smart set with its high-speed urbanization. There are places in this part of the New World where urbanization touches 85 per cent.

The India story is not quite true to this pattern.

One would think that necessity would dictate that poor people on the margins of a village economy should up and leave at the first opportunity. Though India's urban population is growing, yet the rate at which migration is contributing to it is steadily declining. In fact, the rate of urbanization in general went down in the period 1981-2001. Is this because of the uncertainties of urban life on account of the lack of social securities? Or, is it because land ownership is still highly prized even if non-agricultural jobs are being constantly sought? Or, as is more likely, a combination of the two? We tend to overlook the hold of the rural because our towns look over-crowded and filthy. But they are not filthy because they are crowded; they appear crowded because they are filthy. Had they been better planned they would smell different too.

How urban then is urban India? The mere presence of towns does not always indicate development or prosperity. UP, Bihar and Odisha have a fair number of cities of different descriptions, yet they are all fighting for the last place. Half the towns of Andhra Pradesh, Karnataka, Maharashtra, UP, Bihar and MP are really not fully urban, for the remains of agriculture continue to linger on there (Misra 1998). Yet, for the record,

186 Revolution from Above

their residents are town-dwellers, no matter what their real lives are like. If they are not officially rural it is because they inhabit overcrowded spaces with a town hall in the middle. Though one of the criteria in our official definition is that 75 per cent of the working males must be in non-agricultural occupations, yet if it falters on this count it can still be a town. As long as the population density is high and there is a municipal council or cantonment board in the area, the place can still be called urban. This explains why UP with as many as 704 towns still lacks an industrial base and retains its largely rural visage.

Ad Hocism: Taking Urbanization Lightly

Urbanization is an unrelenting process and in its first phase it will draw in the big cities and then gradually move to smaller ones. In the fullness of time, non-metropolitan urban centres will attract investment, primarily because real-estate prices there are lower than in places like Mumbai, Kolkata, Delhi and Chennai. This process is already an established trend in India, furthered to a great extent by the entry of information technology, which lowered the need to set up businesses only where ancillary facilities like banking were present. However, if urbanization is not properly supervised, slums soon begin to appear in the newly emerging smaller towns, and the existing ones in bigger cities get more entrenched, even becoming expensive enough to attract mafia operators. If land prices keep escalating, speculators are happy but citizens, in general, are deprived of their need to live and work in dignified circumstances.

As slums invariably come up in the vicinity of economic activity that requires low-skill and low-wage workers, town planning must play a role in realizing what kind of development we would prefer. When slums are relocated, the poor have to travel long distances, as we saw was the case in Delhi. On the other hand, if they are left at their original sites, shanties lack even the most rudimentary necessities like sanitation and remain blots of squalor on the urban landscape. If migrants come on their own to cities, problems ensue with their domestic lives and the upbringing of their children. If they leave their homes *en famille*, they require adequate health and educational facilities. In the preceding pages these issues have been discussed at length if only to sound the warning bell that urbanization is too important a phenomenon and too closely linked to our collective future, for real-estate interests to take over and be the sole dictator of what form urbanization should take.

Unfortunately, the urban process in India is often perjured for short-term election gains. This is another instance, one that is perhaps the most stark, of maximizing the 'politics of the given'. For example, on 28 August, 2012, Sheila Dixit, the Chief Minister of Delhi, regularized 917 unauthorized colonies in the city. Obviously, this would please those who live in these settlements; but, come to think of it, why were they allowed to stay there for so long in the first place? Clearly, covert administrative support must have been at work, or else something so egregious and out in the open could not have grown to such mammoth proportions over the years. Now that these colonies have been legalized, Mrs Dixit hopes that the Congress will win the upcoming elections.

The opposition Bharatiya Janata Party does not want to be upstaged on this count. Therefore, instead of criticizing the government for regularizing what was irregular, not stopping this process in its tracks, and not bringing the guilty officials to book, this party instead raised the bar by demanding that an additional 301 colonies left out by Sheila Dixit also be favoured along the same lines!

At the end of the day, the Master Plan is in tatters and those who have broken the law have become the ultimate victors. We have not yet touched upon the close connection between urbanization and transport, or urbanization and pollution. A little introspection will tell us almost immediately that these features are all part of one big piece called 'urbanization'. Given the gravity that urbanization entails, it surely deserves a much better deal in India. But our politicians who play on maximizing the given do not seem to be interested.

A fresh start is required: once again the call is out for the 'citizen elite'.

CHAPTER X

The Citizen Elite and Mahatmas: Serving Citizens or the 'Targeted Weak'

Democracy and fraternity can be best served by the citizen elite, or the elite of calling, and not by Mahatmas. The former pushes the frontiers of citizenship, while the latter picks up the pieces of refuse that an uncaring society leaves behind. Mahatmas proliferate in societies where citizenship is weak or missing, typically in the developing world. There are few Mahatmas, if any, in the west, and with good reason. While arguing in favour of this point of view, it is also necessary to clarify the meaning of civil society and rescue it from the view that it relates primarily to NGOs.

'O public road...you express me better than I express myself.'
—Walt Whitman

Planning can be of two types: one that maximizes the given and does not question the ground rules, and the other that changes the rules of the game. The first route is the one chosen by everyday politicians, and some of them can be well-meaning too. They, however, feel that wisdom lies in pragmatics, which is why they are reluctant to think big. The 'citizen elite' believe in challenging the given and are constantly raising the bar as far as democracy is concerned. It is they who have made democracy the way it is today; it is they who have given the world rights and freedoms of the kind that history till then had never known.

We have argued this case at length in earlier pages, but there remains just one other feature that needs to be clarified. We know that the elite of calling are not the same as routine politicians or even leaders of political parties. But to what extent are the elite of calling the same as heroes or Mahatmas (forget the self-seeking politicians), of whom we have a few in our country and in neighbouring ones? While they may be exemplary individuals, it would be a grave error to mistake them for the elite who dig deep to enhance the richness of democracy. It is for this reason that it is necessary to separate the two conceptually.

Mahatmas and Elite of Calling: From Sympathy to Empathy

In societies like India, where there is such a gap between different classes and a general denial of universal services, one naturally tends to equate Mahatmas with the elite of calling. As the overwhelming reality in India is one of want, it is not surprising that some well-meaning and dedicated individuals find it unbearable and reach out to help to the extent they can. One can call them philanthropists, angels of mercy, do-gooders, or whatever, but they try in their way to alleviate some of the suffering of a designated population. Like the elite of calling, these Mahatmas are also few in number, but they are unable to make a difference other than in the little area that concerns them—the targeted population. There are millions who need health care, good education, housing and old-age support; but the philanthropists can make a difference only to the lives of relatively few. While some are helped in this process, society as a whole remains unchanged and in a steady state.

In this case, it is large-hearted people who are serving the needy, but it is not democracy that is delivering to citizens.

Mahatmas are not changing state policy; they are providing help to a few who come within their zone of influence and in areas where they have expertise and commitment. So some may want to educate children, others look after elderly people, still others who help victims of cancer and other life-threatening illnesses, and so on. But in all such cases, it is not a universal programme at work, but specific interventions by specific people in a limited area.

These people are often seen as 'heroes' or 'Mahatmas', and not unjustly so. Yet, since they do not intervene to influence state policies in the direction of universal delivery of public goods, they cannot really be equated with the elite of calling or 'citizen elites'. The heroes (or Mahatmas) and the 'elite of calling' resemble each other at first glance, but they are actually quite different. In the case of the former, they are motivated by 'goodwill' and charity (both laudable virtues) whereas in the case of the latter, the driving force is 'fraternity'. Thus heroes and Mahatmas see their aim as helping the wretched, while for the elite of calling, the goal is to uplift every citizen. In addition, the elite of calling clearly and consciously attack the very foundations of their status and the status quo in order to deliver universally to citizens. Of course, in the long run everybody benefits, but in the short run, the elite are taking a big risk. Heroes, leaders of NGOs, even Mahatmas, rarely ever put their own class interests and social position at stake when they extend their hand to help those in distress.

It is interesting that in societies where democracy delivers to its citizens there are few Mahatmas. The more backward a state, the greater the number of such exceptional figures, and that is not surprising at all. Heroes or Mahatmas come in to fill the gaps in a non-delivering democracy where votes matter but fraternity does not. How many such figures will one find in Europe or the United States of America? Yet, come to India or Bangladesh, and they are not so rare. That is so because there is so much unheeded poverty and want that it drives some of the best individuals to emerge from their privileged surroundings to help. On the other hand, when the state delivers universally,

Mahatmas become a rare feature. Under these circumstances, citizens are proud of, and identify with, what is in the public domain. It expresses the best they can do as a collective. That is why this chapter began with the quote from Walt Whitman.

In the US, people donate quite generously to charity, but these organizations are run in a corporate style, *sans* heroes. Interestingly, many of the donations that ordinary people contribute to causes in the US go to religious organizations and not so much to pure charity or welfare. When these donors give money to entities outside the US, then the money is for organizations helping the poor and the sick and the needy which, very often, local Mahatmas, and imported ones, operate.

The American Peace Corps is a breeding ground for such heroes but so are other international agencies like CARE, Save the Children and so on, though on a less ambitious scale. They come in and help to the extent they can and to the limit their funds will allow, but once they leave, chances of reversals are high; and while they are there, the inefficient state continues to be there as well. This is because in all such cases it is not universal delivery but sectional relief. Jeffrey Sachs believes that foreign aid can do a lot of good; interestingly though, his emphasis is not on universal health, but on public health, sanitation and nutrition (Sachs 2005: 59, 85). This, as we discussed earlier, ends up being low-grade health for the poor because such efforts are not integrated into the universal delivery of medical care. Thus, while sympathy is something that wells up spontaneously, empathy is consciously cultivated for the cause of citizenship. While the first is an expression of anguish and can happen at any point in history, the latter is able to express itself only in the context of citizenship, which is of very recent vintage.

Civil Society: An Inclusive Concept

This distinction between Heroes or Mahatmas and the citizen elite frequently gets blurred because the term 'civil society' is used rather carelessly, perhaps even promiscuously. Drawing on Alexis de Tocqueville's study extolling intermediate institutions in America, Non-Governmental Organizations (NGOs) are often mistakenly called civil societies. This is particularly true of the United Nations, from where many others got their cue. As a result, Mahatmas tend to be considered as agents of civil society, which only adds to the confusion. Civil Society is also equated with being polite and 'civil'; while some other writers use the term to mean that civil society is what the elite enjoy and not the rest (Chatterjee 2001: 165-178, especially 173-178; see also Chatterjee n.d.).

But the term civil society actually refers only to those apparatuses of the state that actually deliver citizenship. Not all intermediate institutions can be grouped under this rubric, for citizenship is something that has a universal quality about it (see Beteille 2002: 69; also Beteille 1996). So a private school or hospital, a philanthropist's NGO, or a sports club, are not proper civil society institutions. This is because they are not intermediate between state and citizens but are organizations that cater to designated people.

Those who, inspired by the UN and other multilateral agencies, identify civil society with NGOs are obviously unaware of the long, intellectual tradition of this concept. From Adam Ferguson, to Hegel, to Marx, to Marshall, to Rawls, the most important feature of civil society is how it enlarges the scope of citizenship. This is why most admirers of NGOs have no compunctions in supporting NGOs in despotic regimes. The rationale behind the activism of such NGOs is much like that of the Mahatmas. They leave the state just as it was, but are lauded for their valuable contributions. When such interventions are repeated often enough, and when they are lavishly funded, these NGOs let these dysfunctional states off the hook!

The institutions that are properly in the domain of civil society are those that enhance the potentialities of citizens and create a status of equality at base. Note, as Marshall clarified, that this is about equality of opportunities and not equality of results or of wealth (Marshall 1950, 1963). The institutions of civil society help citizens lead lives that resemble each other in the most important aspects of their public life. As Durkheim once said, '[O]ne's first duty is to resemble everybody else' (Durkheim 1933). The institutions then that are properly in the domain of civil society are those that provide universal services of public goods. Obviously, the delivery of health, education, public transport, energy and water are the most significant in this connection. Therefore, institutions that deliver these across the board to citizens in general, properly belong to the domain of civil society.

The Expanding Horizon of Citizenship: Putting the Given Under Pressure

Citizenship is never in a steady state. Its limits are constantly stretched because democracy restlessly strives to add to the complement of rights and freedoms. Many of these may not have been imagined even a decade or so before they actually became law. This is true not just in the case of granting women the right to vote, or equal status to minorities, but in more recent times in giving homosexuals dignity and legal protection.

The most important characteristic of citizenship is that it protects in advance a person who may be unfortunately placed at birth. The economic status of a family one is born into, one's race, gender or sexual orientation are all outcomes of a natural lottery against which an individual is helpless. In addition, as John Rawls (1971) argued, such a situation could easily have been the fate of those who believe they are on the 'right side' and with the 'majority'. Had the dice fallen some other way, they might have been scrambling for resources just as the least advantaged do as part of their daily grind. To be fair and just, it is important to examine policies from the point of view of those who are not privileged, and only democracy can do that. This is how citizenship is created.

But every time we take a step forward in this direction, note that all of us prosper. When women, minorities, blacks and gays are allowed to contribute, we are all the richer for it. When some people have privileges and others do not, then the relationship between them will necessarily be governed by extra-democratic norms which can only take the society back.

This is another reason democracy never stands still. After a set of rights is won, the next step is to make for a level playing-field, for the pre-existing conditions are never in tune with this development. This in turn demands not just the legal guarantee of the equality of opportunity, but also the opening up of avenues that are wide enough for everybody to legitimately access socially valuable skills in practice.

If these provisions and rights are not in place then universal law will constantly be undermined. We will not be under one law, but governed by idiosyncrasies, patronage, nepotism and so on. Till the early decades of the nineteenth century there were some lingering romantics who despaired at the idea of formal, universal norms. Georg Simmel, for example, found them to be characterized by 'inordinate hardness' (Simmel 1958: 150) which did not allow delicacy and spiritualism to flourish. What he forgot to add was how these laws, by virtue of being universal, did not let arbitrary norms, favouritism and blocked access to public goods to flourish either.

When such laws do not exist, civil society dies instantly: it does not wobble or gasp—it is dead and gone. The concept of civil society rests on the principle of universal law, which in turn means nothing if it is not bolstered by equality of rights and opportunities that creates an equality of status between citizens (Marshall 1950, 1963). Citizenship and universality are twins; there cannot be one without the other. This is why it is wrong to claim, as Partha Chatterjee does, that in India the privileged have citizenship rights and others do not. Civil society cannot exist if it works for some and not for others.

When Chatterjee argues that only the better-off have civil society rights, he ignores the fact that even these fortunate few actually live off the patronage of those who are still more powerful and are, in turn, patrons to people below them. Those whom Chatterjee designates as full members of civil society also depend on favours and goodwill to get their children into good schools or parents to the most favoured hospitals, and in most cases do their best to evade taxes. They also use their power over those subordinate to them to make them work for below-minimum wages, for longer hours and under unsavoury conditions. Therefore, instead of arguing that there is civil society for some and not for others, it is better to see such societies as bound by a Great Chain of Patronage. This is the given condition and it is this given condition that all those up and down the Great Chain of Patronage are trying to maximize.

In contrast to Chatterjee, but in the same separatist vein, Rajni Kothari believed that civil society was where the poor are to be found. It lingers in their rude huts, in community bonds, and most of all, its vivacity is directly proportional to the poverty of the surroundings (Kothari 1984, 1988). For him, as for Chatterjee, the state has no role to play in the establishing of civil society, other than hindering it. In both instances, civil society's progress is blocked, either at the top end or at the bottom, but it is not something that involves citizens. In this connection, we must insist on the fact that countries like India are not culturally ordained to deny citizenship; what gets in the way is the deep fissures that stratify our society. If we are not clear about this, we would be yielding to a species of cultural determinism, and the culture of poverty is its close cousin. Resignation to what exists is the biggest curse for countries like India, because the odds seem to be so heavily loaded in favour of inequity and injustice.

How does a society break out of these coils and realize substantive citizenship? If the politics of maximizing the given is so compelling, elections too will feed into that logic. Each of us will fight from our own vantage point, from our own perspective, and society will just be a summation of these views, struggles and compromises. But if the whole is to be greater than the sum total of its parts, then it will require an elite intervention; the vanguard of fraternity, the 'citizen elite', to step in to lift people beyond their givens.

As we have seen, targeted approaches fail because they are not universal in scope. Policy directives of this sort play with numbers, get obsessed by them and lose the bigger picture. It is a situation not unlike what Thomas Kuhn had suggested when he segregated normal science from paradigmatic (or revolutionary) science. In the case of the former, there is a near-complete immersion in methodology and methodology alone, as if process is all. From time to time, from within this hardened shell of normal science, paradigmatic breakthroughs happen that change the way we look at the world (Kuhn 1970). This revolution in thought is accomplished by the scientific elite—the ordinary practitioner is incapable of even dreaming of such a step.

It is, then, the 'citizen elite' on whom rests the responsibilities of establishing the foundations and principles of a democracy. It is this category of leaders again who spearhead most advances in society, as the rest are preoccupied with the given. It is this citizen elite, or the elite of calling, who think society and not family, or community, or about the poor. If they have special provisions for the weak, it is always to quicken their entry into the world of universal services that a modern welfare state promises. To be able to do this effectively, the administrations they lead must know the facts on the ground in order to go beyond them.

When, however, the numbers game, or the gathering of information, is utilized for control, it is another matter. For example, if a government wants to know how many members of a particular community live in a certain geographical area in order to persecute them, or deprive them of welfare benefits, then that is 'surveillance'. That term would be completely out of place if the authorities scrutinise a population to figure out how best to deliver state services on a universal basis.

In these circumstances, it would be unfair to label such a task as 'surveillance'—a trend that Michel Foucault started. If it had stopped there one could have dismissed partisans of such a hyper-suspicious view of the state as yet another version of the 'ghost busters'. Unfortunately, there are too many who quote Foucault on this without realizing that society is not a prison, but a place where dreams should be made and realized. Metaphors are good up to a point, but concepts are better.

Briefly put:

1. Civil Society is based on universality and not privilege. It, therefore, cannot work for some and not for others, without damaging its core. Extra-legal measures are not resorted to by the poor, but more so, or equally at least, by the better-off as well. Patron-client relationships can live well with elections as long as we are in the business of playing the politics of the given.

2. Civil Society is never in a steady state for it is constantly enriched by the 'elite of calling' or the vanguard of fraternity. They are the ones who are the first to step outside the politics of the given.

3. Populations are divided on a perennial basis in targeted programmes that do not look at the whole. Universal policies, such as those on health and education, plan for the entire society and not for this or that section of it.

4. Society is more than numbers, but there needs to be an understanding of the gravity of a situation and the constraints that certain sections of people have to face. Without this knowledge it is difficult to deliver welfare on a universal basis.

5. Finally, democracy is what democracy does. It is wrong to judge a state in terms of process and not in terms of outcomes.

CHAPTER XI

The Basque in Spain: From a Basket Case to a Model of Development

If the reader imagines that the building blocks of a welfare state were put in place in a distant historical era and are dim reminders of an age gone by, then a visit to the Basque region of Spain is essential to see how democracy has made a difference in contemporary times. During General Franco's dictatorial rule from 1939 to 1975, the Basque region of Spain was discriminated against; even the Basque language was made illegal. Post-Franco, this region is now a model of development on all fronts and not just in terms of economic growth. The Basque country, in fact, demonstrates how the 'elite of calling' made a difference by changing the given. It also shows how important it is to establish a welfare state especially when the economy is hard-hit. The Basque miracle is not just an economic one, but a democratic one too. It demonstrates how fraternity can be advanced by a committed 'elite of calling' and that it can happen in modern times too.

To prove that thinking citizenship is not unrealizable in the modern era, to prove that utopian thinking is not day-dreaming when fraternity is on the agenda, to prove also that hard, honest decisions work, take a look at what the Basque region of Spain has done in less than a lifetime. If they can do it, why can't we? Why should we yield to the view that citizenship, in the true sense, is something that India cannot aspire to? Why must we necessarily agree with Ernest Gellner when he said that civil society is a product of western democracies and that it cannot be exported (Gellner 1994)?

Come to the Basque region of Spain for a contemporary demonstration of how the elite of calling can make a democracy functional and citizenship-friendly. For a long time Spain could hardly be termed a true member of the western democratic club of nation-states, and its Basque territory was even more distant. To some extent perhaps the language and terrain of this region favoured isolation, but we must not forget the single-minded purpose with which General Franco denied and persecuted the Basques. But the way the Basque country has battled its way to the top is a contemporary lesson on how the elite of calling can make a difference. Democracy has won many victories but most of them were the past, led by figures who are now historical memories. It might seem as if some of the great advances democracies made were possible only in those good old days, but no longer. All this seems true, till you come to the Basque part of Spain.

Beyond Terrorism: The Making of a Democratic Basque

When discussing universal health and education, we have repeatedly stressed that societies embarked on these programmes not when they were rich, but when they were poor. It is because of these interventions that a middle class came up that was independent of patronage and could raise the standards of productivity and citizenship. This, as we said earlier, was true of Sweden, Canada, Austria and Britain. Now take a look at the Basque country.

The history of this region that is significant for us begins as recently as 1980. That is when, post-Franco, Spain became a democracy and the Basque country got its first shot at truly governing itself in the modern era. As most of us might remember, the separatist ETA were till that time very popular with the people of Basque and even had the tacit (sometimes, even active) support of the local Catholic Church.

The ETA terrorists had a certain glamour and halo about them for they went about systematically targeting Franco loyalists. If a few innocents died in the process, that did not take away much of their shine. While some of their feats were admired, it was not as if everybody in the Basque country actively participated in terrorism. Nevertheless, the ETA commanded respect, fear and loyalty in the region. Their most spectacular attack was the one on Admiral Luis Carrero Blanco, Franco's deputy, who was killed when he was leaving church after Mass. He was in his car when the bomb went off. It was so powerful that it tossed his Dodge 3700 to the top of an apartment building near the church from where he had emerged.

There was ample reason for all this anger against Franco's regime. Not only was it brutal, backward and bloody in general, but the dictator's hatred of the Basque was more than pathological. He allowed Hitler and his Italian allies to test their skills with the new splinter and incendiary bomb cocktail, specially selected by Richthofen for maximum damage, on the Basque people.

This payload was dropped in Gernika (or Guernica), a small town in Basque country, also famous for its ancient assembly hall which is now a museum. But over seventy years ago, on Sunday, 26 April 1937, when the faithful had congregated in church, the airstrike happened and the whole place was ripped apart. The mission on the unsuspecting Basques was successful: these bombs did indeed have the deadly capacity to kill and destroy. It is hard to conceive of a leader so cruel that he could allow his own people to be subjects of a test strike by a friendly foreign power. The experiment was a success and Richthofen must have been very pleased with the outcome. The horror of the destruction that followed inspired Picasso's famous painting, 'Guernica', and made Franco the most hated man amongst the Basques. Franco even went to the extent of banning the Basque language (Euskera) from being spoken or written. There are people who went to prison for something as minor as entering their children's name in school with the Basque spelling. In Franco's time, that would be a big mistake.

Yet the Basque region was important to Spain from the nineteenth century onwards for its shipping and steel industries, as well as for real estate. As very little was invested to modernize these units in the early decades of the twentieth century, they could not withstand the sudden rise in oil prices (otherwise known as the 'oil shock') and the recession of the early 1970s. As a consequence, the Basque country spiralled into an economic depression that few thought it would come out of. By the 1980s, youth unemployment had reached 50 per cent (Ploger 2007: 11) and Bilbao, the major hub of this region, bore this damage on its visage—it turned dank, dark and depressing. The river Nervion that runs through this city had but three bridges across it and the water was polluted with industrial waste. It was an ecologically dead river. Health and educational services were hardly of the kind that the rest of Europe boasted of.

The New Basque Region: Breaking Free from Franco's Legacy

In 1980, when Spain turned democratic, Basques agreed to merge with it provided some important conditions were satisfied. The most significant clause they put before Madrid was that the Basque region would raise its own funds and spend them the way it thought best. A fraction of this and no more would be given to Madrid for services rendered to the Basque area in terms of communication and defence. There is, of course, a historical memory that the Basques could draw upon when they signed the 1980 deal with Madrid. When the Basque region agreed to accept the Spanish monarchy in the past, they did so on the condition that their ancient laws, the Fueros, would be untouched. These traditional legal norms in Basque land were very egalitarian in character, which is why a feudal, or seigneurial, system never took hold in this region.

As a Basque intellectual told me, 'We did not have commoners in our history; we were all lords!'[1]

Franco, of course, would have none of that; he had ruthlessly suppressed the Basque part of Spain. But now that he was gone, and Spain was ready for democracy, it was time again that this region could assert itself. Of course, when the post-Franco agreement was struck, the Basques had moved beyond the Fueros, but the passion remained. The 1981 'Concierto Economico' between the Basque government and that of Spain signalled a new federal relationship. The Basque country could now raise its own taxes and use them as it pleased while remitting a part of them to the Spanish government.

Catalonia, another region of Spain that has a distinctive identity, may today wish it had done what the Basques did in 1980. Notwithstanding the grumbles of discontent in Barcelona, the truth really is that Catalonians dithered to take that decisive step at that time. This is perhaps because they lacked the Basque people's historical memory, and this denied them the confidence that such a move would require. The Basques were clearly unequivocal in what they wanted from the Spanish Union, they held on, and eventually Madrid gave in and the 'Concierto Economico' became a formal contract.

Once this happened, the energy and passion that fuelled ETA was diverted to running a legitimate government. In this none of the past was forgotten, but a future was also promised. Pedro Luis Uriarte, who was the first finance minister of democratic Basque country, said in a private interview: 'However splendid a project might look like, it is destined to fail if it does not tune itself to the future' (private interview, July 2010). It was to this future that the new cabinet ministers and administrators of Basque addressed themselves, and what a difference they made in a matter of twenty-five years. They were truly the 'elite of calling' (see also Glass 1997).

It all began with the Guggenheim Museum, which today stands as a symbol of Basque excellence. When it was first

---

[1] According to the Fuero of 1526, Law XVI

envisioned, there were many who did not think it was a good idea to construct such a grand edifice. But as several political office-bearers told me, in one voice, they had to take this chance if only to demonstrate that the people of the Basque region were capable of doing something that was truly world-class (see Crawford 2001). As I was told repeatedly, the call at that time, and it stays true even today, is: 'Bring your dreams to the Basque country and we will make them come true.' Today, Bilbao has more tourists than even the famous San Sebastian sea resort.

A stroll down Bilbao takes one to a three-cornered plaza with an impressive church in the centre, but that is not its most outstanding feature. On the pavement surrounding this building are three near-identical sculptures that stand about four feet high and look like crumpled pieces of paper. These artefacts, the locals will tell you, represent old Basque society: rubbish that is destined for the trash can. The past, in their collective view, is something to be junked so that the future can grow from the present. That is how committed the people in this part of Spain are towards building a new Basque country.

This is the kind of promise that only an 'elite of calling' can make, and the Basques were fortunate to have them when they got both democracy and autonomy in 1980. This elite did not believe in 'maximizing the given' but in changing it, and the evidence of this lies everywhere.

All one needs to be convinced of this is to look at the photographs of Bilbao in 1980 and compare them with what the city is today. Not only is the Guggenheim Museum the centrepiece of Bilbao, but the river Nervion has thirteen bridges across it (where there were only three in 1980). In addition, the water flowing in it has changed colour from grey to blue. The old photographs (see Ploger 2007: 20) give no premonition that very soon the city would become a picture of beauty, elegance and tranquillity. Stand in the centre of downtown Bilbao and look around you. On a clear day you can see cattle and sheep grazing in the distant hills that surround it, unperturbed by the bustle just a few miles away.

The most startling aspect of the Basque area's regeneration was that it did not linger on past cultural injustices. Rather, the attempt of the first generation of the Basque political elite was that they would show the world that they can do it better than most and rival the best. They turned their cultural pride into making demonstrable advances in the economy, not to turn against other cultural groups or seek vengeance for past injustices. This is something that Indian cultural chauvinists should learn from.

Achievements: Investments in Health, Education and Research

Franco did his worst to under-educate the Basques, but today the Basque region stands third among countries in the European Union (EU) region in terms of university graduates and fourth in terms of productivity per worker. The per capita GDP rose dramatically too; from being number seven in this ranking among EU countries in 2000, it climbed to the number three spot in 2008. On all these counts, it does much better than Spain. The Basques number less than 5 per cent of Spain's population but this region contributes over 10 per cent of its export earnings.

After the Basques began to govern themselves, they changed the way industries ran in their region. To begin with, the old shipping yards were dismantled and so were the steel mills as they were wasteful, polluting and not up to current international standards. So they set about establishing state-of-the-art manufacturing in a number of industries. Today, Basque country produces 90 per cent of Spanish steel (Arcelor Mittal is right there in the region) and 80 per cent of the country's machine tools. In terms of foreign trade, Spain depends on its Basque province for 73 per cent of its earnings in aeronautical exports, 71 per cent in automobile parts, 64 per cent in household appliances and 61 per cent in machine tools. This is a high-tech manufacturing region we are talking about.

That the bulk of its exports go to France, Germany and the US only goes to show how developed the Basque country is in technologically advanced production systems. Gone is the old-fashioned grind and grime Basque industrial profile; the new one is absolutely cutting-edge, less polluting and way more productive.

In the 1950s and 1960s the Basque region experienced economic expansion, but the recession of the 1970s forced many industries to close down (including the famous Altos Hornos Steelworks that was set up in 1902). The gravity of this downturn can be gauged from the fact that this left about 340 hectares of industrial wasteland in the heart of Bilbao itself. The recovery began slowly after 1980, but truly picked up about a decade later. The first decade after the Basque country won democracy was spent in planning on how to go about regenerating their economy. From the 1990s it was clear that the way ahead should be with the project method, starting with infrastructural developments.

How did the Basques do all this? Put simply: education, health and research. The members of the first Basque cabinet did not compromise on these, though at that time the province was one of the poorest in Europe. Neither did they ever raise the question: 'Where is the money?' as most contemporary Indian planners do when asked to deliver in these social sectors. The political elite found the money and Basque has never looked back since.

In 2010, the Basque government allocated 35.8 per cent and 25 per cent of its budget to health and education respectively. In India, for a quick comparison, only 2.31 per cent and 4.97 per cent were allocated for health and education, respectively, in the 2012-13 budget (see http://right-to-education-india. blogsport.in/2012/03/union-budget-2012-measly-spending-on.htm; accessed 29 September 2012). Sure enough, in terms of our health and education profile, we are way down on the international rankings. For example, in contrast to the Basque region where there are about 5.2 doctors per 1000, in India we have just 0.5 per 1000 (see www.indiconline.in/health/

Health-Statistics.aspx; accessed on 24 July 2012). And even this figure, as we noted earlier, does not fully reveal the miserable conditions in which patients and doctors interact.

Amazingly, what needs to be emphasized is that figures for the Basque country are well above those of the EU region too. While in the Basque areas of Spain there are 5.2 doctors per 1000, the numbers for France, Germany, the UK and US are much lower; they hover between 2.6 and 4. With the help of the Basque region's impressive doctor/population ratio, the figure for Spain as a whole is 3.2. Not surprisingly, the life expectancy among Basques is 82.1 years and it stands at the top of Europe in this regard. In the background, we should also keep in mind that the government encourages the use of generic drugs, which was earlier resisted by many doctors.

As the Basque government progressed with its social welfare measures, it simultaneously encouraged high-level innovations in science and industry. Towards this end Sociedad para Promoción y Reconversión Industrial (or SPRI) was set up by an Act of Basque Parliament in 1981, roughly a year after they came to power. That is how focused the first generation Basque political elite were. The express intention of setting up this institution was to help in the move away from the traditional shipbuilding and steel-making units to newer technologies. SPRI also gives long-term loans at very low interest rates to encourage investment, but only if the entrepreneurs first commit themselves to using modern technology and investing in R & D.

In due course, Innobasque was established in 2007 in order to keep track of world developments in technology. It was meant to be a centre for innovation and was made up of a number of smaller institutes with special functions. Innobasque, as a whole, acts both as a think tank and as a project mobilizer and catalyst. Very recently, a formal partnership has been forged between Innobasque and Orkestra in order to help raise the levels of competitiveness of Basque industry worldwide. Alongside, it is necessary to mention IK-4 (a member of Innobasque) which helps bring together knowledge that individual industries and organizations may find difficult to access and process. IK-4 receives 50 per cent of its funds from the private sector and takes within its sweep industries as varied as Biotechnology and Mechatrons. This is a good example of public-private cooperation, particularly in the area of Research and Development. Tecnalia is another organization of the same family, but unlike, say, IK-4, its specific focus is to secure projects from which Basque industry would prosper. Since its inception it has been a great success and it gets more business from the European Union than from the Spanish government next door.

Renewable energy attracts special emphasis, for the Basque government realizes that the future is headed in that direction. Today renewable energy contributes only 4 per cent of the Basque region's total requirement, but this number has already gone up by over 24 per cent between 1995 and 2000. Gamesa (a global leader in the sustainable energy field) has a major presence in Basque Spain and has installed the first off-shore wind turbine in Spain. It has set up wind farms in France and its impact is spread across several countries from Brazil to China. Iberdrola, a private energy company, has in 2011 teamed up with Gamesa to provide wind energy to customers in the region. In renewable energy, the Basque region is well ahead of the curve and promises to surge further up on the graph.

Again, the highly regarded European Spalliation Source (ESS) has chosen the Basque country to be a major site of its activities. The ESS is absolutely futuristic in its orientation and is devoted to materials research that uses the neutron-scattering technique. It is hard to get more cutting-edge than that! While the headquarters of this organization will be in Lund, Sweden, the additional one will be in Bilbao in the Basque region. Consequently, Spain will remain Vice-President of the ESS and will own 10 per cent of it. Add to this the accomplishments of Biobasque and Nanobasque and you find an ultra-modern scientific society in place. All of this is a far cry from how the Basque country had fared in the recession of the 1970s. Not only did it come out of a serious economic slump, it became a model for others to emulate. In fact, Bilbao has been shortlisted by the

International Council of Societies of Industrial Development to become the World Design Capital in 2014.[2]

In this surge, Research and Development (R & D) led the way. The Basque authorities are fully aware that if they have to show the world how good they are and how modern and advanced they can be, they must rely on leveraging knowledge. In addition, they are also aware that if they have to be internationally competitive, only R & D can show the way. Techno-Parks are another impetus to R & D. The one near Bilbao allows units in its premises only after they agree to invest as much as 10 per cent of their turnover to R & D. Many enterprises are willing to submit to this requirement because there are certain definite advantages to being located in the Techno-Park. They are now privileged to get state support in terms of market outlets as well as technical and organizational skills: factors that make R & D investments even more attractive.

And all of this shows! In the Basque region the expenditure on R & D is 1.85 per cent of GDP, higher than Spain and equal to the best in the European Union. On the European Innovation Indicator, it ranks higher than the average for EU countries. For the record, Basque Spain has quite an impressive profile in terms of banks; the BBVA is the tenth-largest in the world and its origins are in Bilbao. The Basques have already come such a long way.

Did those who inaugurated the Basque country's tremendous success story ever go to the people and ask their opinion before they embarked on a policy? Hardly ever. From the establishment of the Guggenheim Museum to the setting up of SPRI and Techno-Parks and R & D units in different industries, those in power did what they thought was good for the Basque people. They were focused on how to raise standards of living and working conditions for all. It is this single-minded devotion to these goals that helped them to succeed. Once the region was on

---

[2] Unfortunately, this project is currently in a state of suspension as economic problems have made it difficult for the Spanish government to make the required contribution.

the upswing, many other initiatives came up and grew over time. Mondragon, for example, is the world's largest cooperative; it operates out of the Basque country and is active in a number of fields. Starting as a small engineering unit during Franco's days, it now ranks tenth in terms of economic investments in Spain. One cannot but feel its presence everywhere, for its logo appears on everything from department stores to engineering goods!

Since this progress has occurred only in the very recent past and since one can still meet many of the people who started this engine, their actions have a great degree of immediate relevance. It is not history we are discussing, but something momentous that has happened in our times. As a cabinet minister of the first Basque government said: 'Those politicians who say that they listen to the people before they act, are liars. A good democrat is the one who does what is right and lets the people judge the action and its outcome at election time.'

References

Acharya, Shankar, Robert Cassen and Kirsty McNay (2004), 'The Economy: Past and Future' in Tim Dyson, Robert Cassen and Leela Visaria, eds, *Twenty-First Century India: Population, Economy, Human Development and the Environment*, (New York, Oxford University Press).

Acharya, Shankar (2006), *Essays in Macro-Economics* (New Delhi, Oxford University Press).

Annavajhuila, J.C.B. and Pratap, Surendra (2012), 'Worker Voices in a Auto Production Chain: Notes from the Pits of a Low Road-1' in *Economic and Political Weekly*, vol. XLVII, pp. 46-59.

Bataille, Georges (1991), *The Accursed Share* vol.1, *Consumption* (New York, Zone Books.

Behrman, J.R. and N. Birdsall (1983), 'The Quality of Schooling: Quantity Alone is Misleading' in *American Economic Review* vol. 73, no. 5, pp. 928-946.

Besley, T. and T. Persson (2011), *Pillars of Prosperity* (Princeton, Princeton University Press).

Béteille, André, 'Civil Society and its Institutions' (The First Fulbright Memorial Lecture), Reproduced in *The Telegraph* (Kolkata), 12 March and 13 March 1996.

Béteille, André (2002), *Equality and Universality: Essays in Social and Political Theory* (New Delhi, Oxford University Press).

Béteille, André (2005), 'Distributive Justice and Institutional Well-Being' in Dipankar Gupta, ed., *Anti-Utopia: The Essential Writings of André Béteille* (Delhi, Oxford University Press).

Béteille, André (2010), 'The Institutions of Democracy' in *Economic and Political Weekly*, vol. XLV, pp. 114-133.

Bhagat, R.P. (2011), 'Emerging Pattern of Urbanization in India' in *Economic and Political Weekly*, vol. XLVI, pp. 10-12.

Bondurant, Joan B. (1964), 'Satyagraha versus Duragraha: The Limits of Symbolic Violence' in G. Ramachandran and T.K. Mahadevan, eds, *Gandhi: His Relevance for our Times* (Mumbai, Bharatiya Vidya Bhavan).

Cartright, Nancy, Jordi Cat, Lola Fleck and Thomas E. Uebel (1996), *Otto Neurath: Philosophy between Science and Politics* (Cambridge, Cambridge University Press).

Carvalho, Jose Alberto de and Mary Rodrigues Wong (1998), 'Demographic and Socio-Economic Implications of Rapid Fertility Decline in Brazil: A Window of Opportunity' in G. Martine, M. Das Gupta and L.C. Chen, eds, *Reproductive Change in India and Brazil* (Delhi, Oxford University Press).

Census of India 2001 (New Delhi, Government of India, Registrar General of Census).

Chaddha, G.K., 'Rural Non-Farm Sector in the Indian Economy: Growth, Challenges and Future Direction' (mimeo), Paper presented in the joint Jawaharlal Nehru University and IFPRI Workshop, 'The Dragon and the Elephant: A Comparative Study of Economic Reforms in China and India', held on 25-26 March 2003, at India Habitat Centre, New Delhi.

Chalapathi Rao, K.S. and Biswajit Dhar, 'India's FDI Inflow', Working Paper Number 2011/01 (New Delhi, Institute for Studies in Industrial Development, 2011).

Chand, Ramesh, P.A. Lakshmi Prasanna and Aruna Singh (2011), 'Farm Size and Productivity: Understanding the Strength of Small Holders and Improving their Livelihoods' in *Economic and Political Weekly*, vol. XLVI, pp. 5-11.

Chandrashekhar, S., 'Growth of Slums, Availability of Infrastructure and Demographic Outcomes in Slums: Evidence from India' (n.d., www.iussp.org/Activites/wge-urb/chandrashekhar.pdf, accessed 8 May 2011).

Chatterjee, Partha (2001), 'On Civil and Political Societies in Postcolonial Democracies' in Sudipta Kaviraj, ed., *Civil Society: History and Possibilities* (Cambridge, Cambridge University Press).

Chatterjee, Partha, 'Populations and Political Society' (n.d., www.international.ucla.edu/cms/files/chatterjee.pdf).

Crawford, Leslie, 'Guggenheim, Bilbao and the "Hot Banana"' in *The Financial Times*, 4 September 2001.

Dasgupta, Biplab (1988), 'Urbanization in West Bengal: An Introduction' in Dasgupta, Biplab, ed., *Urbanization, Migration and Rural Change: A Study of West Bengal* (Calcutta, A. Mukherjee and Company Private Limited.

Diwan, Rashmi (2012), *Indian Small Schools: A Review of Issues and Related Concerns* (New Delhi, National University of Education, Planning and Administration).

Desai, Sonalde, Amaresh Dubey, Brij Lal Joshi, Mitali Sen, Abusaleh Shariff and Reeve Vanneman, *Human Development in India* (Delhi,

Oxford University Press, 2010). Also available at the internet link http://ihds.umd.edu/report.html (accessed on 7 March 2011).

Deshingkar, Priya and John Farrington, eds (2009), *Circulation Migration and Multilocational Livelihood Strategies in Rural India* (Delhi, Oxford University Press).

Dreze, Jean, 'India: Poverty Estimates and Food Entitlements' in *The Hindu*, 25 February 2010 (sacw.net/article1351.html; accessed 20 May 2011).

D'Souza, Victor (1975), 'Urban Development in India: Demographic, Functional and Socio-Cultural Perspectives' in *The Indian Journal of Social Work*, vol. 4, pp. 147-160.

Dupont, Veronique (2008), 'Slum Demolitions in Delhi since 1990: An Appraisal' in *Economic and Political Weekly*, vol. XLIII, pp. 79-87.

Durkheim, Emile (1933), *The Division of Labour in Society* (Glencoe, The Free Press).

Dutta, Pranati, 'Urbanization in India', presented at the European Population Conference, 21-24 June 2006; see http://epe2006.princeton.edu/download.aspx?submissionId=60134; accessed on 23 January 2010.

Economic Survey 2005-6, 2006-7, (New Delhi, Ministry of Finance and Economic Division, Government of India).

Economic Survey 2011-12 (New Delhi, Government of India, Ministry of Finance).

Economist 2007, 'India on Fire', 1 February 2007.

Five-Year Plan 2002-2007 (New Delhi, The Planning Commission, Government of India 2002).

Galanter, Marc (1984), *Competing Equalities: Law and the Backward Classes in India* (Delhi, Oxford University Press).

Gandhi, M.K., *My Non-Violence*, compiled by Sailesh Kumar Bandopadyaya (1960), (Ahmedabad, Navjivan Publishing House).

Gandhi, M.K., *Collected Works*, (New Delhi, Publications Division, Ministry of Information and Broadcasting, Government of India, 1967).

Gandhi, M.K., *Selected Writings of Mahatma Gandhi*, Ronald Duncan, ed., 1971 (London, Fontana).

Gandhi, M.K., *The Moral and Political Thoughts of Mahatma Gandhi* (Delhi, Oxford University Press, 1973).

Gandhi, M.K., *The Essential Writings of Mahatma Gandhi*, Raghavan Iyer, ed., 1991 (Delhi, Oxford University Press).

Government of Tamil Nadu, Tamil Nadu Urban Development Fund, Business Plan, Tirrupur Municipality Final Report, Wilbur Smith Associates, Private Limited; (http://tirrupurcorporationtn.gov.in/CCP/CCP_BP_Tirrupur%20-%20Finbal20%Report.pdf;n.d., accessed on 30 April 2011).

Glass, Eduardo Jorge (1997), *Bilbao's Modern Business Elite* (Nevada, University of Nevada Press).

Goswami, Omkar, 'Rural is Much More than Only Agriculture' (New Delhi, CERG Advisory Private Limited).

Gould, Harold, 'In Search of Mahatma Gandhi Today: 51 Years after his Death' in *New India Digest*, September-October 2000.

Gruber, Helmut (1991), *Red Vienna: Experiment in Working Class Culture, 1919-1934* (Oxford, Oxford University Press).

Guerard, Albert (1951), 'Saint-Simon on Horseback: The Economic and Social Policy of Napoleon III' in Ausubel, Herman, ed., *The Making of Modern Europe: Book Two: Waterloo to the Atomic Age* (US, Holt, Rinehart and Wilson).

Gupta, Dipankar (2000), *Mistaken Modernity: India Between Worlds* (New Delhi, Harper Collins).

Gupta, Dipankar (2010), *The Caged Phoenix: Can India Fly* (Palo Alto, Stanford University Press).

Gupta, Indrani, 'Out of Pocket Expenditures on Poverty: Estimates from NSS 61st Round' (http://planningcommission.gov.in/reports/genrep/indrani.pdf, 2009, accessed on 7 March 2011).

Gupta, Kamala, Fred Arnold and H. Lhungdiu (2009), *Health and Living Conditions in Eight Indian Cities, National Family and Health Survey-3* (Mumbai, International Institute for Population Sciences).

Gupta, S.P. (2002), *Report on the Committee on India Vision 2020* (New Delhi, Planning Commission, Government of India).

Habermas, Jurgen I. (1987), *The Theory of Communicative Action, vol. 1, Reason and Rationalization in Society* (Boston, Beacon Press).

Habermas, Jurgen I. (1987), *The Theory of Communicative Action: Lifeworld and System: A Critique of Functionalist Reason* (Boston, Beacon Press).

Hammam, Sonia and Richard L. Clifford, World Bank Presentation: 'India's Urban Poor' (http://wwwpennysleuth.com/bin/z/t/2.16LongWayToGo.jpg, 2007, accessed 21 February 2011).

Handbook of Indian Statistics 2011 (Mumbai, Reserve Bank of India, 2011).

Handbook of Statistics on the Indian Economy 2010-11 (Mumbai, Department of Statistics and Information Management, Reserve Bank of India, 2011).

Hardiman, David (2003), *Gandhi in his Time and Ours* (New Delhi, Permanent Black).

Heredia, Rudolf C. (2007), *Changing Gods: Rethinking Conversion in India* (New Delhi, Penguin Books).

Hutton, J.H. (1931), *Census of India, 1931* Vol. 1, *India*, Part 1, *Report* (Delhi, Manager of Publications).

Hutton, J.H. (1961), *Caste in India* (Delhi, Oxford University Press).

India: Key Data Incorporating Budget Analysis: The Red Book (Mumbai, Kay Nirnay, Sumangal Press, 2007

Jagirdar, Brinda, (http://iobbancon2011.com/uploads/CEDocuments/Compdm/Article13.pdf, 2011, accessed on 21 July 2012).

Jhabvala, Renana (2005), 'Work and Wealth' in Alyssa Ayres and Philip Oldenburg, eds, *India Briefing: Take Off At Last* (London, M.E. Sharpe).

Kothari, Rajni (1984), The Non-Party Political Process' in *Economic and Political Weekly*, vol. 19, pp. 216-224.

Kothari, Rajni (1988), 'Integration and Exclusion in Indian Politics' in *Economic and Political Weekly*, vol. 23, pp. 2223-2227.

Khera, Reetika (2011), 'Trends in Diversion of Grain from the Public Distribution System' in *Economic and Political Weekly*, vol. XLVI, pp. 106-114.

Kolata, Gina, 'Knotty Challenges in Health Care Costs' in *The New York Times*, 5 March 2012 (http://www.nytimes.com/2012/03/06/health/policy/an-interview-with-victor-fuchs-on-health-care-costs.html; accessed on 4 July 2012).

Kuhn, Thomas (1970), *The Structure of Scientific Revolution* (Chicago, University of Chicago Press)

Kundu, Amitabh (2009), 'Trends and Patterns of Urbanisation and their Economic Implications' in *Urbanisation and Migration: An Analysis of Trends, Patterns and Policies* (Asia Human Development Research Paper Series, vol. 16).

Kundu, Amitabh, and P.C. Mohanan, 'Employment and Inequality Outcomes in India', (http://www.oecd.org/dataoecd/54/51/42546020.pdf, 2010, accessed on 23 December 2010).

Kundu, Amitabh, and Lopamudra Ray Saraswati (2012), 'Migration and Exclusionary Urbanization in India' in *Economic and Political Weekly*, vol. XLVII, pp. 212-227.

La Porta, R., F. Lopez-de-Silanes, A. Schleifer and R. Vishny (1999), 'The Quality of Government' in *Journal of Law, Economics, and Organization*, vol. 15, no. 1.

Lee, Roland D., Andrew Mason, Tim Miller and Steven W. Sindig (2001), *Population Matters: Demographic Change, Economic Growth and Poverty in the Developing World* (New York, Oxford University Press).

Lee, Derek Byer, Xianshen Dias and Chris Jackson (2005), *Agrarian Rural Development and Pro-Poor Growth* (Washington D.C., The World Bank).

Lee, Roland D. and Andrew Mason (2011), *Population Aging and Generational Economy: A Global Perspective* (Cheltenham, Edward Elgar).

Levi Strauss, Claude (1966), *The Savage Mind* (Chicago, University of Chicago Press).

Maiti, Diyendu, and Arup Mitra (2010), *Skills, Informality and Development*, Institute of Economic Growth Working Paper No. 306 (Delhi, Institute of Economic Growth).

Mannheim, Karl (1936), *Ideology and Utopia: An Introduction to the Sociology of Knowledge* (London, Routledge and Kegan Paul).

Manpower Profile of India, 2005, 2008, 2009 (New Delhi, Institute of Applied Manpower Research, Concept Publishing House).

Marius-Gnanou, Kamala and Francois Moricano-Ebrard, 'Urbanization in India: From Megacities to Urban Villages' (http://www.ifpindia.org/ecrire/upload/press_ifp_website/indiapolis_articlerelu.pdf) accessed on 5 January 2011).

Marshall, T.H. (1957), *Citizenship and Social Class and other Essays* (London, Syndics of Cambridge University Press).

Marshall, T.H. (1963), *Sociology at the Crossroads and Other Essays* (London, Heinemann).

Marshall, T.H. (1975), *Social Policy in the Twentieth Century* (London, Hutchinson University Library).

Mehta, Arun C., Analytical Report 2008-9: *Elementary Education in India, Progress Towards UEE* (New Delhi, National University of Education, Planning and Administration, 2011).

Ministry of Agriculture Yearbook 2003 (New Delhi, Government of India (in collaboration with All India Report on Agricultural Census and Fertilizer Corporation of India and Agricultural Statistics at a Glance, 2003).

Misra, R.P. (1998), *Urbanization in India: Challenges and Opportunities* (Shillong, ICSSR Northern Regional Centre).

Mosca, Gaetano (1939), *The Ruling Class* (New York, McGraw Hill).

Mukherji, Shekhar (2006), *Migration and Urban Decay: Asian Experience* (Jaipur, Rawat Publication).

Mukhopadhay, Abhiroop and Soham Sahoo (2012), *Does Access to Secondary Education Affect Primary Schooling: Evidence from India* (Delhi, Institute of Economic Growth Working Paper No. 312, Institute of Economic Growth).

National Commission for Enterprises in the Unorganised Sector *Report on Conditions of Work and Promotion of Livelihoods in the Unorganised Sector*, New Delhi: Government of India, 2007)

National Family Health Survey-3, *Family Welfare Health and Living Conditions in Eight Indian Cities* NFHS-3 (Deonar, Mumbai: International Institute of Population Studies, 2005-6).

National Sample Survey, *Some Aspects of Operational Land Holdings in India, 2002-03* (New Delhi, National Sample Survey Organization, Ministry of Statistics and Implementation, Government of India, 2006).

National Sample Survey, *Employment and Unemployment Situation in India*, Report No. 537 (New Delhi, Ministry of Statistics and Implementation, Government of India, 2010).

National Sample Survey, *Migration in India 2007-2008*, Report No. 533 (New Delhi, Ministry of Statistics and Implementation, Government of India, 2010).

NASSCOM-IDC 2006 Domestic Services (IT-ITES), *Market Opportunity* (New Delhi).

Nayyar, Dhiraj and Shravya Jain, 'The Job Squeeze' in *India Today*, pp. 20-23, 17 September 2012.

Panchmukhi, P.R. and Santosh Mehrotra, 'Assessing Pubic and Private Provision of Elementary Education in India' in Santosh Mehrotra, P.R. Panchmukhi, Ranjana Srivastava and Ravi Srivastava, eds (2005), *Universalizing Elementary Education in India: Uncaging the 'Tiger' Economy* (New Delhi, Oxford University Press).

Parel, Anthony J. (2007), *Gandhi's Philosophy and the Quest for Harmony* (Cambridge, Cambridge University Press).

Ploger, Jorg (2007), *Bilbao: City Report* (CASE Report No. 43), (London, Centre for Analysis of Social Exclusion).

Rai, Himanshu (2009), 'Towards New Poverty Lines for India', (http://planningcommission.gov.in/reports/genrep/himanshurai.pdf, n.d., accessed on 7 March).

Ramaswamy, K.V. (2009), 'Global Markets: World Export Opportunities and Local Labour Market: A Study of Indian Textile and Apparel Industry' in *Indian Journal of Labour Economics*, vol. 52, pp. 607-630.

Rani, Uma (2008), 'Learning Processes and Learning Skills in Auto Component in Auto Component Firms Supplying to Global Production Networks' in J. Unni and Uma Rani, eds, *Flexibility of Labour in Globalizing Economies: The Challenge of Skill and Technology* (New Delhi, Tulika Books).

Report of the Committee on Indian Vision 2020, (New Delhi, Planning Commission, 2002).

Robson, W.A. (1957), *The Welfare State*, L.T. Hobhouse Memorial Trust Lecture, no. 26 (Oxford, Oxford University Press).

Rothstein, Bo (2006), *Social Traps and the Problem of Trust* (Cambridge, Cambridge University Press).

Rothstein, Bo, Marcus Samanni and Jan Teroell (2010), *Quality of Government, Political Power and the Welfare State*, Quality of Government Working Paper Series (University of Gothenburg, The Quality of Government Institute, Department of Political Science, ISSN 1653-8919).

Rothstein, Bo (2010), *Corruption, Happiness, Social Trust and the Welfare State: A Causal Mechanisms Approach*, Quality of Government Working Paper Series 2010:9, April 2010 (University of Gothenburg, The Quality of Government Institute, Department of Political Science).

Rothstein, Bo (2011), *The Quality of Government: Corruption, Inequality and Social Trust* (Chicago, University of Chicago Press).

Rawls, John (1971), *Theory of Justice* (Cambridge, Massachusetts, Harvard University Press).

Rich, Norman (1977), *The Age of Nationalism and Reform, 1850-1890* (W.W. Norton and Company,)

Russell, Bertrand (1958), *Unpopular Essays*, (London, George Allen and Unwin).

Sachs, Jeffrey (2005), *The End of Poverty: How We Can Make it Happen in our Lifetime* (New York, Penguin Books).

Sen, N.B., ed., *Wit and Wisdom of Mahatma Gandhi* (New Delhi, New Book Society, n.d.).

Sengupta, Devina and Sreeradha Basu, 'Why Cos Ignore Masters in Engineering Institutes' in *Economic Times*, p. 8, 14 December 2012.

Shiva Kumar, A.K., Lincoln Chen, Mita Choudhury, Vijay Mahajan, Amarjeet Sinha (2011), et al., 'Framing Health Care: Challenges and Opportunities' in *The Lancet* (37), no. 9766, pp. 668-679

Saxena, N.C. (2009), *Recommendations for Methodology for Conducting BPL Census* (New Delhi, Ministry of Rural Welfare, Government of India).

Seventh All India School Education Survey (7th AISES), *Schooling Facilities in Rural Areas* (New Delhi, National University of Education, Planning and Administration, 2006).

Shaw, Annapurna (2004), *The Making of Navi Mumbai* (New Delhi, Orient Blackswan).

Shiva, Kumar (2006), *Towards Faster and more Inclusive Growth: An Approach to the Eleventh Five-Year Plan (2007-2012)* (New Delhi, The Planning Commission, Government of India).

Shiva Rao, B.D. (1968), *The Framing of India's Constitution: Selected Documents*, 4 vols. (Delhi, Indian Institute of Public Management).

Simmel, Georg (1978), *The Sociology of Georg Simmel*, Kurt H. Wolf, ed. (Glencoe, The Free Press).

Singh, D.P. (2009), *India: Urban Poverty Report* (New Delhi, Ministry of Housing and Urban Poverty Alleviation, Oxford University Press).

Sinha, Koutelya, 'Indians Pay 78% of Medical Expenses from their own Pocket' in *The Times of India*, 13 January 2011.

Srinath Reddy, K., Vikram Pate, Prabhat Jha, Vinod K. Pant, A.K. Shiva Kumar and Lalit Dandona (2011), 'Towards Achievement of Universal Health Care in India by 2020' in *The Lancet* (37), issue 9767, pp. 760-68.

Srivastava, Ranjana (2005), 'Review of Elementary Education in the Selected States' in Santosh Mehrotra, P.R. Panchmukhi, Ranjana Srivastava and Ravi Srivastava, eds, *Universalizing Elementary Education in India: Uncaging the 'Tiger' Economy* (New Delhi, Oxford University Press).

Statistical Outline of India 2006-7 (Mumbai, Tata Services Limited, Department of Economics and Statistics, 2007).

Stevens, Philip and Martin Weale, 'Education and Economic Growth' in Geraint Johnes and Jill Johnes, eds (2003), *International Handbook on the Economics of Education* (Northampton, Massachusetts: Edward Elgar Publishing).

Terchek, Ronald J. (2000), *Gandhi: Struggling for Autonomy* (New Delhi, Vistaar).

Tendulkar, Suresh C., R. Radhakrishnan and Suranjan Sengupta (2009), *Report of the Expert Group to Review the Methodology for Estimation of Poverty* (New Delhi, Planning Commission, Government of India).

The Bilbao Declaration on Eco-Innovation: Fostering Eco-Innovation in SMEs (Bilbao, Eighth ETAP Forum on Eco-Innovation, Departmentio de Medio Ambiente Planifacacion Territorial, Government of Spain and European Commission DG Environment, 2010).

Thompson, E.P. (1958), 'Agency and Choice-I: A Reply to Criticism' in *New Reasoner*, no. 5, pp. 89-106.

Thompson, E.P. (1963), *The Making of the English Working Class* (London, Victor Gollancz).

Thompson, Gavin (2009), 'Health Expenditure: International Comparisons' Standard Note, SN./SG/2584 (London, Library of House of Commons).

Venkateswarlu, Umakant (1998), *Urbanization in India: Problems and Prospects* (New Delhi, New Age Publishers Limited).

Yeatts, M.M.W., *Census of India, 1931*, Vol. 14, Madras, Part 1, Report (Madras, Government of India, 1932).

Index

Forest Rights Act, 101
Foucault, Michel, 196
Franco, General, 199
fraternity and democracy, 3-5, 9
Freud, Sigmund, 139

Gadkari, Nitin, 103
Gandhi, Indira, 80, 104
Gandhi, Mahatma, 34
  beliefs, 46-47
  on charkha and khadi, 50
  as a 'citizen elite', 65
  contribution to democracy, 65-67
  as India's elite of calling, 47-49
  on inter-faith relations, 61
  legacy of, 48
  on liberal secularism, 57-59
  on non-violence and liberal democracy, 52-54, 64, 66
  objection to socialism, 51
  and public policy, 63-65
  response to industrialization, 49-52
  on socialism, 51-52
  on swadeshi movement, 50, 64
  view on brahmacharya, 60, 62
Gandhi, Rajiv, 35, 83, 104
gems and jewellery exports, 121, 123
George, David Lloyd, 140-141
Ghodawat, Sanjay, 176
Gorwala report, 113
Goswami, Omkar, 126
Gould, Harold, 48
Gowda, Deve, 93
Gram Panchayat, 64
Gray, Thomas, 8
Great Chain of Patronage, 195
Grey, Earl, 27, 29-30

Gujarat pogrom, 2002, 32, 66
Gupta, Indrani, 146

Habermas, Jurgen, 52, 61
Hammam, Sonia, 169
Hazare, Anna, 93, 111
health care, 137-139, *see also*
  universal health, programmes for realizing
  in Britain, 140-141
  in Canada, 141
  Europe *vs* USA, 141-145
  in India, 146-150
  in Spain, 140
  in Sweden, 140
  in USA, 141
  in Vienna, 138-139
Hegel, G.W.F., 61, 192
Hill Burton Act, 1946, 141
Hindu Marriage Act, 34
Hitler, Adolf, 7
horizontal mobility of labour, 126-129
household industries, 122
household investment in terms of savings, 118-119
human agency, 14
Human Development Report, 147

India, *see also* economic growth
  aging population, 152
  as an example of dystopia, 44
  consensus in Indian politics, 105-108
  difficulties in realizing citizenship, 33-34
  elite classes of, 37
  'elite of calling' in, 34-37, 39-41
  health expenses, 146

Nehru, Jawaharlal, 34, 64, 68
  advocacy of secularism, 73
  advocacy of socialism, 51
  as an 'elite of calling', 78-79
  on capitalism, 70
  development of public sectors,
    77
  establishment of centres of
    learning and industries,
    72, 77
  Five-Year Plans, 80-83
  on health and education, 79-
    80
  impact on urban India, 77
  policy of non-alignment, 70-
    71
  relation with America, Britain
    and USSR, 70-71
  on secularism, 69
  shortcomings, 78
  in urban planning, 79
non-agricultural units, 126
non-violence, principle of, 52-54
  centrality of, 54-57
Nuclear Bill, 101-102

Owen, George, 43

Panchatantra, 36
Panchayati Raj, 35, 64
Pandit, Vijayalakshmi, 71
Pankhurst, Emmeline, 28
parliamentarians
  perks of, 98-101
pastoral professions, 99-100
Paswan, Ram Vilas, 103
patronage, 108-110
patronage-based politics, 33
Pawar, Sharad, 107
Peel, Robert, 27, 29
Planning Commission, 82-83, 87,
  89

Plimsoll, Samuel, 29
Police Reforms Act, 101
politics in India, 32-33
  consensus in, 105-108
'The politics of the given', 41
Poona Pact, 63
Poor Law of the Speenhamland
  system, 29
poverty, 13, 20
  in India, 87
  measurement of, 87-89
  targeted approaches to
    removing, 89-92,
    137-138
  in United States, 88
Premji, Azim, 175
Public Distribution System, 24
Public Health Act, 29

Radhakrishnan, Sarvapally, 46
Radiatorwala, Nafisa, 175
Raja, A., 112
Ramrajya, fables of, 36
Rani, Uma, 123
Rao, Narasimha, 83
Rashtriya Janata Dal (RJD), 102
Rashtriya Samajwadi Party (RSP),
  101
Rau, B.N., 71
Rawls, John, 13, 192-193
Reddy, K. Srinath, 87
Reforms Act, 1831, 28, 30
religious demonstrations,
  prohibition of, 30-31
remunerative professions, 99-100
Right to Information Act,
  111-112
Roman law, 61
Rongzhen, Nier, 28
Rothstein, Bo, 38
Rudy, Ravi Pratap, 36
rural labour force, 177